A CROWN OF REVERIES

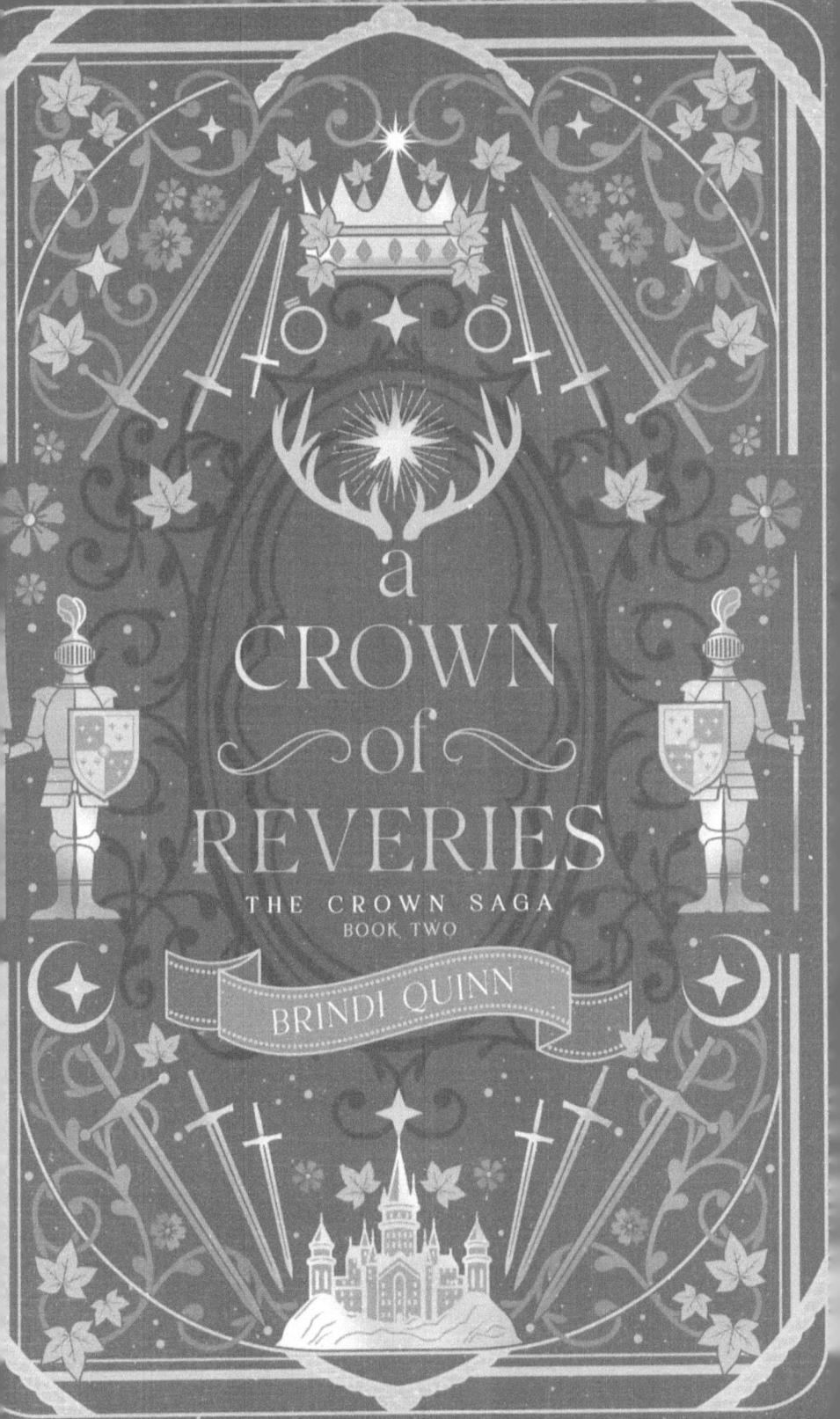

a
CROWN
of
REVERIES

THE CROWN SAGA
BOOK TWO

BRINDI QUINN

N & E

Published by Never & Ever Publishing | @neverandeverbooks
Edited by Meg Dailey | @thedaileyeditor
Cover and title by Saint Jupiter | @saintjupit3rgr4phic
Artwork by Natascia Mora | @moranatascia
Maps by Centaur Maps | @centaurmaps
Interior by Brindi Quinn via Vellum

ISBN (Paperback): 978-1-967709-02-1

Originally published November 13, 2020.
Lovingly revised, refreshed, and re-crowned in 2025.

SERIES READING ORDER

Book One: *A Crown of Echoes*
Book Two: *A Crown of Reveries*
Book Three: *A Crown of Felling*
Book Four: *A Crown of Dawn*

For those who walk boldly into darkness—and shine brighter for it.

CONTENT WARNING

The Crown Saga contains references to child abuse, child trafficking, and exploitation, which—though not depicted in graphic detail—may still be distressing for some readers. The series also features moderate to graphic violence, large-scale battles, and occasional body horror, including monstrous transformations. Romantic and sexual content ranges from mild innuendo to explicit scenes. Additional sensitive topics include coarse language, alcohol use, magical coercion, emotional manipulation, and pregnancy depicted under perilous circumstances.

DRAMATIS PERSONAE

THE QUEENS & THEIR COURTS

- **Merrin Iralore (22)** — Queen of **the Crag**. Compassionate, irreverent, increasingly audacious; channels shadow-kissed magic and an alchemist's deft hand, bona fide Nemophilist, in love with the Clearing's naughtiest knight.
- **Beau Lysavere (23)** — Queen of **the Clearing** and Merrin's sister-in-crown. Regal, sharp-witted, unfailingly composed; no longer hears the hush of roots in the Scarlet Wood. Expecting a child with a grumpy knight.
- **Sestilia of the Cove (nearly 26)** — Tempestuous sea-queen with silver hair to the floor and a mind as broken as the tides. Equal parts lonely and lethal; swears Merrin is her *best friend*—consent optional.

KNIGHTS & ALLIES

- **Sir Windley of the South (25)** — Beau's most infamous guard with a dark, forgotten past. Hue-shifting hair; his wicked tongue hides wolf-loyal depths. Utterly (and forbiddingly) devoted to Merrin.

- **Sir Rafe of the North (20)** — His blade sleeps since he severed vows to Luna, yet his silence still cuts true. Quietly hunts a new patron goddess while carrying a tender, secret ache for the freckled queen who once outranked even the moon in his heart.
- **Sir Albie (pushing 70)** — Merrin's senior knight. Weather-worn, fatherly, disapproving of Merrin's current choices.
- **Sir Saxon (27)** — Knight of the Crag. In charge of the army while Sir Albie's away.
- **Mother Poppy (ancient)** — Royal tome-keeper, former regent, grandmother in all but blood. Helping Merrin's cousin look after the court while she's away.

OTHER POWERS & PRESENCES

- **The Widowbirds** — Long-tailed messengers bonded to royal blood; summoned by a filigreed whistle, each note attuned to one of the Ten Northern Queens.
- **The Echoes** — Shadow-hands that obey only the Nemophile's Crown, glimpsed behind closed eyes and heard at the mind's edge.
- **The Scarlet Wood** — Living forest of blood-red leaves.
- **The Emerald Wood** — Night-bright sister-forest.

- **The Four Goddesses** — Principal deities of the realm, each holding her own mercies—and grudges—toward humes.
- **Luna** — Goddess of frost, tides, and the silver moon. Once bound to Rafe by oath, she now circles above like a spurned satellite—casting drama whenever cloud-cover permits.
- **Soleil** — Goddess of dawn-fire. She lifts the sun, blushes the sky at dusk, and spares her favor only for lovers who can stand the burn.
- **Exitium** — Shadow-sovereign bound to the Nemophile's Crown. Speaks through the Echoes, hungers for ruin, and tempts Merrin with power that always costs more than it gives.
- **Wraiths** — Shiver-thin fiends that haunt the hinge between worlds and lust after the hearts of those adjacent to goddess power.

NEW FRIENDS & FOES

- **Charmagne "Charm" (mid-20s)** — The rose-haired Spirite tangled in Windley's shadowed past, all burnished-copper beauty and razor-edge temper. Calls humans "pets," covets Merrin's crown, and loves jealousy almost as much as blood-sport.
- **Edius "Edi" (late-20s)** — Broad-shouldered Spirite mimic who can steal a face after draining a soul. Reluctant accomplice to Charm, protective of Pip, yet still kneels to Ascian—for reasons he keeps buried.

- **Pip "Pipsqueak" (appears ~18)** — Moon-pale prodigy whose cotton-candy hair shifts with every heartbeat he "tastes." Torn between childhood devotion to Windley and terror of Ascian's leash.
- **"Master" Ascian (age unknown)** — Lavender-eyed puppeteer who once owned Windley. Hex-weaver, life-leech, collector of pretty things; cracks a triple-tailed whip and nurses a grudge as old as sin.
- **Meraflora "Flora" (late-20s)** — Warm-hearted herbalist from Windley's past. Honey-voiced and braver than she looks; her forest cottage offers visitors a brief haven.

Nemophilist

Noun. A wanderer drawn to the enchantment of forests; one who finds solace among trees and deep woods.

THE Queendoms

SNOWY
NORTH

QUEENDOM
OF THE
CLOUDFALL

QUEENDOM
OF THE
CACTI

QUEENDOM
OF THE
CANYON

DESERT

QUEENDOM
OF THE
CRATER

WILDERNESS

QUEENDOM
OF THE
CRYSTALLINE

THE CRYSTAL
SEA

QUEENDOM
OF THE
COTTONWOOD

QUEENDOM
OF THE
CURRANT

THE SCARLET
WOOD

FOREST
FORTRESS

QUEENDOM
OF THE
CLEARING

QUEENDOM
OF THE
CRAG

INN

QUEENDOM
OF THE
COVE

THE
Queenless
LANDS

THE FORGOTTEN
QUEENDOM

THE
EMERALD
WOOD

DR
W

GIANT'S
NECROPOLIS

WOODCU
CAB

HERMIT'S
ABODE

BEETLEWOOD
FOREST

MERAFLORA'S
COTTAGE

THE
TRADI
POST

THE
HEXED
CITY

ASCIAN'S
MANOR

THE
WILLOW
GROVE

THE GOLDEN
FIELDS

THE
EDGE OF
NOWHERE

THE BLUE
FLOWER
FIELDS

SOUTHERN
SPIRITE
CITIES

CONTENTS

PREVIOUSLY IN A CROWN OF ECHOES...

T he night after retrieving Beau, we made camp deep in the Emerald Wood, the chill of approaching autumn heavy in the air. Everything seemed lighter—as though the burden of what we'd endured had finally eased.

I stroked Ruckus's silky fur, amused as Beau, now dressed in one of my riding outfits, tugged uncomfortably at the seams of her trousers.

"I look like a boy," she muttered.

"Yes, but a cute one," I teased.

She huffed, adjusting the waistband. "I feel...indecent."

"You'll get used to it," I promised, nudging her gently. "Britches let you ride faster. Just imagine the footraces we'll have in the Scarlet Wood."

Beau shot me a dry look, pulling at the fabric again. "Sometimes I swear you were born into the wrong body, Merrin."

I'd always believed bodies were wonderfully versatile.

Despite everything—the horrors she'd survived, the loved ones she'd lost—Beau held herself together admirably. She'd grieved in solitude, then alongside me. Now she stood strong for those who remained, a true queen. Yet beneath it all, I knew her pain hid.

She gazed up through the canopy, blinking away moisture that had glistened in her eyes all day. "The moon will turn gold soon," she murmured softly. "We won't return in time for the lunar festival."

I looped my arm through hers. "Then next year's shall be twice as grand to make up for it."

But as I followed her gaze skyward, my insides gave an uncomfortable squirm.

I doubted I'd ever look at the moon the same way again. I'd made an enemy of the goddess trapped within, and only time would tell whether I'd truly broken the hex upon Rafe's heart.

For now, at least, he seemed well. But I noticed things now I'd been blind to before—the subtle lift at the corner of his mouth when Beau spoke, the fleeting touches of his hand as he passed by her.

Perhaps someone had to know love themselves to recognize it in others.

Speaking of—

A finger trailed down my arm.

"Thinking of ways to misbehave, Your Majesty?"

I turned—to find Windley, his come-hither smirk far, far too obvious for this setting—and I quickly checked around to make sure none of Beau's other guards saw.

Rafe was discreet.

Windley? Not so much.

Had his actions always been this obvious? Had they gotten worse? Or had I truly been that oblivious?

Maybe our monster was simply more unruly than theirs.

I could hardly wait to return home—to escape these

watchful eyes. Drinks on the veranda. Stargazing in the belvedere. Secret walks through the wood...

But if I was honest, little else about going back appealed to me.

Things felt simpler out here.

A wandering soul was a free one.

I toyed with my mother's necklace, wondering if she had ever felt that same draw—if she'd hidden a quiet yearning behind her regal composure.

Around us, the night grew merry, with the cavalry elated at having recovered their lost queen. Albie stayed nearby, watching me closely, openly disapproving of the way Windley's hand brushed my back whenever he thought no one else was looking. The betrayal in the woodcutter's cabin felt like a distant memory now. I knew my wrinkled knight had acted out of love, however misguided. And to be fair, I hadn't exactly told him I suddenly possessed insurmountable power.

Ever my protector, he fed the cavalry my fabricated tale: the moon goddess had rescued Beau from an unknown captor.

And that story—the lie of it, the legend—would be recorded forever in the royal archives of both our queendoms.

For now, my secret was safe. I would carry the echoes for Beau until she was ready to take them back. Bartolomew's sacrifice had proven their destructive potential. And Windley—

Windley was proof of mine. Proof of what my own reckless heart could unleash.

Beau was the responsible choice for such power.

The fire crackled, its glow illuminating the weary faces of those who had survived. Albie sat nearby, nursing a tin cup of liquor, watching over me through a drunken haze. Beau curled beside me, her fingers carefully threading through my tangled hair, coaxing out the knots.

A feather drifted into my lap—pure white, almost luminous in the fire-glow.

"Another one!" Beau breathed, eyes widening. "That makes four tonight. Where in the Emerald Wood would a bird this pale even come from?"

I twirled the quill between my fingers. "Maybe a widow-bird's down feather?"

She shot me a look. "Widowbirds are black as pitch, Merrin."

Undeterred, she raked gently through the rest of my hair, as if the phantom dove itself might be nesting there.

I chuckled and flipped the feather into the flames, watching it curl to ash.

Yes.

For a fleeting moment, all was right with the world.

But only for a moment.

The cavalry was drunk.

Albie was drunk.

My head rested comfortably in Beau's lap, Rafe and Windley observing us from across the fire. The warmth from the flames felt like a gentle warning, quietly urging me to remain where I was—to not retire for the night.

I didn't listen.

"Lion queen?"

A naughty voice was at my ear.

I opened my eyes to darkness. "Windley? What are you doing here? This is the queens' tent."

Beside me, Beau purred quietly in her sleep, curled like a kitten.

"Was Albie right?" I accused. "Are you a bounder?"

He snorted. "If I were, you'd be my first target."

I sat up, rubbing sleep from my eyes. "Are you all right? You look...strained."

He exhaled a thin stream of air, pinching the bridge of his nose. "Sorry, I didn't think you'd be asleep yet. I have a strange headache, and I feel the urge to take a walk."

I frowned. "A headache?"

"I've been getting them the past few days, but tonight's especially brutal. I'll clear my head—find a stream, perhaps." He rolled his shoulders with a grimace. "I would've told Phylo or another guard, but most are dead-drunk. Don't let them leave without me. I'll be back by morning."

I kicked off my blanket. "I'll come."

Windley shook his head. "No, you should rest. You've just defied the heavens, haven't you? That had to have taken a lot out of you."

"I've already got my cloak." I grabbed said cloak and seized his shirt collar. "Besides, I've been waiting to get you alone."

His dark eyes glinted in the shadows. "Oh? And what exactly do you plan to do with me? Can't wait to find out. Truth be told, I might've come here hoping you'd follow."

In the dead of night, we slipped past the dying fire—fingers entwined, footsteps glowing faintly behind us.

His palm was warm.

His knuckles strong.

Desire crept up my neck at the realization we were truly alone—away from camp, away from watchful eyes.

Windley kept glancing at me, as though afraid I might vanish with the sunrise. I wanted him to look at me that way forever.

We wandered through the trees, chatting easily, gloriously at peace, until nearly an hour had passed.

That was when Windley made a sudden, pained noise and pressed a hand to his temple.

I stopped abruptly. "Windley?"

His blackstone ring glinted as he rubbed his forehead. "I'm fine," he said, voice tight. "Walking really does help, but it's determined to disrupt our night. Shame—I finally have you alone, and I'm impaired."

I cleared my throat lightly, concern edging into my voice. "I wonder what's causing it. You said it's been happening for days?"

He gave a low hum. "Mm. But never like this. Before it was dull—tonight, it's sharper."

Instinctively, I scanned the darkened woods for something helpful. "Over there," I said, pointing toward a patch of tangled underbrush. "Moth rose—it's good for aches. If we find some vera, I can brew a remedy."

I tugged his hand, but he resisted. "Not that way."

I paused, blinking. "Not that way?"

He hesitated, pressing harder against his brow, wincing.

Unease goose-bumped my skin. "Windley? What's happening?"

"I don't know. It feels like something's battering against a locked door inside my head." His brow furrowed deeper. "But walking this direction eases it somehow."

My pulse quickened. A headache relieved only by traveling a specific direction? That wasn't natural.

I planted my feet. "Something's wrong," I urged, tugging him swiftly. "Let's turn back." The woods pressed closer, shadows thickening around us, heavy and suffocating.

Windley faltered beside me. "...Shit." His grip tightened

painfully around my hand as his gaze darted through the encroaching darkness. "I didn't realize we'd strayed so far."

We'd barely pivoted to head back before I saw it—

A mound of tangled forest growth, shaped too precisely like a human silhouette.

My fingers dug into Windley's palm, nails biting his skin.

"What is it?" He whipped around. "What do you see?"

Before I could answer, the mound straightened—

And stepped forward.

Windley's hatchets were instantly in hand. "Stay where you are," he snarled, voice edged with threat. "Unless you want to lose a limb."

A figure draped in a long, hooded cloak.

My breath caught, my mind racing to identify who else could possibly be this far out in the wilderness.

The figure didn't stop.

Windley stepped in front of me, arm braced across my waist.

A lone figure emerged between the pines and began to clap —slow, deliberate—each echo rolling through the trees.

"Well, well..." crooned the stranger—velvet voice gliding from honeyed baritone to lilting alto. "The instant your little tricks sparked in the Emerald Wood, we felt the pulse clear down south."

"Halt!" Windley barked. "Name yourself—state your purpose in this wood."

The clapping stopped. Moonlight caught a flash of teeth.

"Eight years gone, and the prodigal still bites." A soft chuckle. "And look—you've collared something potent for a pet. Clever boy, Windalloy."

Windley drew a sharp breath; his fingers tightened on the hilt at his hip.

Windalloy. It couldn't be coincidence. *Eight years*—that was exactly how long Windley had been with us.

And by "collared pet," they meant...

Windley didn't respond. His entire body went rigid, breath carefully controlled—but his knuckles whitened dangerously around his hatchets. "Who are you?" he demanded.

"Come now." The figure tilted their head, amused. "The effects of that crude elixir must be fading, now that you've stepped foot on southern soil. Surely you remember your *master.*"

Windley visibly flinched as the figure lowered their hood, revealing a strikingly handsome face—pale skin, elegant features.

But the eyes chilled me most: gleaming, intoxicating lavender.

A Spirite.

Windley staggered, a sharp cry tearing from his throat. "Argh! No...I—"

Panic flared through me. I clung to him, preparing to summon the echoes. Whoever this was, I wore the Nemophile's Crown—I could end this now!

Darkness surged at my fingertips—

"MErrIN?"

"Merrrrin."

But when it had passed, Windley merely jerked upright, his breath steadying. And calmly—too calmly—he remarked,

"Oh. I forgot about all that."

He turned, just enough for his lips to brush my ear—a breath-light caress, pulse-quick beneath its restraint.

"Run, lion queen. Back to camp. And don't look back. Ever."

The force of his command cut through every instinct I had

—to stay, to fight—because I recognized, in the pleading timbre of his voice and the anguish searing his eyes...

He wasn't asking.

I'd barely made it a few lighted steps when three more hooded figures erupted from the trees. Rough hands seized my arms, dragging me back into suffocating darkness.

As shadows swallowed me, my last image was Windley—unmoving, resigned—facing his forgotten history as if awaiting judgment.

It seemed Windley's dark past had finally caught up to us.

I

WIND

This story would be better if Beau were the one telling it. *Beautiful, regal, freckled Beau.*

Actually—no. This one is all mine.

Hello again, captive ones. Oh, how I've missed you. Did you miss me?

Fair warning: things might get a little sticky this time. But I promise, as always, it will all be worth it.

Ready?

"Run, lion queen," Windley had just choked out. "Back to camp. And don't look back. *Ever.*"

From the darkness—speckled with Luna's rays and drifting threads of forest light—three sets of hands seized me as I turned to flee. Unfortunate for them, these rogues had no idea who they were dealing with.

"*MerRin?*"

I tipped my head back, leaning into the shadows, letting those unseen hands weave me into their embrace—

Until Windley's voice pierced the void:

"Don't!"

I snapped to attention, catching his frantic gaze.

He didn't want these assailants to witness my power?

"Rip them from their bodies! Send them to hell!"

Not yet, I warned the eager darkness, forcing myself still as three hooded figures seized me. They dragged me downward, pushing me into the plush, glowing moss—unaware they held their own deaths in their hands, should I choose to unleash my wrath.

"She smells different," murmured the man above me, his voice a deep rumble edged with intrigue. Powerful hands pressed against my shoulders, pinning me down with measured strength. He leaned in closer, his breath warm and disturbingly intimate against my ear, as if he knew exactly how much pressure I could withstand. *"Interesting."*

My skin prickled rebelliously beneath his firm grip.

"That's because she's a royal," a woman purred, venom and amusement thickening her voice.

"Oooh," chimed another—a younger male, bright with genuine curiosity. "How'd Windalloy manage that?"

"He's good at pretending," the woman remarked coolly. "Always has been."

I ignored their taunts. Whatever darkness lay in Windley's past didn't matter. Eight years was enough to know the truth of someone's soul.

But as it turned out, Windley's dark past *did* matter—and it was plunging me into greater danger than I could ever have known.

Ahead, in a moonlit clearing, Windley stood locked in a

tense standoff with the lavender-eyed man—the handsome stranger who'd introduced himself as Windley's master.

"Release her, Ascian!" Windley snarled, his voice almost feral. "I'll come without struggle if you just let her go."

"Aw," Ascian drawled, lips curving into a cruel smirk. "She must be quite the pet if you're willing to trade her leash for yours."

"You'd *best not* disrespect her by calling her that," Windley hissed through clenched teeth. Moonlight flashed off his twin hatchets as he gestured sharply toward the rogue holding me captive. "Tell your lackeys to back off, or I'll carve them to pieces."

"Oh-ho, testy," rumbled the deep-voiced man above me, flexing his grip on my shoulders as if to remind me who was in charge.

"If not a *pet*, then what *is* she, Windalloy?" The woman behind me sounded haughty. "Sorry to tell you, *cupcake*, but it's not in our nature to love humans—even if he's convinced you otherwise."

A lie.

I'd seen, felt, and known Windley's love a hundred times over. Even now, he stood defensively between Ascian and me, shielding me from the cruelty in those lavender eyes.

The echoes stirred impatiently, waiting just beyond my fingertips, eager to strike.

Ascian's calculating gaze studied us. "Tell me, Windalloy, why does the ground glow beneath her?" He tilted his head thoughtfully. "A hex, perhaps?"

"Maybe," Windley challenged, stepping protectively closer to me, "one designed to poison her life force and ward off parasites like *you*."

"No," interrupted the younger lackey, crouching beside me, studying the moss with unsettling fascination. "It looks more like a magical reaction to me. Master Ascian, let me taste her and find out? *Please?*"

Windley's fury ignited instantly. "Anyone tastes her, it'll be the last thing you ever do."

He once claimed his people had evolved past their predatory roots—but the growl deep in his throat suggested otherwise, and the rogue's breath at my neck felt downright primal. Cold menace rolled off Windley in waves, and—goddess help me—I liked the spark it lit down my spine.

"*Interesting.*" The rogue leaned closer, voice dripping with temptation. "Forget the rest of this. Why not come with me— slip into the woods and get good and lost?" His thumbs skimmed my shoulders. "Must taste damn good if he guards you so fiercely."

A surprisingly gentle offer, delivered by such brutish hands.

The woman beside him let out a cutting scoff. "Oh, spare me. Whatever she tastes like, it's probably syrup-sweet. Curves like that always come dripping with sugar."

"*Tear her limb from limb!*"

Dangerous of her to provoke the echoes like that. If Windley didn't act soon, I might not be able to hold them back.

Across the clearing, he remained locked in bitter stalemate with Ascian—his former master.

"Play nice now, Windalloy," Ascian crooned, eyes glittering. "I'd hate for history to repeat itself." He raised his chin mockingly. "You do recall what I did to the last pet you brought home?"

Windley went utterly still, Ascian's wicked smile deepened, and it told me more than words ever could.

Perhaps that was the moment—the exact moment—I realized Windley's past was far darker, far more horrific, than I'd ever imagined.

The echoes stirred, anger surging in response to whatever pain Ascian had dredged from Windley's memories.

"Enough of this," Ascian commanded curtly. "Get her up."

The deep-voiced rogue obeyed, hauling me upright. "Still waiting on that answer, hon."

Answer, *hon?*

As to whether I would run away with him here and now?!

"Clearly it's a no!"

"Too bad." My captor's rough grip grew rougher, while the female twisted my wrists painfully behind my back.

Meanwhile, beside me, the lackey with the youthful voice lowered his hood.

Not what I'd expected.

Not predatory. Not menacing.

He looked younger than Rafe—moon-pale skin, round cheeks, vacant eyes, and pastel-lilac hair. A youthful face, yet something about it felt slightly off, like a portrait hung unsettlingly askew.

"Wow," he breathed softly, light eyes widening in surprise. "No wonder Windalloy likes you. You look a lot like Flor—"

"Don't talk to her, Pip," snapped the woman.

My heart lurched. "Wait—who do I look like?"

The woman yanked my hair viciously. "Did you not hear me, *worm?* Don't speak to Pip. He's impressionable."

Across the clearing, Windley's head whipped toward us, eyes narrowing dangerously. "Did you say *Pip?*"

"Obviously," the woman sneered. "Who'd you think we were?"

Windley's expression shifted—from disbelief to recognition, then darkened into something worse.

"*Charmagne?*"

The woman laughed harshly, followed by scorn dripping

from every syllable—"Took you long enough. Don't you recognize your own sister and brother, *idiot?*"

It took a moment for her words to fully register.

Even then—

My voice stumbled, gracelessly failing like a fish floundering on land, as surprise snagged in my chest. "Windley...is this your *family?*"

I searched Pip's youthful face for some resemblance—but aside from those sharp-tipped Spirite ears, I found nothing. If these truly were Windley's siblings, did that mean Ascian was their father?

Wrong.

On all accounts.

Windley's response sliced the air like a blade:

"*I have no family.*"

The declaration hurt, a dull ache blooming in my chest—but Windley didn't hesitate. In an instant, he lunged forward, hatchets poised to strike.

But before he could reach Ascian, a brutal snap shattered the air.

Thwack!

Windley froze mid-step, weapons falling slack at his sides. My eyes darted toward the sound—and for the first time, I noticed the whip in Ascian's grasp. Three cruel tails gleamed beneath Luna's cold rays, coils shimmering like serpents poised to strike again.

A flicker of naked fear flashed across Windley's features, rare on him and unbearably painful to witness.

I loathed it. And I loathed the man who put it there.

But loathing was dangerous when nurtured by darkness.

Within the strongest rogue's grip, I began to tremble violently—a tempest of emotion brewing beneath my skin, pressure building until I could no longer contain it.

"Windley!" I cried desperately. "Duck!"

Power surged from my core as my neck wrenched back—

And when my lips parted, darkness burst forth.

"Pip, watch out!" Windley shouted, diving to the ground as my vengeance billowed toward Ascian like storm clouds overtaking the sea.

"He has no merit!" My voice mingled with the echoes, warped and savage, as shadows swallowed the forest in an opaque, roiling fog.

Pip heeded Windley's warning, cowering beside my glowing feet. Charmagne and her brutish companion released me, startled by the sudden eruption of my power.

I didn't pause to see what had become of Ascian or his cruel lavender eyes. Seizing Windley's arm, I pulled him into the swirling darkness, taking advantage of the chaos. We ran blindly, slipping away beneath the veil of shadows as it consumed everything behind us.

"Wait!" Windley protested. "Camp is the other way."

"They're dangerous, aren't they? Then we're not leading them back to Beau."

I wouldn't let them near her—not even one taste.

Windley cursed under his breath. "Then follow me—I recognize this place."

He took the lead, guiding us expertly through dense tangles of greenery. The only sounds were our rapid breaths and the quiet snap of twigs beneath our feet.

Eventually, the shadows behind us began to thin, darkness giving way again to pale, silvery moonlight. For a moment, the forest fell silent—just the steady rhythm of our breathing, and Windley's grip on my hand.

Until—

"Ugh," he teased, casting a wary but playful glance my way. "Must you always be so damn magical?"

My glowing feet made me a beacon in the night.

With a forced smirk, Windley scooped me into his arms, like some damsel from a storybook. But the smirk was a lie. That confrontation had cut him deeply. I could see it in the tightness between his brows and the careful swallow at his throat.

All I wanted was to find someplace private, someplace safe —to soothe the hurt away.

"Windley?" I tested hesitantly.

"Queenie?" he echoed, pressing a tender kiss to the crown of my head.

"Has your memory returned?"

His jaw flexed, eyes clouding. "I'm afraid so. That headache—it was my memory elixir breaking. Now I recall exactly why I chose to forget." His voice grew strained. "Ascian's power... I should've known it would eventually call me back."

My arms curled more securely around his neck, holding him close. "I won't ask you to relive anything painful, but... when you're ready, I'm here."

"I know," he hummed. His hold strengthened—a little possessive, a lot protective. "You're the only one I'd trust with it anyway."

This time, his smile was genuine. The tension eased.

Thank goddess.

We pressed onward, creating distance between us and the dangers behind, moving deeper into the safety of the woods. But Windley glanced back just once, to whisper—

"Pip...he never escaped..."

Eventually, he slowed, sharp ears straining for signs of pursuit. When satisfied we were alone, he carefully set me down, immediately burying his face in his hands—as if that simple gesture could erase the nightmare we'd just survived.

"You shouldn't be caught up in this, Majesty," he murmured bitterly. "But it's too late. You've been seen, your glow's been seen. And after that display of shadow puppetry, you've certainly piqued Ascian's interest." He cast uneasy eyes toward the surrounding darkness. "Our best bet now is finding shelter. I know a place."

"But can we really hide?" I asked. "That man said they 'felt' your power. Won't they sense where we are even now?"

Windley shook his head. "It was my power they tracked, yes. Because I've been using it recklessly down here—if only I'd remembered to be careful." His jaw tightened as he glared angrily at his blackstone ring, glittering ominously in the night. "That's what was pulling me toward them, too—Ascian's energy. I didn't realize it until now. It's been too long since I've felt another Spirite's ripples. I guess I never expected to come back this far south."

"Ripples?"

"That's how it feels to us when another Spirite uses their power—like ripples of energy. Stronger near the source, weaker with distance."

"Can you still feel his now?"

Windley exhaled tiredly. "No," he admitted, grim. "But not for the reasons you're hoping. More than likely, Ascian's shut it off completely. Unfortunately, by shouting my warning, I betrayed your attack. I doubt your spell reached him."

I'd feared that. But—

"I'm not sorry I used it," I insisted, firm—maybe even *defiant*.

Windley chuckled quietly. "Sorry? Why should you be?" He captured my fingers, bringing them to his mouth with gentle reverence. "I was foolish to imagine you'd just sit there silently. You're hopelessly incapable of it."

Love.

It was love shimmering in his eyes as he laughed down at me.

Love etched into his brow as he mapped a plan to keep me safe.

Love lingering on his lips as they brushed against my skin.

Charmagne—or whoever—had no idea what she was talking about.

"Our ride home will be slower," Windley warned, caution threading his usually cocksure tone. "Just you and me this time. Can you manage that?"

A scatter of images flickered:

My empty bedroll beside Beau's; Albie's mustache whitening by the day; the council chamber I'd abandoned, drought charts still unsigned.

I pressed my thumb into the gold of my signet ring. A young queen, yes—*reckless*, perhaps—but the crown still sat firmly on my shoulders. Hard sums and harder choices were nothing new. And this one was simple: shielding Beau, her unborn heir, and the scraps of her cavalry from Ascian's horrors mattered far more than any ledgers languishing in the Crag.

Supporting Windley as he faced his past tugged at me with an ache I couldn't quite name.

"My mettle isn't on trial," I said, steady but with a spark. "Lead on, Windley—try not to lose me."

Oath and heartbeat fell into step together. I would follow him—monsters in tow, shadows nipping at our heels—because some crowns are carried farther than a council hall.

I tried to remember, even then, that monsters cornered do not whimper.

They bite.

2

THE PROOF OF SCARS

Windley's destination lay somewhere in the west, and he kept glancing upward between the trees, charting our course by the stars.

As we walked, I pressed the filigree whistle to my lips and gave it breath, hoping to summon one of the widowbirds that had swarmed Beau upon her release from Giant's Necropolis—each bearing one of my outdated messages on its ankle. If one appeared now, I would immediately send it onward—to Albie, to the others—to tell them to return home. That we would follow soon. That we had to be certain no evil trailed us.

I still didn't fully understand the danger posed by the lavender-eyed man and his lackeys, but I knew enough—I couldn't risk leading them to Beau. Not while most of her cavalry lay incapacitated.

So I followed Windley, granting him the silence he needed to sift through the memories now flooding his mind. I saw them clearly behind his eyes, reflected in the steady rise and fall of his chest, and I traveled quietly beside him, fighting the urge to offer to share the burden.

As the sky shrugged off its cloak of darkness, dawn revealed the first signs of Windley's destination. The forest floor, once untouched, became speckled with slabs of stone—weathered relics half-swallowed by moss and ivy. At first, they lay scattered. Gradually, they gathered—walls broken by tree roots, archways shattered by time—a city long abandoned, overtaken by the forest.

"You've been here before, Wind?"

He stood gazing out over the fallen queendom, dappled in shifting forest light, looking more pensive than I'd ever seen him.

I reached up to tuck a piece of rose-colored hair behind his ear, but he caught my wrist before I could finish.

"You called me that before, too—*Wind*," he murmured. "It seems you only call me that when you're worried." His gaze softened, drifting somewhere distant. "I have been here before. It was my home, briefly." Shadows flickered across his face, memories weighted. What a strange existence. It was like his wounds were covered but never fully healed. "Don't worry, darling. I'll make sure they don't find us."

That wasn't what worried me, and he knew it. But Windley was a bottler. And if he was going to uncork at all, today wouldn't be the day. He was focused on the mission of keeping me safe, and it was a fine mission to occupy him.

Besides, he was wrong—I didn't call him that only when I worried. I called him that because it felt good on my tongue.

"Well, then, Wind," I said, reclaiming my hand and sliding it up to his collar instead. "Since you've shown me to your old home, you must at least show me to your old bed."

The shift worked as intended. His throat bobbed as his gaze found my grip. "Our bashful queen says things like that now?"

If it meant bringing him back to himself, then yes.

"I'm accustomed to being tucked in."

"Careful, queenie. I'm still a predator at heart." With a confident tug, he slipped an arm around my waist and led me deeper into the ruins.

If only it truly were that easy to distract him. Eight years was enough time to know precisely how to handle him. This was all a shallow game for his sake. If I hadn't learned, our monster might have died.

They were fickle things—the monsters created with those closest to our hearts. They could wither just as quickly as they bloomed. It took careful understanding to nurture a monster, and ours wouldn't survive without missteps.

I let the keeper of my monster lead me through the deserted queendom, over stone and scree, until we reached what seemed to be a courtyard overtaken by debris. Overhead, broken arches suggested an arcade long ago reclaimed by ivy, winding elegantly around cracked stone columns.

Windley unbuttoned his cloak and spread it neatly across a dense pile of leaves.

"No beds, I'm afraid. This will be the most rugged night you've ever spent in the wilds, Queen Merrin. Will your royal sensibilities survive it?"

Normally, he'd tease, bowing low and mocking my station. But now he wore a different expression altogether.

Poorly masked shame.

He was ashamed of making me sleep in a place like this. Ashamed to be the reason I wasn't curled comfortably back at camp in the queens' tent beside Beau.

He should have known me better.

Mirroring him, I unbuttoned my cloak and laid it beside his. "You're forgetting the night we fell asleep on the tree fortress's veranda. It took Beau forty minutes to pick the bugs from my hair."

He stared at me, and when he blinked—

Love.

That was persistent love, chasing away the shame.

"Yes, I forgot who I was dealing with. Queen of sticks and squalor—lest we forget the state of your own chambers."

"I didn't realize you'd noticed."

He reclined onto our makeshift bed. "I've seen cooks' pantries tidier than your royal quarters."

"I like it that way!"

"I didn't say it was a bad thing. Now rest, twiggy queen— I'll keep watch." With a catlike grin, he reached to coax me down beside him.

Good. He was himself again—for now.

But that hand of his was suspicious.

"You need sleep too, Windley." Arguably more than I did. And I certainly wasn't letting him subdue me with cuddle powers.

Caught, he withdrew his rejected hand. "I'm not letting you sleep unguarded, Merrin. You're still a queen. I'll be fine."

Luckily, I was no longer just a queen—but a *magical* one.

I placed a finger to my lips—"One moment"—and leaned back into darkness, blocking out whatever protest Windley had prepared.

The shadows greeted me more calmly than usual, their aggression spent on Ascian mere hours ago. Invisible hands skittered against me, carrying me through airy darkness, awaiting my intent.

"Hello, little terrors," I whispered, surprised by the fondness creeping into my voice. "I'd like a favor, though I'm not certain it's possible."

"MerriN?"

"Those without merit skulk in the brush. I need protection from them."

"We will tear them limb from limb! We will pull the flesh from their bones!"

"We don't need to go that far! Not yet. Can you just keep watch for those without merit and wake me if they enter this place?"

Inside my head, a chorus of non-human whispers debated the request as though it were something new and thrilling. They sounded inquisitive, eager, sloshing about in the unseen world. I let them mull it over, turning a deaf ear to one particular voice hovering at the outskirts—clearer than the rest and fighting for my attention.

Exitium.

The one who'd caused me to kill Bartolomew.

I didn't want their advice.

But I wasn't offered a choice.

In the absence of a solution, the swirling darkness parted like a curtain, giving free rein to Exitium's influence.

"Hello, Merrin," they purred, slipping into my ear like a serpent.

The shadows tightened around me.

"What you seek is possible. Release the ones you call echoes and hold them there. They will do as you command."

They? Not we? So, Exitium considered themself separate from the rest of the darkness?

Uneasy, I waited for them to speak again, but Exitium withdrew, dissolving into the swirl of shadows. The remaining echoes stirred, as though sensing the promise of secrets yet to be revealed.

"MerRIn!"

"*mERriN!*"

"*MErrIN?*"

What kind of villain was I? I had sworn never to use them again, yet already, I'd called on them twice since.

"Merrin."

That last one was real. I opened my eyes to find Windley squinting at me.

"What are you scheming in there? I told you to go to bed."

"Ordering me about now, are we?"

He groaned, rubbing his eyes. "Merr, please, you're very cute, very hard to resist, and this is a lot of responsibility for me —you are a foreign queen, after all. I'll be fine."

"Sorry, *Sir* Windley. This is what you get. Admitting this to ourselves means I get to take care of you just as much as you take care of me. You should know me well enough to realize this won't be a one-sided thing." I tipped my head cleverly. "And besides...I think I found a way for us to sleep protected."

His frown softened into amusement, a playful spark dancing at the edges of his mouth. "What, with your little shadow tricks?"

"Little?" I scoffed.

"I'm all eloquence tonight."

"And every night," I giggled.

A drop of forest light caught in his gaze as he studied me sidelong, humor and intrigue flickering there.

And maybe...a little pride.

Now I knew how Rafe felt all those times I'd gawked.

"Who am I to deny a queen's command? Go on, then."

I tipped my head back, inhaling deeply as I pulled the echoes closer. When I exhaled, darkness spilled forth in a trembling cloud. It hovered around us until I guided it downward with a thought, settling it into a pulsing haze that rolled outward like mist, creeping across the arcade before spilling farther, spreading like ink over the ruins' floor.

"If anyone enters this place, I'll know. The echoes will shout at me."

Windley prodded at the smoky haze with the toe of his boot. "How certain are you of this?"

"It's wholly untested."

"A pleasant rest it will be," he said dryly. With a shake of his head, he took my arm as if hauling me up a cliff—only to sweep me down beside him.

"Like a tripwire snapping, I'll be able to tell if the ground is disturbed by anything large enough to cause concern. I felt it just now, when you pushed it with your toe. I won't let harm befall us."

Smirking at my heroics, he cast one last cautious look around before pulling me closer. "You may be a fine ruler, Merrin, but I've said it before—you would've made one hell of a guard."

I had no response. Even without the use of his power, his arms wrapped around me set my blood racing. I nuzzled into him so he wouldn't see the heat coloring my cheeks.

This was our first night sleeping alone together, but there'd be no "canoodling," as Windley liked to call it. Instead, he hugged me tightly to his chest, using my warmth as comfort while he silently chewed over the events with Ascian and his so-called family. Though his body felt reassuring against mine, his thoughts were somewhere far away. I waited for his breathing to slow and deepen before finally allowing myself to drift.

Some hours later, I woke to find Windley sleeping as heavily as if we were safely back at the fortress, his hair a spill of black-blue silk, eyelashes dark against his cheeks.

So, he trusted my power after all. It was gratifying to see him relieved of the weight of his memories—and satisfying to see him surrender to my protection.

Perhaps he'd been right. Maybe I truly was better suited to guard than to rule.

The early morn was cool enough to turn the embrace between a wayward queen and her borrowed guard from inappropriate to necessary. His warmth was my shield, his steady breaths my comfort. And while birds settled into the ruins, attempting to stir him with their morning song, Windley remained determined to sleep off the exhaustion of the previous night.

He lay turned on his side, the small of his back exposed and chilled from an untucked shirt. I reached to pull it down for him, but curiosity held my hand hostage. Careful not to wake him, I eased the fabric farther—not for any promiscuous reason, but to confirm a theory.

As my fingertips brushed against the disfigured strips of flesh hidden beneath, my throat closed tightly. The scars were clustered in groups of three—matching perfectly the three-tailed whip the lavender-eyed man had cracked through the air.

Trauma lingered within those wounds. Horrors etched deep into his flesh.

Now I knew.

The lavender-eyed man—Ascian—had been Windley's tormentor.

"We will scorch the skin from his muscle!"

Yes. We would end him.

Whatever else lay ahead, of this I was certain.

When sleep reclaimed me, I drew Windley closer than ever before, heart racing frantically, hoping to shield him from nightmares I couldn't yet understand.

"Argh! Why must you insist on spooning *me*, Merrin?"

We stirred slowly in the afternoon warmth, golden sunlight dancing lazily over the rubble. Windley looked significantly less bedraggled now, though one cheek bore the distinct imprint of a leaf.

"Because it feels right?" I offered.

"But I'm twice your size!" he complained, anguish thickening his voice theatrically. "It defies all laws of ergonomics. You're like a stubborn little turtle shell clinging to my back."

I scoffed indignantly. "Excuse me? Men have perished dreaming of a turtle queen clinging to their backs."

No man had ever perished for such a reason.

He turned toward me with mock severity, hair tumbling forward as he hovered close. "In all the ways I imagined us in bed together, I was never once the little spoon." He groaned dramatically, rolling over me as I sank deeper into our leafy nest, my breath catching with delightful anticipation. "You think you're adorable—" He stopped himself mid-complaint, his voice softening warmly. "Well, it's true."

He leaned in, brushing the gentlest kiss to the tip of my nose before nuzzling against it, breath fluttering over my skin.

Self-indulgent queen that I was, with Windley poised above me, pinning my hand against ivy, biting his lip as he studied my mouth with sinful intent, I wanted nothing more than to forget his wounds, my darkness, and fall headlong into ecstasy with him.

But that was not meant to be.

"*MeRRin!*"

At that moment, the echoes and their carpet of fog surged urgently, alerting me that someone without merit had breached our refuge.

3

TWO BIRDS

Windley's hatchets were drawn, blades thirsty for blood they hadn't yet tasted.

"Can you sense which way, Merrin?"

"Over there!" I thrust a finger toward the far side of the ruins.

"Over there?" His brows furrowed as he lowered one hatchet. "Why would Ascian approach from that direction?"

"I don't know, but this time, I'll be ready." I began tipping my head back, summoning the dark currents already rising within me, but Windley caught my chin with careful finesse.

"No, lion queen. I'll handle it. You don't need more blood on your hands." He raised his brows. "But back me up?"

I suspected this was about more than sparing me guilt—Windley wanted to shield me from the darkest parts of his forgotten past.

With the echoes pounding against my temples, he drew me stealthily behind the remnants of a crumbling wall that had once guarded the courtyard's entrance. His pointed ears twitched, listening intently.

"What the hell?" he muttered, head tilting in confusion. "That doesn't sound like—wait, is he—?" His brows lifted in surprise, then he cast me a bemused sidelong glance. "Chap's got quite the mouth on him."

"Chap?" My pulse leapt. "You mean it's—?"

Windley stood abruptly from our hiding place, hatchets dropping to his sides as his voice carried easily across the ruined courtyard. "Oi, chap! Queen Beau lets you kiss her with that mouth?"

"*You!*" snapped a distinctly familiar, tightly wound voice. "*Finally!*"

I scrambled to my feet, relief flooding through me as Rafe emerged from the trees, looking spectacularly rumpled and sour-faced beneath an emerald cloak. He wasn't alone. He clutched a length of string—the other end tied to a flustered black bird with an absurdly elongated tail.

"Rafe!" I stared incredulously. "You leashed a widowbird? They don't exactly thrive in captivity."

"You think?" Rafe retorted tersely, immediately paling with horror at the tone he'd taken. He sank to one knee at once, voice contrite. "A-apologies, Your Majesty. It's been a frustrating morning, stumbling blindly through the forest after this creature. Beau insisted it would lead me straight to you, but it spent more time pecking itself free than guiding."

Probably because he'd tethered it like an errant kite.

Windley raised a hand to hide his amused grin. "Queens— they think they can get away with anything because they're cute."

Rafe was clearly not in the mood. He swatted irritably at the bird as it swooped at him again, then waved an exasperated hand toward Windley and me. "And what exactly is this? An elopement? I'd expect this sort of reckless escapade from *him*, Your Majesty—but from you? What of your subjects?"

"It wasn't intentional, Rafe. We merely went for a walk and encountered some trouble in the woods." I paused, glancing toward Windley. It was his choice how much more to share.

Windley hesitated, carefully scanning the shadows behind us before speaking. "Something unfavorable is after me," he said, eyes serious, "and now it's caught wind of our rantipole queen."

Rafe folded his arms skeptically. "Something unfavorable?"

I crossed mine too. "*Rantipole?*"

Windley ignored my protest, holding Rafe's stare. "You said Merrin's magic surpasses even the elders of your clan, yes? Mine too, as it turns out. But what if there existed a being who could steal such power—and worse, it's now seen hers?"

So that's why he hadn't wanted Ascian to witness the echoes.

Rafe's expression grew impossibly drier. "Nothing's ever simple with you two, is it?"

"Yet it was *your* affair that sent us out here in the first place," Windley retorted smoothly.

"And it was *you* who stole Her Majesty away in the middle of the night. *Again*," Rafe shot back without hesitation.

"Enough," I interrupted, stepping between them and gently freeing the bird, which perched gratefully upon my shoulder. "You both sound like bickering fogies. It doesn't matter whose fault it is. Rafe, return to camp and tell Beau and Albie not to wait for us. We'll ensure our trail is clear before heading back."

Rafe frowned, uneasy. "Respectfully, Your Majesty, you'd be safer returning with me. Beau's guards could help defend against this threat."

Absolutely. Not.

Windley interjected before I could object. "Chap does have a point, queenie. If you return with him, I can lure Ascian away by turning on my power. If your safety is our priority, it's not a bad plan."

"But why would we resort to that when it's my power that can end him?" I argued.

Windley's gaze warmed, a quiet sadness flickering through his eyes as he carefully set his hands on my shoulders. "Are you truly so eager to kill...?"

Again.

I knew he'd nearly said "again." A Bartolomew-shaped lump formed in my throat.

But beneath Windley's shirt were scars I could never forgive—and they fed the darkness now pulsing hotly inside me, a darkness finally finding purpose.

Beau had been right to warn me.

"The one pursuing you caused pain, didn't he? To you and others? His death will be worth any defilement to my soul."

"Admirable, Merr—but as I said, if Ascian gets his hands on you, he'll try stealing your power for himself."

Why was he resisting me so fiercely on this?

There was something else—something he wasn't telling me.

"Windley," I said, my voice hesitant, "have your feelings for me... If they've lessened since regaining your memories..."

People often tell stories in the absence of understanding...

Sometimes even me.

He seized my hand with sudden precision, pressing it firmly to his chest, where his heartbeat thudded beneath my palm. "Don't start with that. If anything, they've..." He shook his head, a flicker of conflict in his eyes. "Never mind." His frown deepened, his voice gentler yet fiercely sincere. "No, lion queen, this isn't some crude attempt to ditch you, if that's your worry."

Then why did it feel as if, once he left, he would never return?

As if reading my thoughts, Windley offered his most impish smirk. "Do you really think I'd give you up after all that?"

But "all that" had happened before he regained his memories. Would he have still stayed near me, professed his love, if he had remembered that something "unfavorable" was after him?

A creeping heaviness settled in my stomach at the thought that he might do something rash to shield me from his dark past —even if it meant erasing himself from my present.

"The other option is to take her back by force," Rafe proposed.

"Rafe!" I scolded.

His expression remained stony as ever. "It's my *job*, Your Majesty."

Windley's smirk vanished instantly. "No. Never again. Your job may be to keep her safe, mate, but mine is to keep her happy. While I agree it's best she returns with you, that's her choice." His keen eyes pierced mine. "So—what's your decision, Queen Merrin?"

I'd learned from years of ruling that responding to a question with another question was an effective way of subtly highlighting flawed logic.

"Can you honestly tell me you have a better way to defeat Ascian than using my power?"

A long, long pause.

Then Windley exhaled a thin, frustrated breath. He flicked a dismissive hand at Rafe. "Could you just—step away for a moment?"

Rafe stared without smiling longer than was necessary before turning away, petty as ever.

Windley leaned in, lowering his voice. "Listen, Merrin. This isn't easy to say because, truthfully, I'd love nothing more than to steal you from your world and hide you somewhere no one could ever find you. But—I also know if I want to keep you, you have to return with Rafe. There's a good reason I took that elixir. I've done things I'm not proud of, and I'm not sure a queen who fights injustice will forgive them. If you keep following this path with me, your opinion will change."

So that was it. Not about ditching me, nor sparing me guilt, nor even shielding me from Ascian—though perhaps those too. Mostly, though, it was about preserving my image of him. Protecting the feelings woven around it.

Buying time, I looked away, gathering thoughts scattered by nerves. "As I've said before, Windley—what makes you think my opinion of you is favorable now?"

"I'm serious, Queen Merrin."

"Don't call me that—it feels too distant now."

When Windley first arrived at the Clearing, he was still a youth. Whatever he'd done before that, he'd chosen to change. He'd traveled far to escape his past—something undeniably admirable.

"My feelings aren't so fragile, Windley. I'll return with Rafe only if you genuinely believe there's a better way to defeat Ascian than my echoes."

He groaned. "This card again? While your power is likely the only thing strong enough to kill what Ascian's become..." He looked at me as if I might disappear with the sunset. Only this time, there was no quiet reverence—mere worry. "We'll need to be strategic. I have to explain what makes him dangerous. Can I have a few more days with you before I do?"

"Of course."

His dark eyes lingered over mine, carrying a depth of emotion I couldn't yet grasp. Before I could reach for him—

Rafe came barreling toward us, startling the widowbird off my shoulder. Windley shot it a sour look before stiffening at the sight of Rafe's drawn sword.

Something much larger than a wind stag was tearing through the forest, snapping branches in its wake.

And it was heading straight for us.

"Damn!" Rafe cursed. "I thought I'd shaken it off!"

"IT?" Windley demanded, already shifting into a defensive stance.

"Something's been tracking me—off and on—for hours."

"And you led it directly to the queen?!" Windley's voice hardened.

"I wouldn't have had to come find her if you hadn't stolen her in the first place!" Rafe snapped irritably. "Besides, it went quiet hours ago—I thought I'd lost it."

"Waiting for you to drop your guard, *clearly*." Windley's grip tightened around his hatchets.

Rafe lunged forward. "Don't blame me that your southern forests are home to unknown barbarism! Need I remind you, this is *your* motherland, Windley?"

"Whatever is large enough to topple trees isn't native, *Rafe*. If it's after you, then you're the reason it's here."

"Enough!" I commanded sharply, watching the trees splinter closer. "We don't have time for this."

"You're right." Windley's fingers circled my wrist, suavely guiding me into a crouch. He and Rafe exchanged quick, guard-like signals, but my attention snagged on Rafe's sword. It lacked its familiar frosty glow—Luna's exile had clearly stripped it of enchantments.

Some would argue an easy price to pay for a freed heart.

It must have been why Windley took point. With hatchets at the ready, he whispered, "Listen to Rafe," before slipping from our shelter to gain a clearer vantage.

Rafe nodded tightly, directing in a low voice, "Stay here, Your Majesty," before darting toward a fallen spire, his focus locked on the splintering branches ahead.

I strained my own ears, but my listening stretched beyond the physical realm.

"Ones without merit!" seethed the darkness, sloshing around me like a boat on stormy seas. *"Let us eat them! Scald them! Melt them!"*

"How many?" I hissed, words tight with alarm.

"Hundreds! Crawling, swarming, flying!"

"H-hundreds?!"

"Coming for the conjurer!"

"For Rafe? Why?"

The darkness churned in confusion, unable to answer—until, like before, the turmoil parted, releasing the voice I least wanted to hear.

"A pact-less conjurer is as ripe as the fertile grounds of spring," Exitium murmured eerily. *"Until he finds another celestial, vile things will hunt him. One draws near—a crow. Defeat it, or watch it devour his heart."*

"A crow?" I echoed, bewildered.

A sudden, harsh cry from Windley pierced the air beyond the ruins.

"Go now!" Exitium roared, ferocious. *"Or it will consume both their hearts!"*

Ignoring Rafe's startled protests, I broke from the shelter, sprinting toward Windley's defensive stance in the sunlit courtyard.

"Lion queen?! I told you to stay back!"

I skidded to a halt. "What is THAT?"

I'd expected a simple crow—not this towering fiend looming over him!

Vaguely human, it stood unnaturally tall, its gray skin bristling with jagged black feathers. A cloak of dense plumes dragged behind like a sinister pelt, and coal-black hair framed a pale face set with milky, vacant eyes. Those haunting eyes locked onto mine, pinning me in place with immediate, *magical* dread.

"Hold your ground and speak your intent," Windley growled, blocking its path.

"*Bold*," hissed the crow, its voice a rustling autumn breeze. "I seek the conjurer. Where is he? I hear his heart beating nearby, unchained."

"It's after Rafe," I whispered. "The echoes said it wants to eat his heart—and yours."

"Mine?" Windley flashed a savage grin, baring sharp canines. "That's curious. Surely you know what I am, wraith."

"I do. I'll settle for your liver instead." As the crow's gaze slid toward me, Windley shoved me behind him with a protective motion, never taking his eyes off the creature. "Just a human," he lied with practiced ease. "Not suited for refined tastes."

"Something tells me her heart might be. Why else guard her so closely? *Your* kind isn't exactly known for companionship."

"Come now," Windley purred, voice low with challenge. "Someone as ancient as you should know better. She is my companion—and the only way you'll taste her heart is over my corpse."

"Fine by me. You first, then the conjurer, then the sweet-smelling girl for dessert." The crow spread its shadowy shroud wider, and darkness pooled at its feet.

"Wait!" I cried. "You really want to fight?"

"Fight?" The crow's beak twisted into a cold smile. "This won't even qualify."

I held my ground. "Are you sure? Leave now, and I won't have to destroy you."

"You?" Amusement rippled through the wraith's voice.

"How presumptuous. For that insult, I'll eat you first—and slowly."

Shadows began to seep across the ground—trickling at first, then faster, devouring every patch of sunlight until the ruins drowned in darkness.

"Merrin?" Windley's voice was urgent. "Now would be a good time to crown-up!"

"I—I can't! My eyes won't close! They're stuck!"

"What?" Windley spun toward me. "Stuck?"

Yes—I'd been desperately trying to summon the echoes for some time, but those milky eyes held mine open, locking me out of my own darkness. "I need to close my eyes to reach the echoes, but I can't seem to break contact!"

Windley pressed a palm over my eyes. "Does that help?" I shook my head. He cursed under his breath. "We need a distraction!"

But the distraction came from the crow instead. Its feathers rustled violently, launching razor-sharp quills toward us. Windley lunged forward, twin hatchets flashing. Steel clashed with feather in a shriek of impact, driving him backward. Teeth gritted, he planted his feet, muscles straining against the unrelenting barrage.

Precisely as the creature had intended. "Shall we wager how long he can remain standing?"

At this rate, it wouldn't be long.

Luckily, another ally had already heard Windley's call.

"Hey!" Rafe's voice sliced through the chaos, halting the fiend's assault. "I'm the one you're after—my heart's the one you want!"

The crow paused, letting out a dark chuckle. "When dinner marches willingly onto the plate... Plucky."

But Rafe's diversion worked. The crow's chilling gaze flicked away from me, as the magician stepped from the shadows, brandishing his enchantment-less sword, giving me the opening I needed.

In a fraction of a heartbeat, I squeezed my eyes shut—

And fell into darkness.

The echoes surged eagerly, clamoring for my command.

"Now," I urged. "End the one without merit!"

But instead of lunging outward, the shadows hesitated, swirling restlessly.

Then—a voice.

"Speak my name."

My spine went rigid. "No."

The shadows constricted around me like tightening vines. *"The others cannot defeat this wraith alone,"* Exitium coaxed. *"Your enemy is too powerful. Speak my name—or witness the conjurer's end."*

My pulse raced, Beau's warning echoing vividly in my mind: *We train our whole lives to resist their pull. Be careful, Merrin—they're dangerous.*

Exitium felt most dangerous of all. Was this a trick? A calculated cornering? Yet Rafe stood defenseless, his sword stripped of power, and Windley's strength faltered under the relentless assault. Once again, no time remained to deliberate. Once again, it seemed I had no choice.

I clenched my fists—

And surrendered.

"EXITIUM!"

The name tore from my throat like a curse, and darkness erupted in answer. A surge of blackness burst from deep within me, flooding outward, swallowing ruins, sky, and wraith alike.

A deafening shriek split the air, driving me to my knees as the world tilted sickeningly—

Then silence.

Slowly, the darkness receded, dissolving around us like ink

in water—and from my throat in ribbons of black vapor. I gasped desperate breaths, fingers clawing weakly at the stone beneath me as the last strands of darkness melted into nothingness.

The wraith was gone.

Rafe crouched nearby, hands clasped tightly over his head, breathing heavily.

And Windley—

Windley held me in his arms, chest heaving, lips warm against my hair. "That," he panted shakily, "was entirely too close. Perhaps we shouldn't ever look anyone directly in the eyes—ever again, yes?"

"You said 'ever' twice."

"On purpose."

I pressed my ear to his chest, fingers gripping instinctively into the fabric at his back. He noticed, tipping his head down curiously.

"Windley...you do have a heart, don't you? Earlier, the way you spoke made it seem almost like—"

His lips brushed against my forehead, voice meant only for me. "Haven't you felt it yourself? Of course I do. Just not the kind he was after."

"Oh."

He smelled wonderful, felt comforting beneath my touch, his chest rising through the fabric of his travel-worn shirt. My fingertips drifted lightly upward, grazing flushed, inviting skin at his neck.

"Merr..." Windley murmured cautiously, carefully—

But before he could finish, Rafe let out an exhausted sigh and nudged the feather-strewn wraith remains with his boot. "Thank Luna that's over."

Windley lifted his head slightly. "*Luna?* Still holding onto that, chap?"

Rafe paused, reconsidering. "Habit. Though I suppose I should really thank the queen instead."

I finally pulled away from Windley, blinking up at Rafe. "Don't thank me yet. The echoes said that thing was after your heart. Until you pact again, more will come. Hundreds, perhaps."

Rafe's expression darkened grimly.

Windley released an exaggerated breath. "Yet another beastie chasing us down, courtesy of you." He rested his chin comfortably atop my head. "Nothing's ever simple *with you*, is it, chap?"

Rafe replied with a deadpan stare.

"It seems you're stuck with us awhile," I told him, voice pitched to a calm reassurance. "We can't risk sending you back to Beau with hundreds of—whatever that creature was—trailing behind you."

"A wraith," Windley muttered, reluctantly loosening his hold on me.

Rafe's frown deepened.

"And what exactly is that?" I asked.

"Nothing we want to tangle with," Windley said, rolling his shoulders and warily scanning the aftermath. "Dead things that siphoned scraps of power from a goddess—not enough to ascend, but enough to linger, twisted between realms."

I swallowed nervously. "Then why are they after Rafe?"

Windley studied Rafe. "Consuming the heart of someone capable of channeling a goddess's power likely strengthens them."

Rafe's knuckles whitened around the hilt of his sword. "You're saying that unless I pact again quickly, more will hunt me down?"

I nodded. "That's exactly what the echoes warned."

Rafe hesitated, troubled. "But my clan is bound to Luna. I

was hers from birth. I wouldn't know how to pact with another celestial." His gaze dropped lower, worry clear. "If my pact's broken, what about my people? Will these wraiths come for them too?"

Windley let out a low breath, lifting one shoulder in a reluctant shrug. "Unlikely. A goddess's power transcends realms. Luna's exile only means she can't create minions here. But your personal pact being severed—she must've known the consequences for you."

Rafe's jaw tightened. "And now you're an expert on goddesses?"

Windley studied his nails. "I've remembered a thing or two."

A memory sparked.

"That steward at Sestilia's," I cut in. "He was a magician too, wasn't he, Rafe? His belt had a glow—different from yours. Perhaps you could pact with his goddess?"

"Soleil," Rafe supplied. "The sun goddess. I don't know much about her."

Windley tilted his head thoughtfully. "Soleil, eh? In that case, perhaps we could kill several birds with one stone."

"Windley, no!" I gasped, leaping protectively before the widowbird, who'd just dared flutter down from a nearby tree.

Windley blinked, confused. "What—oh. No, Merrin. It's a southern expression." He eyed the widowbird with obvious disdain as it nestled in my hair. "All I mean is, we've got several pressing issues at once."

A new goddess for Rafe. Ascian and his minions. Windley's murky past.

Those were surely at the forefront of his mind.

But there were others here too.

Exitium's whispers, growing stronger. The Crown's mysterious "long-awaited purpose" Luna had cryptically mentioned.

And...

It's not in our nature to love humans—even if he's convinced you otherwise.

Your kind isn't exactly known for companionship.

Windley's gentle voice broke through my troubling thoughts. "You all right, lion queen?"

He and Rafe both watched me curiously.

I blinked quickly, realizing I'd drifted.

Luckily, I had years of practice daydreaming through royal conferences. The key was confidence, as if lost in important deliberation.

I raised my chin decisively. "Very well. Rafe, send the widowbird back to Beau, informing her we've gone to find you a new celestial and that I've temporarily taken charge of Windley while he resolves personal matters here. She and the others should head home without delay. With danger pursuing each of you separately, we must put distance between us. Windley, proceed with your 'multiple birds, one stone' plan."

"Multiple birds, one stone?" Windley smiled playfully. "You heard our queen, Rafe. I assume you have parchment handy?" Then he darkened his voice, brushing his lips teasingly against my ear. "You'll be protecting us then, Merr? With your shadowy forces? And what exactly do you mean by 'taking charge' of me?"

"No," Rafe cut in tersely. "Enough of that. I endured enough of your boundless flirtation on the way down here."

On the way down here? But we'd been so discreet.

Windley chuckled roguishly, eyes briefly flaring emerald. "Oh, that was nothing. I'll show you flirtation so masterful it should be illegal."

Rafe's tone was arid as desert sand. "Please don't."

I, meanwhile—"Windley! You just used your power! Ascian will sense our location!"

"Relax," he assured casually. "It was just a whisper—only enough to give him a general direction. The idea was to draw him away from Queen Beau and Sir Albie, wasn't it?" He gestured impatiently toward Rafe. "Better hurry with that letter, chap. And then the feathers."

The feathers? I'd clearly missed something.

"Nice cover," Windley whispered smugly, eyes glinting with knowing amusement. "But you missed my entire brilliant plan, didn't you? Hmph. I've watched you for years, Merrin—I recognize all your *tricks*. Fine by me; you didn't object." He grinned briefly, then leaned closer, expression softening to concern. "I also know when something's troubling you. You don't have to say anything, but if you feel the need—"

I pressed my finger to his lips. "You're already the one I'd go to."

4

THE EDGE OF NOWHERE

"If you're screwing with me, so help me—"

"Chap, why's it so hard for you to believe I'm on your side? Go on, then. Take them off. Good luck with the wraiths."

Feathers.

They were arguing about feathers.

Windley had theorized crow feathers stuffed into Rafe's clothing might mask his scent from the wraiths hunting him. The logic was sound enough—at least in theory. But Windley was only eighty percent confident it would work, and Rafe was one hundred percent annoyed by the prickly, musty plumes now invading every crevice of his wardrobe.

That was the first part of the "brilliant" plan I'd missed.

The second was our destination.

"The Edge of Nowhere," Windley recapped as we left the ruins behind. "Legendary coastline, vivid with colors of sea and sky you won't find anywhere else in the realms. Believed to be the handiwork of a goddess, so, naturally, perfect for us."

"I've never heard of such a place. How far?"

"They say if you follow the coast long enough, you'll reach it," he replied with a casual shrug.

"'They say'? So it can't be marked on a map? Are you even certain it's real?"

"Says the woman with glowing footprints and shadowy whispers inside her head. Southerners believe it exists as surely as your northerners believe the southern mountain does—well, *did*." Windley nudged me. "It's one of our staples. Like your otter and crane tale."

Ugh. Mother Poppy's favorite—and decidedly not mine.

"Fine. If it's real, Rafe could contact a new goddess there," I conceded. "But what other 'birds' are you planning to stone along the way?"

"Goddesses aren't particularly fond of my kind, but they adore Rafe's. If he charms her right, we'll secure an ally strong enough to help finish Ascian once and for all." Windley leaned in, mischief at the corner of his mouth. "Think I should offer him pointers?"

I pressed a palm to his chest, easing him a step back. "And why wouldn't goddesses like Spirites?"

He frowned, clearly displeased that lore interested me more than his advances. "Because we aren't their children."

"No?"

"No, our foremothers were...something else."

"Oi!" Rafe barked impatiently from ahead. "Which way?"

"Well, definitely not that one," Windley called, like it should be obvious.

"Then come up here and guide us!" snapped Rafe. "You're lagging when you're supposed to be navigating! How did I get stuck with you again? Your Majesty, of all the guards in the queendom, you want this one?"

"You're the one who crashed our honeymoon," Windley

drawled. "If you hadn't interrupted, I surely would've devoured our virtuous queen by now."

I flicked Windley's neck. "Says who?"

He feigned a wounded pout.

At least Rafe's arrival had distracted him from his troubled memories. If anything, Windley seemed even more himself—maddeningly so.

Unbearable, Beau had once called him.

Yes, perfectly, wonderfully unbearable.

I'd promised Windley a few days before we tackled Ascian's mysteries, and he seemed determined to fill them with playful avoidance. It was the best way to help him cope: humor him, tease him, and let him process on his terms.

We traveled along the overgrown trail leading away from the ruins toward the forest beyond, moss devouring the stones beneath our feet. As daylight waned, our pace quickened. Provisions were limited, and we needed to leave the Emerald Wood to resupply soon.

Windley, however, didn't seem overly concerned.

"Why's chap so sullen, anyway?" He murmured, elbow resting heavily on my shoulder as he nodded toward Rafe. "Worried about Beau's wrath when she gets our message?"

"Hmm. Might it be because he's only just been reunited with her after weeks apart, they haven't spent but a night together, and now we've dragged him away, this time even farther from home?"

"Ah, right." Windley acted as though it was a sudden revelation. "Though if we hadn't, that wraith would've attacked a significantly less magical queen, yes?"

True. A genuine sudden revelation for me.

"You realize Sir Albie won't let this go easily," Windley mused, watching Rafe slash irritably at unruly branches. "If

Rafe found us using that bloodthirsty bird, your knight might try the same."

"In my letter, I specifically ordered them not to follow. Beau will enforce it."

"I don't know, Majesty. Guards have been known to break oaths for you."

His tone was light as ever, but the look he cast me tingled my skin. I recognized that look now—understood it differently.

I hesitated, unsure how to respond. Should I embrace my queenly duties and refocus our attention on the mission? Or perhaps fall back into our familiar banter, keeping my head held high and resisting his antics? Most tempting of all—should I inch closer, hoping his arm might find its way around my shoulder?

How did one properly shift from friends to...whatever we'd begun to become?

I couldn't imagine calling him "darling," or holding his arm at some formal gala. Instead, I pictured teasing him mercilessly. Challenging his wit. Racing beside him through the Scarlet Wood. Meeting his devilish grin with one of my own. Or...letting my hands slip beneath his shirt as he pulled me onto his lap—

"Merrin?" he interrupted, scattering my thoughts.

His moss-colored hair ruffled in the evening breeze, softly illuminated by fading sunlight. Desire tugged insistently at my chest, driving the rhythm of my heartbeat.

His gaze drifted into the trees, evading mine. "Would you think me a coward if I took another elixir?"

"Of course I wouldn't!" I said swiftly, recalling his scarred skin. "But..."

His brow lifted, curiosity piqued.

"It doesn't seem like something you'd do," I finished honestly.

He hesitated, lips curving into a faint, self-deprecating smile. "Don't let me fool you, queenie. Even the strongest of men are weaker than they pretend."

I tilted my head skeptically.

He chuckled, plucking a twig from my hair. "Fortunately, I've never technically qualified." He studied the stick briefly, then tossed it aside. "By the time we find civilization, you'll look positively feral."

"*Southern* civilization," I revised. A curious concept, as anything beyond the queendoms was considered barbarous back home. "How far?"

"Walking? Week or two."

"'Walking,' he says, as if there's another option," Rafe interjected, perpetually grumpy.

"There is, actually," Windley said airily. "I'll show you tomorrow when we reach the golden field. Tonight, let's find shelter for our queen. I'll catch dinner. You...relax."

Normally, Rafe hunted, but Windley had likely volunteered because of Rafe's lost enchants.

"I can still—" Rafe began, but Windley had already disappeared into the amber dusk, ignoring sentences once they ceased being interesting.

Rafe sulked impressively, hacking at brush to fuel a fire. I busied myself loudly snapping branches, giving him the space from conversation he clearly desired.

After dropping an armful of sticks at his feet, I turned to gather herbs and trumpet bulbs—the bulbs weren't particularly flavorful, but they held enough moisture to sustain us until we found a proper stream.

"Your Majesty," Rafe said, stopping me before I'd fully stepped away. "I'm sorry."

Surprised, I glanced back.

He knelt by the fledgling fire, hair more disheveled than usual. "I'm sorry for being ill-mannered. I have no excuse."

"Firstly, you're far better mannered than Windley, who makes you look like a saint. Secondly—" I placed a friendly hand on his shoulder. "You do have an excuse. I hate leaving Beau too, especially so soon after getting her back. I understand why you're frustrated."

He said nothing, so I proceeded with care.

"But...Beau is precious—and Windley's pursuers are dangerous, and now you have wraiths on your trail. Beau's strong, but she's...shiny. Too shiny for all this. We must protect her."

Rafe stared into the fire's dancing flames, clearly weighing his words. "Beau isn't the only one worth protecting, Your Majesty. You shouldn't underestimate yourself." An earnestness crept into his voice that was rare for him. "I'll do better tomorrow."

"Let off steam when you need to, Rafe. I've always wished you'd be yourself around me."

I left him to his preferred solitude, warmed that he was opening to me, wary of pushing too hard—

"He's right, you know."

I nearly jumped out of my skin. Windley had been waiting —no, *lurking*—behind a nearby tree. Before I could scold him, he whisked me out of sight.

Ambush, indeed.

"If anyone sparkles, it's you, my queen."

His fingertips skimmed my jaw, tipping my chin until our gazes caught—dark, intent, dizzying. He played this game too well. My traitorous heart thudded.

"I'm afraid I'll dull you if I get too close."

"You could always test that theory—closer, I mean." The words escaped me in a hush.

A velvety laugh. "You're staring at my mouth again. Hoping I'll kiss you?"

"Certainly not," I lied, lifting my chin like an invitation.

"Shame," he whispered, honey-warm against my cheek. "It's all I've thought about since you woke me."

A shiver rippled through me. With a theatrical sigh I relented. "Fine—but only because you groveled so prettily."

He leaned in. My palm found his chest, fingers curling into the heat of his shirt just as his lips brushed mine—

Of course I do. Just not the kind he was after.

I couldn't help myself.

"Checking for a heartbeat again?" he teased.

"Of course not," I murmured, though heat flooded my cheeks.

His hand covered mine, pressing it firmer to his chest until that steady rhythm pounded against my skin. "Didn't know they could race like this until I met you."

The world fell away. Campfire crackle, distant voices, all dissolved into the charged air between us. My lips parted, drawn inexorably toward his, hungry to erase the last breath of space—

"Fire's ready." Rafe called from the clearing. "Dinner?"

Windley let out a noise of quiet reluctance, his forehead nearly touching mine. "Impeccable, *always*. Hold that kiss for me, lion queen—I'll be back for it."

With a teasing peck against my brow, he stepped away, leaving me flushed, breathless, and utterly frustrated beneath the shadowed canopy.

Windley tossed Rafe his catch—grouse, naturally.

"Is this meant to be a stand-in for that widowbird?" I asked over dinner, watching him across the flickering fire. Windley looked far, far too smug while he ate.

"For all you know, it *is* the widowbird."

I snorted. "I'd like to see you try catching one."

"That sneer suggests you doubt my hunting prowess," Windley said, pressing a hand to his chest in mock offense.

"You couldn't," Rafe cut in. "I spent an afternoon with one of those bastards."

"I don't understand your hostility," I huffed. "Widowbirds have served as companions to royalty for generations."

Windley cocked his head, tugging at his forest-hued hair. "Your definition of 'companion' might differ slightly from mine, lion queen."

Companions.

Your kind isn't exactly known for companionship.

I shook off the troubling echo.

We slept beneath a coverlet of shadows set to guard against those without merit. Rafe was bundled miserably in the crow's feathers, while I was comfortably wrapped in Windley's cloak. With our fire now reduced to a soft, ember glow, the campsite was illuminated only by the nocturnal shimmer weaving through the trees. The air was flavored like a serene autumn in the Scarlet Wood—familiar, nostalgic. The night breeze drifted politely across the clearing, rustling foliage and reminding us we were nearing this forest's edge.

Sleep eluded me—not from discomfort, but because comfort had never felt so intoxicating.

Windley was solid and grounding. Unlike last night, exhaustion hadn't robbed us of tenderness. I burrowed my face against his chest, inhaling deeply. Warm pine resin and ever-green sap, sweet and heady, with just a trace of amber-musk—his scent lingered like magic.

I marveled at the strangeness of this closeness.

These arms holding me—warm, steady—were Windley's. His touch. His embrace. Never would I have imagined him holding me like this, so open and endearing.

Not Beau's bastard of a guard whose origins had turned out to be so much more complicated than I ever guessed.

"Shhh," he murmured softly over my head, tightening his embrace.

"I didn't say anything," I whispered back.

"It's not your mouth; it's your mind. I can practically feel your musings." His voice was sleepy but amused. "Rest, lion queen. We have an early start tomorrow."

Stupidly perceptive incubus. I nestled deeper into his cloak.

Five peaceful minutes passed before he sighed—a long, drawn-out breath signaling surrender. "Alright, queenie. What is it? What's stopping your lungs from growing heavy?"

I tilted my face upward in the dimness, feeling him tense when I finally admitted, "This feels peculiar."

"This? Our embrace?"

"Mm."

His frown was slight, concern threading quietly into his voice. "You mean it feels unnatural?"

Oh—I hadn't considered how that might sound.

"No," I quickly amended. "Quite the opposite. It feels completely natural. That's precisely what's so strange. My body relaxes into yours as though we've always done this."

His muscles immediately eased. "Goddess, queenie, don't scare me like that."

Comfortable silence followed. Then slowly, his hand traced the curve of my back, fingertips grazing along the hem of my shirt, toying idly with the fabric as if debating whether to lift it or let it fall aside.

He had a gift for subtle, maddening touches. I tried—and failed—to keep my breathing steady.

He cleared his throat. "Maybe it feels natural to me because I've imagined it since the moment we met."

"Are you implying love at first sight?"

He chuckled. "Funnily enough, down here it's called love at first scent."

Blood flushed hotly beneath my skin. "You smelled me first? Exactly how keen is your sense of smell?!"

"Shhh. You'll wake the grumpy one." His fingers moved upward, lightly tracing between my shoulder blades, his voice dropping to a low hum. "I can't say why it feels natural with you. But—I'm glad it does." His tenor changed fractionally, as did the nature of his touch, becoming more careful. "It gives me hope," he whispered, "that maybe you'll withstand what I have yet to tell you."

His dark past. The things hidden in his memories.

Perhaps the cork in his carefully bottled truths was beginning to shift, loosened by pressure only he could truly release.

"I don't understand what you're worried about, Windley. Whatever happened in your youth isn't who you are now. I'm reasonable enough to accept that a person's soul can change."

His response was immediate, quiet, and unsettlingly sincere. "And if a person has no soul?"

My throat tightened involuntarily at the ease with which he'd voiced such a thought.

He must have noticed, because he quickly added, "Teasing, love. Just thought I'd give you something new to puzzle over after the heartbeat discovery."

Playful deflection—typical Windley.

I searched his eyes; he gave the slightest shake of his head, asking me to leave it there.

I'd allow him as long as he needed, as promised.

"Wouldn't matter," I murmured, settling into his reassuring warmth and solid contours. "Always suspected you were a soulless devil anyway. Somehow I'm sure it would only make me love you more."

A faint grin twitched at his mouth. Eyes closed, he winced softly and drew me nearer.

The embers crackled, throwing warm gold across his lashes. I followed him into the soothing dark behind our eyelids—but the night wasn't quite done yet.

Just as sleep tugged me under, he spoke again, his words drifting like a phantom through my hair:

"It was wrong of me, Merrin, to steal your heart. If you decide you want it back, I wouldn't blame you. You deserve to know you have that choice."

His confession carried a quiet honesty I'd never heard from him before.

"But rest assured, my lionhearted queen—every stolen beat was worth it. Whatever comes, you're the only one who has ever truly held my heart—and you always will."

My breath caught, and I inched closer, pressing my cheek to his chest where his heartbeat thrummed—steady, sure, entirely mine. In that rhythm, I heard a promise far older than either of us.

I was beginning to understand how right Beau had been when she offered her advice.

It's easier than you'd think...and also more painful.

5

WALLOPS AND GAZELLES

U nder the morning sun, it was as if last night's confession had never been spoken. Windley was lively, flirty—normal.

"Hand me that knife, chap?"

"You sure you want the knife?" Rafe drawled. "Wouldn't another utensil better suit you?" Though all other utensils remained back at camp with Albie and the cavalry.

"Damn it, Merrin! Do you see what your spooning has done to my reputation?" Windley protested dramatically. "We can't let Rafe think you're in charge!"

"Her Majesty is queen," Rafe pointed out dryly. "She is in charge by default."

"He's always like this," I said, folding my arms. "What's wrong with a woman spooning a man? I see nothing improper about it."

"It has nothing to do with you being a woman!" Windley threw up his hands. "It's simple logistics! The taller person should always be the biggest spoon—it's literally in the name."

He jutted his lower lip in an over-dramatic sulk. "Besides, you feel lovely to cradle. How am I supposed to smell your neck if you're behind me?"

Smell my *neck*?

"You're the one who rolled away," I reminded him archly. "I didn't force you into submission."

"Oh, believe me, queenie, you forced me." He lifted his chin darkly, stretching his neck in a way that accentuated his sharp jawline and toned physique. "Next time, I'll take charge by whatever means necessary."

Effective.

Windley was—as always—nearly insufferably hot. It was difficult to reconcile this teasing, cocky version of him with the Spirite who'd held me so tenderly the night before. Not only was his past more complex than I'd imagined—everything about him was.

"Just let me know if you'd like me to cut off his hand, Your Majesty," Rafe deadpanned.

"Start with a different appendage," I suggested sweetly.

Windley smirked, shirt lapping dangerously in the wind like an attractive sea rogue. "So that's what you're daydreaming about?"

"It's going to be much worse this time, isn't it," Rafe grumbled, "without Sir Albie to maintain order?"

Windley had deliberately withheld details from Rafe about our encounter with Ascian and the others. He'd explained only that using his powers now acted as a beacon, drawing something unfavorable from his shadowed past.

Rafe remained oblivious to the pain hidden beneath Windley's casual bravado—and Windley clearly intended to keep it that way. Charmagne had been right about one thing: the Clearing's incorrigible guard was remarkably adept at playing pretend.

I did see the cracks. Lingering glances, prolonged silences, looks he stole when he thought I wouldn't notice—as though imprinting my image permanently into his memory, convinced our relationship was to end soon. He was certain I wouldn't love him once I knew the truth, yet I was equally certain he wasn't the villain he believed himself to be. In fact, I suspected quite the opposite—that Windley had been a victim.

I knew his bold, magnetic nature was armor. My imagination tormented itself, wondering what horrors had forced him to forget his past and flee to a land where his kind was scarcely known.

These dark musings stirred my companion shadows.

"The lavender-eyed man has least merit!" they seethed. *"Least among all two-legged creatures. We shall punish him most harshly!"*

It sounded like a fine plan. Even without knowing Windley's full story, the omens spelled disaster for the man with lavender eyes.

We emerged from the trees into sprawling golden plains as though birthed anew into open, endless space. The breeze, temperate beneath the canopy, was wild and free here, tugging playfully at our clothing, beckoning us deeper into the rhythmic sway of grass.

I forced away memories of crimson-stained blades and the life ended by my own hand.

"We're here." Rafe shifted impatiently. "What's this miraculous new mode of travel you promised?"

Windley pointed toward distant gray creatures lumbering lazily, small-horned gazelles prancing nearby. Wallops, he'd called them last time.

"You intend to catch one and ride it?" I asked.

"I wouldn't say catch."

"Seduce?" I guessed.

"*Entrance*," Windley corrected indignantly.

Rafe shot me a sidelong look. "Seduce," he confirmed.

"Seduce," I echoed.

"I liked you better when you were afraid of her," Windley griped at Rafe, who merely rolled his eyes.

Windley turned back to me. "I'll need to expend considerable energy, meaning others might sense our location."

"Then we'll need to move quickly afterward," I said.

"And I won't be able to do it alone," he continued meaningfully.

Then I'd once again be sustenance for an insatiable fiend.

"Fine." I nodded, trying not to seem eager. "How do we proceed?"

His smile betrayed his delight. "My power doesn't affect all animals, but Wallops—the larger ones—are easy enough to tame. They're also much quicker than they look and strong enough to carry three at once. I just need to lock eyes with one, close enough through the grass." He indicated a thicker patch. "Follow me quietly."

"They look rather intimidating," I whispered as we crept forward. "Will they bite?"

"Bite?" He chuckled. "No, they use their tusks defensively, but they prefer to flee."

Despite his reassurance, their enormity grew more apparent as we approached—gigantic creatures towering over us. Mounting would be impossible without their compliance.

Windley, confident as ever, singled out one solitary wallop feeding lazily on grass. "He'll do. Ready, Majesty?"

Perhaps too ready.

I gave a shaky nod, and with exaggerated care, Windley lifted my fingers toward his mouth—then reconsidered, releasing them with a sly grin.

"Wind?" I questioned.

"This will be better." He cupped my face, pausing for the briefest moment, before leaning in to press his mouth to mine.

My heart jolted—first from surprise, then from the warmth of discovery, and finally from an overwhelming tenderness. His fingers were respectful yet possessive, restrained yet longing— as though fearing he might break me. My own hands found his hair, pulling him closer as fire raced through my veins.

Then everything intensified.

That initial sweetness transformed into something more potent as Windley began feeding from my affection. Waves of pleasure and longing pulsed outward through every inch of my being, overwhelming me. My soul yearned to melt into his.

I loved him—utterly, fiercely.

"Ah!" Windley wrenched himself away, his breath ragged. "C-careful, lion queen. I haven't... Your feelings..." He swallowed hard. "I took too much. Are you all right?"

I was in no state to answer, too lost in his eyes—mesmerizing, candescent apricot.

"Chap!" Windley hissed urgently. "Mind taking her shoulders? I'm afraid she'll collapse when I let go."

"Don't look at me with those things," Rafe spat, shielding himself with his forearm. "I'm not interested in becoming your lover."

"Shame," Windley managed a weak quip, gaze still locked on mine with undisguised longing. "You're missing out." His grip tightened on my shoulders, attention entirely focused on me. "Merr...I want more, but I've already taken too much." His hands slid slowly along my shoulders, up my neck, and back again—shaking with obvious restraint.

"Get on with it," Rafe prodded, taking hold of me. "You've a beast to 'entrance.'"

Windley reluctantly let go, and the second he did, my knees weakened—but Rafe steadied me. My eyes remained fixed on Windley, hypnotized, noting a peach-colored glow trailing behind him. I felt compelled to follow, and would have if he hadn't clearly instructed,

"Stay with Rafe," before cautiously approaching the wallop.

As Windley grew closer, the other wallops bolted, their massive feet pounding like drums, leaving only one behind— his chosen target, caught in a trance as compelling as my own. It froze, a single eye locked onto Windley as he spoke in a soft voice, as if narrating a story meant to lull a child into dreams—his hand coaxing. The creature wavered, stepping backward yet reaching forward tentatively with its trunk— torn between instinctive fear and the irresistible desire to draw nearer.

I recognized the struggle—and, like mine, the wallop's own curiosity ultimately won.

The instant the creature's trunk touched Windley's palm, all tension evaporated. It nuzzled him eagerly, as affectionate as an oversized kitten. I might have found humor in the sight had I not been enveloped in Windley's lingering spell.

A moment later, the wallop knelt obediently, allowing Windley to grasp its massive ear, place a foot onto its bent knee, and hoist himself up gracefully onto its back.

"Like that, Rafe," he called smoothly. "Can you bring the queen? Looks like she's deep under my spell. Just hold her waist, I'll summon her." His luminous stare softened upon finding mine again. "Still with me, my queen? Come to me now." He reached his hand toward me, glowing, inviting.

"Hell, that guy's scary," muttered Rafe, but I barely registered it, too absorbed in Windley's beckoning.

I took a hesitant step forward, legs still wobbly, so Rafe

guided me to the creature's side, boosting me upward into Windley's waiting arms.

His gaze returned to normal as he positioned me, yet remnants of the apricot warmth stuck, clinging to my senses long after golden fields transformed into an ocean of rich blue blossoms—a sight both foreign and breathtaking. Each bloom was delicate yet unified, rippling endlessly toward the horizon like an unbroken floral sea.

Windley had been right: the wallop moved with astonishing speed, turning the scenery into a blur once he commanded it to run.

I sat securely between my guards, cheek resting dreamily against Windley's back, Rafe steadying me from behind.

"How long will she be like this?" Rafe asked.

Windley hesitated, voice tinged with mild guilt. "...A while."

"Next time, contain yourself."

"Right," Windley said, rubbing the back of his neck. "Won't let it get that far again. But with her, it's..." He paused, jaw tightening as his gaze slipped toward me, drawn like iron to a magnet. "It's nearly impossible. You have no idea. But I'll handle it better next time."

Secretly, I wanted it to go even farther.

It was evening before I could manage coherent speech, and even then, my words weren't especially impressive.

"Windley," I murmured weakly, voice rasping against his shirt.

"Majesty!" He whirled around instantly, gripping my shoulders and examining my face. "Has it finally left you?"

"I believe mostly so. At least enough."

"Thank goddess." Relief swept across his face, chased almost immediately by remorse. "Merrin, I'm sorry—I took far more than I meant to. You deserve better. My self-control seems to vanish around you, but next time I'll be ready."

He'd clearly spent hours berating himself for that lapse.

"It did give me a few blessed hours with my thoughts blissfully quiet," I confessed, voice gentle. "You've muzzled that gift for years just to stay near me, so one slip was bound to happen. But next time—*just a sip, not a draught.* I'd like to stay upright long enough to...enjoy it."

I slid his hand to my waist, grounding us both. "Because, Windley—knee-buckling euphoria or not, you nearly toppled me." The corner of my mouth quirked. "One more thing: why apricot this time?"

His brooding melted into a sly grin. "Wondering why not *emerald?*" He leaned closer, voice low and intimate. "That shade is reserved for you alone, my queen."

A pointed *ahem* came from Rafe behind us.

Windley wrinkled his nose, turning forward again. "We'll travel through the night. Any objections?"

"Not if it means breakfast," Rafe said, rubbing his stomach.

"We'll have to hunt or forage," I pointed out. "Sir Albie has all our money."

"Or," Windley suggested artfully, "if we find a town, I could simply...coerce supplies."

"We aren't bandits!" I chided.

He waved it off smoothly. "Trust me, they'll consider the experience worth the price."

Rafe shot me a sidelong glance, one brow raised. "Seduce?"

"Seduce," I agreed.

Windley *tsked.*

"And if the next settlement is full of men?" Rafe asked, skepticism thick in his voice.

Windley shrugged. "The plan stays the same."

I blinked. "Wouldn't that feel...odd? Using your gift on men?"

An unmistakably Northern question, yet Windley didn't flinch. "Not at all. You saw me use it on Phylo, remember?"

True—back on the road to the Necropolis.

Catching the puzzle still in my eyes, he added, "I connect with spirit first, body second. Looks matter—granted—but what draws me is the soul. The last person I want to touch is someone with a rotten spirit; their shape is irrelevant."

Then his gaze slid back to mine, voice dropping to a purr. "But don't worry, my queen—yours is irresistible on both counts."

My eyes drifted traitorously to his mouth again.

He noticed, lips quirking upward at the corners.

It truly was unfortunate Rafe sat so near.

The sun's last rays faded to one side as, from the opposite horizon, something else ascended. None spoke it aloud, yet we all watched anxiously, waiting to see if Luna's glittering face would appear.

"Phoo," Windley exhaled finally. "You're in the clear, chap."

But he'd spoken too soon.

As if summoned by his taunting words, Luna's giantess eyes flicked open, gazing directly upon us. Though logically she might look anywhere, it felt chillingly personal—as if the moon goddess had marked our tiny, scandalous trio atop a Spirite-charmed beast.

"Oop. Nope, there's our gal," Windley noted. "Who do you think she hates more—the man who rejected her or the queen who banished her to the sky?"

"*Not helping, Windley!*" I scolded.

But Rafe had paled for another reason. "Wait—what day is

it?" The magician knit his brows tightly. "Shouldn't she be gold by now?"

Rafe was right. The Gilded Lunar Festival occurred at autumn's dawn, when the moon blazed golden for three nights straight.

"You're right," Windley mused. "Tonight would mark the second night of the Clearing's festival."

Yet Luna's moon shone its usual silvery hue, unchanged from the previous night.

"Perhaps destroying her physical body prevents her from turning gold?" I ventured hesitantly.

"Or she's simply that furious," Windley countered darkly. "I'll breathe easier once we reach the coast and our dear chap here has secured Soleil's favor."

Curiosity nudged me again. "I've been meaning to ask— why are you so certain it's Soleil who awaits us at the Edge of Nowhere? Is southern lore truly that specific?"

"Simple deduction," Windley explained breezily. "Rafe identified Soleil as the sun goddess. The Edge of Nowhere is famously painted by a goddess. Tell me, my clever queen— what typically paints a horizon?"

I felt faintly foolish for not realizing it sooner. "A sunset."

"Or sunrise," Windley added prudently.

"Not bad," I conceded. "You do have your moments."

Windley flashed a wink over his shoulder. "Let's hope Lady Sun finds our chap charming enough."

Rafe, perhaps nursing similar worries, fell silent, maintaining a wary vigil on Luna's gradual ascent.

Making an enemy of a goddess wasn't ideal, yet I reassured myself it had been necessary.

For Beau.

For her child.

I tried to remain alert, tracking Luna's steady path until she passed her apex and began drifting toward the western horizon —exactly as expected. Only once I was certain the moon goddess intended no immediate harm did I allow Windley's presence, the cool night air, and our mount's steady sway to lull me toward sleep—still failing to grasp just how dangerous it was to anger a goddess.

Foolish of me, truly.

6

LUNA'S TREACHERY

"**H**old the queen!"

Those words jarred me awake. The voice belonged to Windley, while Rafe's arms cinched tight around my waist, and the wallop beneath us was hurtling faster than ever.

"What's happening?!" I squirmed, twisting in Rafe's stalwart hold.

"Luna!" he shouted, tightening his grip to prevent me from tumbling off our charging mount.

Luna?

Confusion flashed through me as my gaze swung upward—and froze. The moon, stamped with Luna's eyes and lashes, hovered impossibly at the center of the sky, though I'd watched her clearly begin descending toward the western horizon before I slept. Somehow, she had reversed course and returned to her apex, lingering overhead and spilling a fuzzy beam of golden light behind us, marking our position precisely.

Windley snarled curses skyward. "That jealous moon-hag stretched the night! She's tracking us with that beacon *thing*!"

"Beacon?" My heart skipped, panic rising.

But before he could answer, a chilling cacophony erupted behind us—guttural snarls, savage screeches, and flapping wings flooded the darkness. Wraiths poured from the shadows, hundreds strong, crawling, surging, and flying after Luna's golden shaft of light.

"That beam is guiding them straight here?!" I gasped.

"That's why she didn't turn gold?" Rafe realized.

"Exactly!" Windley spat, spurring the wallop faster. "She must've conserved power—saving it just for us. Great job, Rafe. Court a celestial, ghost her, and now the night itself is stalking us."

There was no time for banter. "Rafe, switch places with me! You hold me secure—I'll hold off the wraiths while you take a moment to commune with Luna directly!"

"There are too many of them, Your Majesty!"

"I mean only to buy us time! Try to reason with her, Rafe! You cannot give her your heart as promised, but maybe she will take mercy on you if you appeal to her! Explain to her what it is to be a reborn mortal!" I used his shoulder to balance myself, already maneuvering myself toward the back. "Windley, keep us steady!"

Windley dutifully leaned forward, gripping the wallop with his knees, corded muscles taut as he pressed our mount onward. Rafe slid into my former spot, anchoring me securely with a firm arm around my waist. Stabilized by his hold, I drew a deep breath and fell into a cool, shadowy world.

The echoes caught me with a soft bounce.

"*MeRRin!*"

"*mErrIN?*"

Their excitement flurried close, awaiting permission.

I gave it swiftly. "Now!"

Their eagerness distorted into rage. *"Tear them apart! Rend their souls! Destroy the unnatural!"*

We moved as one—Windley guiding the charging wallop, Rafe fastening my body, and my hands thrusting toward the darkness behind us. The echoes surged, shadows erupting like arrows into the monstrous swarm. Wraiths sizzled and exploded, yet countless more came forward, undeterred.

"Rafe?" I shouted desperately over my shoulder.

His voice was tight, strained with urgency. "She either can't hear me—or refuses to listen!"

Windley swerved the wallop, dodging a group closing in from the east. "Try your magical babble—lift your sword! Maybe she'll notice that!"

"Do it!" I urged.

Keeping me pinned securely against him, Rafe unsheathed his now-frostless blade, pointing it skyward. But Luna's stubborn spotlight remained fixed.

A fresh wave of wraiths emerged from the shadows. The echoes barely slowed them this time.

"Not working!" Rafe lashed bitterly. "She's ignoring me!"

Only one option remained. Pulse roaring, I shouted toward the front, "Windley, slow down—let Luna's beam catch us!"

He shot a look over his shoulder, eyes flaring. "This better be one of your brilliant tricks, queenie."

"Trust me!"

"Always have." He hunched over the wallop's neck, muscles bunching. "Hold tight!" With a low growl, he reined the beast back just enough for Luna's golden spotlight to sweep over us.

Instantly, the wraiths erupted into frenzied shrieks, excitement doubling as their prey was illuminated. The sound scraped against my nerves, panic spiking.

Windley shouted, "Make your magic sing, Merr—now!"

I snapped my focus upward, locking onto Luna's blinding column of gold. My shadows alone couldn't defeat hundreds— but the swarm wasn't the real enemy. It was the beacon drawing them near.

Gathering every ounce of strength I possessed, I dove inward, plunging into my deepest reservoir of power. Dread coiled in my stomach even as determination pulsed through me, and I released my control in a raw cry:

"EXITIUM!"

Darkness erupted from me, a torrent of searing night exploding upward to collide violently with Luna's light. The golden beam shuddered beneath the force, glasslike cracks racing along its surface. For a moment, darkness fought against divine luminance, vibrating dangerously—

Then it shattered.

Glittering shards of starlight burst apart, scattering like celestial embers over the meadow in a dazzling rain.

"Brilliant, love—absolutely brilliant!" Windley cheered fiercely, his voice triumphant amid the bedlam.

Stripped of Luna's guidance, the wraiths reeled, disoriented. Growls turned to confused murmurs as they dispersed blindly, chasing sparks that flickered harmlessly into the grass.

My chest heaved with shaky breaths, exhaustion dragging at my limbs even as relief flooded me.

Windley maintained our swift pace until silence was absolute, until Luna—now subdued—resumed her journey westward, finally ready to relinquish the night to day.

Rafe murmured an awkward apology for failing to persuade Luna, but I waved it away. My attention remained fixed on the retreating moon, ensuring she intended no further betrayal.

Windley let out a long, relieved breath. "Looks like she finally got the message."

"Thank goddess."

We rode on until Luna dipped behind the treetops, her perilous glow at last receding. Only then did we rein in our mount and slip into a secluded grove.

There the hush settled—uneasy but complete. The echoes fell silent, the night stilled, as though the past hour's chaos had been no more than a passing nightmare.

Another evening spent outrunning magic-spawned terrors. How far away those days of choosing festival sashes felt now—when the greatest worry was the shade of a ribbon or the gossip of a court. What is a royal protocol beside vengeful goddesses, ruinous power, and creatures I can scarcely name?

Life had grown very strange indeed.

"Safe for now," Rafe assessed warily, eyes scanning the darkness. "But we need proper shelter. And water."

Windley patted the wallop's thick trunk. "Just an hour's rest, pup. Then we move again. Same goes for you, chap—I know you're exhausted."

Rafe glanced at me, seeking approval.

I nodded gently. "Rest, Rafe. I caught a little sleep earlier, and Windley—"

Windley raised a guilty hand. "Still overflowing with your stolen energy, love."

I mustered a resigned smile—life with his magic would take some getting used to. "Precisely."

With an exhausted sigh, Rafe murmured something unintelligible, then slumped beside the wallop. Moments later his breathing settled into sleep.

The wallop nudged Windley with its broad muzzle; he chuckled and scratched the creature's ear.

"Who knew you were so good with animals," I said, amused.

"*Some* animals," he replied. "Depends on their spirit—same as people. This one's sweet. *Unlike your troublesome stag.*"

"Ruck is merely misunderstood!"

"Whatever the queen says."

We sat shoulder to shoulder in the grass while my adrenaline ebbed. Above us Luna continued her slow descent, and for the first time all night the air felt calm.

After a long, companionable silence, Windley spoke again. "Rafe's had abysmal luck with exes." He shot me a sideways look. "Though, on second thought, being *your* ex might be the most terrifying fate of all."

"You should be so fortunate. Men have perished for that honor."

No one had perished for that honor.

He laughed—low, rich, reassuring after the chaos. "Someday I'd love to meet these unfortunate fellows."

"Haven't you been listening? You'd need to visit their graves."

His grin sharpened into pure rogue's delight. "Death as the only escape—duly noted." He shifted closer, casting a quick look at the sleeping Rafe. "Still, I do feel for the poor chap. Lucky you were there to save him yet again." A theatrical cough. "Queen show-off."

"It's easy to show off around those with lesser skills," I teased.

He edged nearer, the heat of him brushing my arm. His voice dropped to a velvet hush. "Careful, lion queen. Match your skill against mine and you won't be smug—you'll be *molten.*"

This moment was perfect—genuine, untouched by shadows from Windley's past. I wanted to preserve him like this forever.

Yet my curiosity tugged, tempting me closer toward the mystery of his strange, inhuman heart.

"Earlier," I ventured, guiding our playful banter toward... something else, "when you said spirits matter more than appearances, did you truly mean it? Could I let myself go completely—fill my hair with twigs, devour endless pastries—and it wouldn't matter to you?"

Amusement danced in Windley's eyes. "Firstly, you should devour as many pastries as your heart desires. Secondly, your hair is already full of twigs. Thirdly—is this you fishing for compliments? You already know how I look at you. I'd have thought my attraction painfully obvious."

He was right. My insecurities sought reassurance I already held.

Or perhaps I was just a glutton.

Likely both.

He sighed, as though humoring a very demanding queen. "Alright, I'll indulge you, silly royal." Then his tone softened, warmth glinting in every word. "Yes, your exterior is breathtaking, Merrin, but it's never the first thing I notice. What hits me is the fire beneath it all—grounded and stubborn as a storm-root, blisteringly quick, treating every soul as an equal, and leaping to defend anyone who can't defend themselves. You've got the courage to show your scars and still laugh anyway. Clever, playful, and—goddess help me—still too modest to see how that makes you utterly irresistible."

Each word sank into my chest, melting into an ache I hadn't known was there.

"Now..."—he leaned closer, eyes gleaming with private mischief—"what exactly draws you to me?"

I hesitated, pride tangling with a flicker of uncertainty.

"Stubborn," he purred.

"I'm getting there. Rulers aren't meant to be this

unguarded. I've little practice, and it isn't always easy being gentle with you, Windley."

"And yet," he murmured, "you manage beautifully."

Often it was embarrassingly easy; slipping from friendship to something deeper felt as natural as breathing, even if it sometimes left me fumbling.

And other times...

He chuckled, studying me. "It's entertaining, watching everything unfold behind your eyes. You're usually so sure of yourself. Tell me—you wouldn't call me a weakness, would you?" Chin propped on his knuckle, sparks dancing in his gaze, he hummed, "I'd give anything to step inside your head, just for a moment."

Heat bloomed in my cheeks. I tucked my face against my knees. "You're confident too—strong, witty. You see me exactly as I am, push me when it counts, and never care what anyone else thinks. You say what you want, do what you please. You're playful, fearless, always ready to risk—"

Had he drawn closer? His breath felt warmer, his gaze softer.

Mustering courage, I lifted my eyes. "Yes, I'm capable on my own, but...with you beside me," I whispered, "it feels like I can do more than I ever dreamed."

It wasn't my imagination. Windley leaned in, fingertips sweeping a strand behind my ear; his lips hovered a breath from mine.

"It isn't easy for a Spirite to fall in love," he admitted, voice low but steady. "Yet with you, my queen...it felt inevitable."

My heart kicked. I dragged him closer, kneading the iron-taut muscles along his spine, urging him on without a word. His lips tilted with a reckless vow—then met mine.

Maybe it was the rush of surviving the night, but goddess, the kiss detonated through me.

Those spoken truths only proved what I already sensed: Windley's past would never sway my heart. Eight years of teasing, laughter, and quiet loyalty had forged something unbreakable.

Yet the confession struck him differently.

When he finally drew back, a new shadow crossed his features—not weakness, but a raw uncertainty he rarely showed. He framed my face in one sure hand, thumb mapping the curve of my cheek as though setting it to memory.

"Thank you, lion queen. This is exactly what I wanted in my veins before..." His gaze flicked to the paling horizon—steel tempered with worry, not defeat. "Whatever tomorrow throws at us, know that having your heart today was worth every risk."

His tone carried a thread of finality—as if he'd already prepared to pay some costly debt.

Only then did it hit me—Windley wasn't merely afraid of my judgment; he was convinced he didn't deserve love at all.

When we remounted the wallop, I pressed tight to his back, fingers hooking into his shirt as if I could anchor that doubt away. If I held on long enough—fiercely enough—maybe he'd start believing what his strength had always merited.

7

A HERMIT'S ABODE

"Your Majesty."

The next time I awoke, Rafe's calm voice eased me awake as dawn crept over the horizon.

We were no longer atop the wallop. The beast rested a short distance away, beside a small pool shrouded in fog, reeds glistening silvered in the pale dawn. The wildflowers cushioning me were cool and dewy, but Windley's cloak had been thoughtfully stretched underneath, keeping me dry.

Thank goddess the night had passed.

Again, any goddess except *that* goddess.

The landscape had transformed since I'd last closed my eyes. Though still draped in that endless blanket of blue petals, the plains were now dotted with short, gnarled trees whose brittle branches cascaded with flowers like delicate vines. The scene had a dreamlike quality—ethereal and untouched. A gauzy mist drifted lazily through it all, scented sweetly with renewal and promise.

"I never dreamed the south would be so beautiful," I murmured to Rafe.

Beau would have loved this place. Her prettiness would have blended seamlessly into its beauty. Perhaps Rafe was thinking something similar, for he remained silent as stone, eyes faraway.

Windley, meanwhile, was—

He was—

"Wait—where's Windley?"

"Scouting that place out," Rafe said, adjusting his shoulders as a loose feather drifted from his sleeve.

He nodded toward a small dwelling nestled between twisted branches, which I'd entirely overlooked while admiring the scenery.

"A home! Does this mean we've reached southern civilization?"

"Not yet," said Rafe. "Seems more like a hermit's abode. Windley told us to give him ten minutes to check it out."

Minutes passed quietly in the soothing rustle of leaves and distant birdsong. Then Windley reappeared, waving us forward with an easy gesture.

The hermit's dwelling proved sparse and musty, nearly as web-coated and abandoned as the woodcutter's hut—but after the chaos of our journey, even this humble shelter was a welcome relief. A chance to rest, wash, and fill our stomachs.

Rafe busied himself preparing breakfast from the pond, while I wandered nearby, gathering edible vegetation. Windley sat thoughtfully, stitching wraith feathers into Rafe's cloak with skilled precision, his fingers easily working needle and thread.

Though dawn had fully arrived, the fog remained stubbornly, blanketing the blue-stained meadow in a moody aura. I found myself appreciating its mystery even more.

Windley was finished mending Rafe's garb by the time I returned with breakfast. He may not have appeared the type, but Windley was an excellent seamster. Most guards were, given they spent their days tending queens.

"Anything else need mending, lion queen?"

"My sleeve," I said lightly. "Could you stitch it while I bathe?"

Windley didn't reply immediately, merely watched as I unfastened my cloak and slipped my outer layer off over my head.

"I'm leaving before you offer to wash her," Rafe muttered, bowing exaggeratedly. "I'll tend to the fire, Your Majesty."

Down to my modest undershirt, I balled up my torn garment and tossed it toward Windley. He caught it deftly, raising a skeptical brow.

"In the fishpond, Merr? Did you see the slimy things Rafe pulled from there?"

I smirked at his concern. "Relax. There's a warm spring around back—I found it gathering amaranth. Likely why there's no tub here. The hermit had no need for one."

That suited me fine. Heating bathwater took too long. In the queendoms, most used luxurious bathhouses, bursting with steam, slippery with scented oils. I'd snuck away from Albie's watchful eye to visit them occasionally—even convincing Beau to join once.

"Remember when you helped me sneak Beau out to visit the Clearing's fanciest bathhouse?"

Windley held his needle between his teeth, snapping my shirt straight like shaking dust from a rug. "Ah, yes. Your visits always make for delightful corruption of the others."

Visits.

I've spent years petitioning Albie for a transfer he keeps burying just to serve at your side...

Our monster nudged at me.

"Windley...when we return, I intend to secure your transfer to my queendom."

He stilled, shoulders locked.

"I—only if it's still what you want," I added.

For a heartbeat, melancholy swept over his features—resolve warring with some buried pain. His lips parted to answer, then pressed shut again as he looked down at the shirt in his hands.

"Want isn't the problem." His jaw flexed, voice low and controlled. "Ask me again—after you know everything."

That same note of finality from the night before clung to him, heavier now. I decided to give him space.

I had just turned for the door when his voice caught me. "Merrin...I will tell you. Soon."

Holding back—resisting the urge to press—felt like a wound I couldn't tend. If I pushed too hard, I might break the very thing I was trying to protect.

I steadied my breathing and nodded. "Whenever you're ready."

Then I stepped outside.

Earlier, along with amaranth, I'd gathered lavender and fae's cradle—an herb from the Crag, said to soothe troubled spirits. I blended them into a calming bath.

Surrounded by steam and a meadow of cobalt blooms, I soaked, letting the water draw every mile of travel from my pores. When my muscles finally loosened, I filled my lungs, exhaled, and slipped my mind into the waiting dark.

Shadows whirled up, catching me with a hundred eager hands.

"*MErrIN.*"

"*merRin.*"

"*MeeeerriN.*"

"Exitium," I called into the shifting void, "are you there?"

A ripple of black pulsed outward, spreading like smoke under polished quartz—slick tendrils knotting together until a single column reared up before me, faintly glowing at each seam.

"I am always here, within your soul."

"This isn't my soul," I countered.

"You deny what you know to be true. It is your soul. The false layers are already peeling away. Blood-hunger skims your edges. I needn't ask if you feel it—I know you do."

"I'm not interested in your talk of corruption. I'm only sheltering the echoes; they return to Beau. I will not become what you claim."

I shoved against Exitium's presence—harder than before—but it didn't budge.

"Too late, Merrin. I warned you the first time you spoke my name. The path is forged; you will not wander from it. Together we will speak destruction. Together we will rewrite the world."

A single shadow-arm, denser than the rest, slid upward and closed around my throat.

"Together, we will kill everything!"

"No!" I tore myself free of the abyss. I had meant to ask about the painted coast, Soleil—anything useful for our quest—but that chance was gone. I would not return to that darkness unless desperation forced me.

"We shall see..."

Exitium's final whisper thinned to nothing. Heart pounding, I pushed the void away until only the meadow's hush and my unsteady breathing remained.

Yes, defeating the stags and wraiths had felt undeniably powerful—exhilarating, even—but it wasn't something I wanted to dwell upon, wasn't something I wished to crave again.

To face such power was inherently dangerous.

Windley, Rafe, and I—each of us was battling demons, and our current plan was to have those demons cross paths.

Was that really wise?

Maybe I should've questioned it more.

When I returned from the bath, damp-haired and refreshed, the men sat near the fire.

"We shouldn't tarry too long," Windley said. "Take repose now, and depart at nightfall."

Rafe grunted agreeably.

"I left extra herbs in the spring for you," I said, eyeing their dirt-smudged faces. "Go wash."

Rafe went first, grudgingly scattering a fresh layer of crow feathers across the water to mask his scent.

"Perfect. Now I'll reek of bird and broody swordsman," Windley groaned in mock dismay.

His grumbling coaxed a small smile from me—welcome levity after another brush with the darkness skulking at the edge of my mind.

"Maybe the scent will lend you some of his manners," I teased.

"The wraith's manners?"

"*Rafe's* manners."

He flashed a playful, sharp-toothed grin and tossed my shirt back neatly mended. I pulled it over my wet hair, strands clinging rebelliously to my skin.

"I'm worried," I admitted, tugging at the long ends. "Albie has my brush. It'll be chaos when it dries."

He patted the ground before him invitingly. "Come. I'll use my fingers."

I blinked, briefly surprised by the sincere offer. "You don't mind?"

Yes, guards and handmaids brushed queens' hair regularly, but Windley wasn't my guard—he was Beau's. Yet, the way he gazed at me now, it felt entirely different—more intimate, more earnest.

"Let me take care of you, my queen."

I surrendered willingly, tilting my head back as his careful fingers combed through my damp tresses, slow and gentle.

"You've combed someone's hair before?" I guessed.

A breath of silence, then—

"Long ago," he said, almost haunted.

My shoulders stiffened. "Not Beau—?"

"No." His fingers halted. "My keeper's daughter."

I remembered the brief mention.

"Your keeper... Ascian?"

Windley shook his head, breath catching. "Ascian was my master."

Master.

Just when I thought I understood—

He lifted his hands from my hair and buried his face in them, shoulders bowing as though he'd sentenced himself.

"Windley?" I swallowed a knot. "What is it?"

Slowly his palms fell; storm-dark eyes met mine.

"You."

"Me?"

"Your confidence," he rasped. "You're so sure your feelings won't change. You think it helps, but it terrifies me, Merr."

I gripped his shoulders as though fine porcelain. "I can't help being certain, Wind. You speak of reading spirits. I've read yours. I don't see how that could shift."

When he stayed silent, I ventured, "If you need more time—"

"No." He lifted his gaze; will had replaced uncertainty. "After last night I realized I can't let this go farther without the truth. I need to tell you today."

"What if you shared only what I need for Ascian?"

He gave a single, resolute shake of his head. "Half-truths would be an insult. From the moment my memories returned, I knew I owed you everything. What terrifies me is watching your eyes change after."

"What if...you didn't have to see them?" I suggested.

He went very still, attention fixed on me, waiting.

"I meant every word last night. You're not broken—you don't need salvation, only someone to listen. We could sit back-to-back. Tell me as much—or as little—as you can. Skew it if that eases the telling. I'll keep my 'frightening stare' hidden until you're ready—minutes or days."

Love.

There was love in the way his lashes lifted.

Love in the hand that framed my cheek.

Love in the warmth of his brow against mine.

"Back-to-back, then," he murmured, a vow more than a concession. "But the truth, lion queen. You deserve nothing less."

Under a slate sky in a meadow of blue blossoms, devil and queen pressed our shoulders together.

Then he spoke, and I listened—until I understood.

And the face I wore afterward was, indeed, one of horror.

8

THAT DARK, FORGOTTEN PAST

"Where to start?" Windley clicked his tongue, then exhaled—a weary sound that gave away how long he'd carried this weight, even if only just remembering it. "The beginning, I suppose. Far back."

I stayed silent, thinking only: *It's all right, Wind. I'm here.* Listening was the least I could offer.

"I've told you Spirites outgrew their predatory instincts ages ago. That's...mostly true. But every race has bad eggs, and fate cracked me into a rotten nest."

Fog curled in, cocooning us from the world and softening his words to a private hush.

"My mum died of eternal cough when I was a youngling. Pop raised me alone—quiet man, kind soul, a painter. Landscapes, portraits when the purse ran thin. We scraped by, happy enough...until a fire took him, too."

A raw ache flared in my chest—another orphan, like me.

"The city collected its strays. They shipped me to a boarding school in Farrowel. It wasn't awful. I found other lost kids, started to feel like I belonged—until a 'distant uncle' appeared, papers in hand, claiming guardianship. Only...he wasn't family. He was a man who'd been watching, waiting for me to reach the right age." Windley's breath snagged. "That was Ascian."

He paused, steadying himself. "To understand, you need some geography. The South is mostly human, but you'll find Spirites like me, Naiads, Seelie—and the occasional rarity, like Rafe.

"Spirites wield beguiling. It's outlawed in some public spaces, but behind closed doors, humans pay dearly to feel it. Most want a mild lift—something to ease the nerves. Others crave more...something darker." His voice roughened. "The way your Cove friend did. People chasing carnal extremes.

"The beguiling I've used on you—that's different. There's affection between us, which makes the pull deeper, intimate. But some seek the sensation for twisted ends."

Windley drew a long breath, bracing himself.

"A Spirite's beguiling shows up around puberty—earlier for some, later for others. Pip bloomed early. That's who Ascian hunted: kids whose powers were just waking.

"At first we could only give people a feather-light euphoria —harmless enough. But some clients..." His voice snagged again, thin as breaking glass. "They wanted children precisely because it felt illicit, 'purer.' Ascian sold that thrill and made a fortune off those appetites."

Horror cinched my chest.

"We learned to protect ourselves—little tricks to fend off their hands—but it didn't always work. The first life I took..." His voice cracked. I inched closer, letting him anchor against my calm.

"The money was one thing; power was the point. Ascian loved hexes—curses that siphon a victim's magic. A hex drains the caster too, unless someone else pays the price. We became the conduits."

He fell silent, drawing one slow breath as though sorting memories like scattered splinters of ice.

"This is the worst of it, Merrin."

Guilt rippled through him, yet he pushed on.

"Ascian fitted us with stone rings—gems he swore were cut from the first cave. They let us plant permanent hex-anchors in anyone we beguiled. The marks withered while Ascian drank them dry. We were children—tools—forced into sin before we even knew the word, evil made normal a day at a time.

"He's had other strays—at least one more since I escaped; you saw him, that oversized berk who dared lay hands on you in the forest. Power on power, spirits ground to dust. When he saw your shadow-magic I knew you'd be his next obsession." His voice thinned to a blade. "That's why I tried to send you off with Rafe. The thought of him touching you..." He broke off, breath ragged. "There's nothing worse."

Heat flared at my back—Windley's silent claim.

I braced myself for whatever followed.

"You asked about my keeper," he began, his voice raw and sand-edged. "One of Ascian's clients—rich, ruthless. He didn't just want beguiling; he liked pain."

My nails bit the damp earth.

"I was a mouthy little hellion—Ascian whipped me plenty—but this...this was something else." Windley's head tipped back against mine, a breath leaving him as though he'd just taken a blow. "Ascian spotted another payday and sold me to that man."

I felt his shoulders bunch, the subtle scrape of knuckles tightening against cloth. "Those were the worst years."

I didn't ask how many. I doubted I could bear the figure.

"Once a week Ascian let me visit the others. I took it for

mercy—really, it was another leash. Whenever I begged for freedom, he'd remind me I was maxed-out on hexes, only good for coin."

His fingers twitched, a fine tremor betraying the memory.

"I tried to run—caught. Tried to stab him—failed." He swallowed. "I wouldn't have survived if not for..." His voice lost its edge, dropping to something almost gentle.

"His daughter. The one kind thing in that house. She'd wrap my wounds, sneak food, spin stories on the worst nights. One evening she found the courage to unlock my cell—and gave me my life back."

A short, bitter laugh escaped him. "I bolted—rides, hideouts, whatever I could find. Once I reached open country, I revoked every hex, downed the elixir I'd pinched, and never looked back." He breathed the next words so softly I almost missed them. "Not even for Pip."

He straightened, but tension rippled along his shoulders. "Pip was with Ascian even before me—good kid, timid-hearted, like a brother—and I left him, Merrin...too scared to go back."

The shiver that ran through him then was quiet but unmistakable.

"So there it is, Majesty," he finished, voice rough as gravel. "Villain. Coward. I'm sorry I forced my way into your world. My hands are filthy, my spirit worse. No man deserves you—and certainly not me."

The words fell between us like cooling embers.

So much pressed at my throat—horror, grief—but none of it was for Windley.

"Windley, may I look at you?" When he didn't answer, I whispered, "Wind?"

A faint nod.

Turning, I met his eyes—and my stomach drew tight. I'd never seen him so stripped, so exposed.

His gaze was hollow, shame carved deep. Brows pinched in silent misery, jaw rigid, holding back a flood. The sight speared straight through me.

"Windley." I knelt in the blue flowers, resting a steady hand on his shoulder. Fog still hugged the meadow, thick with the weight of all he'd confessed. "You were right," I said, offering the tears he would not. "My opinion has changed."

He nodded, resigned—until I added, clear:

"In all honesty, you're stronger than I ever imagined."

His breath faltered; he slapped my hand away with a brittle *tch*.

"Don't condescend, Your Majesty." Anguish split his voice. "Maybe you didn't hear me—I set hexes that *stole lives*. Spirits like yours—fed to a monster. I was some noble's toy, locked up like a cur. I abandoned Pip to save myself." His teeth ground. "Don't turn me into the victim."

How could he not see?

I caught his face, ignoring the flinch, and made him meet a blade-bright compassion.

"You're wrong," I said—low, but unshakable. "I've watched countless lives in my realm, and none carried a weight like yours. A hammer isn't guilty when a careless hand swings it. Those sins belong to the wielder, not the *tool*."

Emotion roughened my voice.

"You're no villain, and you're finished being a victim. You survived, Windley—and that takes grit."

Disbelief widened his eyes, as though acceptance were impossible.

I touched my brow to his. "Whether you believe it now or later, I'll champion you until you do. You don't need saving—you already saved yourself. I'll stand beside you anyway, as fiercely as you've stood by me. I'll keep loving you, especially on days you can't. Just promise you'll stay."

We remained like that—only breath and heartbeat—his arms slack, as if the fight had gone out of them.

When I finally shifted to leave, his fingers circled my wrist, drawing me back into the crushed blossoms. He folded himself around me, face buried in the curve of my neck.

Some battles aren't conquered by strength, but by the courage to yield—letting tenderness finish what sheer force never could.

Side by side, we breathed.

Side by side, we grieved—until even sorrow fell silent.

Windley's pulse finally eased, but mine drifted elsewhere, sliding toward the shadows. A low fury coiled in my chest, dark as a starless void, winding itself around every wrong done to my favorite knave.

And amid the storm of revelations, one detail remained unspoken—something Windley never thought to mention, yet crucial all the same.

9

BEGUILING

W indley and I stayed that way for the better part of an hour. I was certain Rafe must've seen us at some point—surely his baths weren't that long—but he didn't interrupt. With our knees pressed in the petaled ground, Windley held me tighter than ever, as though trying to fuse his aura with mine.

And there, in the depths of my soul, was the echoing growl, relentless:

"We will make them pay for what they did. We will tear the flesh from their bones. We will crush them into dust. Our fury shall be so great that none will withstand our wrath. We will destroy all without merit, for we are she who wears the Nemophile's Crown."

And frighteningly, I wasn't sure if it was the echoes speaking...or me.

"Merrin? You okay?"

I raised my head from Windley's chest, finding his eyes filled with concern.

"I should be asking that of you," I murmured.

"No, I mean..." He motioned at the air between us, where shadows misted outward, roving and searching. "You're leaking."

Indeed, faint traces of darkness seeped from my wrist, twisting like smoke before fading into the cold air.

I jerked my arm close to my side, fingers clamping over the spot. "I'm fine!" I lied. "The echoes just don't like being this far from the forest."

Windley was faster. He caught my hand before I could fully tuck it away, his grip firm but careful. "Really?"

I tore my wrist free. "What else would it be? More importantly, how are you feeling?"

His fingers raked through his hair, strands deepening to blue like the petals beneath us. He hesitated.

"Look, Majesty...I'd understand if—"

I didn't let him finish. Before he could distance himself, before he could turn this into something heavier than it needed to be, I pressed a finger softly against his lips.

"I almost forgot. You owe me an answer."

He blinked. "For which question again?"

"As I told you, I intend to endorse your transfer to my court when we return. Will you have it?"

His eyes fixed onto mine, searching, bracing. He seemed to be testing me, waiting to see if I'd flinch—if I'd second-guess my own words now that I knew everything. But I wasn't bluffing. I'd never been more certain.

And after a moment, he seemed to accept it.

Slowly, deliberately, he nodded. Once. Then again, quicker this time. Then again—his gaze finally breaking as his cheeks flushed pink. "Yes, I'll 'have' it. But don't think you'll get to start ordering me around."

"In that case, I revoke my offer."

For the first time in hours, his mouth twitched. "Too late. You're stuck with me now, queenie."

There was no one I'd rather be stuck with.

As he took my hand to lead me back toward the hermit's abode, I offered quietly, "If ever you want to talk about it, rationalize it, grieve it—"

This time, his finger pressed gently to my lips. "I know, lion queen. Thanks. What I need is time."

The rest of the day passed in quiet, the sun stretching long shadows over the plains. Windley bathed longer than usual, as if washing away remnants of the story that clung to his skin. I hoped that in telling me, he could free himself, if only a little. And I hoped he knew my acceptance wasn't because I was great or merciful, but because he deserved it. There would've been no justice in blaming him for sins coerced from him as a child.

Rafe prepared a meal, the wallop napped lazily, and I surveyed the sky anxiously, fearing Luna might pull another stunt.

But as night fell across the plains, Luna didn't show—not that night, nor the next. She hadn't seemed the type to sulk—only to scheme. Perhaps Exitium's power had weakened her.

I didn't dare enter the darkness to ask.

We maintained an even pace, journeyed by night, rested by day. Windley gradually eased back into his old self, and Rafe grew progressively grouchier the farther we traveled from Beau —until, after trekking long and far across several sunrises and sunsets, we reached the first of the southern cities: a cobblestoned country village, reminiscent of the outskirts in the north.

"I spy a meadery, a trading post, and an inn," I said.

"Right then, to the meadery," said Windley.

He was only needling Rafe for sport, though Rafe didn't take the bait. Instead, he folded his arms and leaned against the inn's wall beneath a large sign featuring sharp, unfamiliar lettering.

I turned to Windley. "Can you read this language?"

Windley released an ironic chuckle through his nose. "It says: NO UNSOLICITED BEGUILING."

I raised a brow at him. "So that *'flirting so masterful it should be illegal'* line wasn't just talk, after all?"

Our plan was to stock up on supplies before heading to the coast in search of the legendary painted shore, where the sea and sky burst with colors unseen elsewhere—where Rafe would pact a new goddess, and Windley would lure Ascian for his final penance.

"So, you're going into the trading post to seduce the shop-keep into giving us food, canvas, and whatever else we need?" Rafe asked in a wry tone.

"That's plan B. Plan A is to offer my services in exchange for goods. If they refuse, I'll do it anyway. Good enough?"

We had little choice.

"Once you use your power, we'll have to leave quickly, won't we? Because Ascian will sense your location?" I guessed.

"Afraid so." Windley drummed his fingers thoughtfully in the air, his blackstone ring catching the fading light. "I'd prefer you two wait out here. I don't want our queen getting jealous."

"Wait—" My eyes caught on the ring. "Is that the one Ascian gave you, Windley? Could that be why you sense each other's power?"

"Good thought, but it's not that simple." He flexed his fingers. "We sense each other because we've beguiled each other. When a Spirite beguiles another, it leaves an imprint that resonates whenever power is used. The closer you are, the stronger it feels. Too far away, and you sense nothing at all.

That's why they only started sensing me when I used my power on southern soil."

Ripples, he'd called them.

Absently, Windley twirled his ring. "I haven't felt Pip, Charm, or Ascian use their powers since we last saw them, though."

"Because they're too far away?"

"No, my guess is they're making that new bloke do the heavy lifting so they don't have to." He meant the one with the deep voice and iron grip who'd helped Charmagne restrain me. "I've never met him before, so I definitely haven't beguiled him."

"So we're essentially blind to their location?!"

"This is why I didn't say anything earlier." He patted me with an easy, affectionate tap on the head. "Don't worry; we've been careful. I haven't used it since I tamed Dandelion." He gestured toward the wallop resting lazily nearby.

"You named the wallop?" A name entirely unfitting for a massive, tusked beast.

"Of course. Isn't it cute?" Windley wrinkled his nose. "Dandy is my second-favorite lion."

"Enough flirting," Rafe deadpanned. "Go bat your lashes at someone else."

"Boo." Windley stuck out his lip, then tossed us a lazy wave before slipping into the trading post.

He seemed steady again—unburdened, as though his mischief was no longer just a mask. The last few days atop Dandelion had been good for him. Good for us both. The longer I rode pressed against his back, the stronger my resolve became—and the more he seemed to accept that I didn't see him as a villain, that I didn't hold him responsible for sins that weren't his.

More than anything, I felt for him, forced to shoulder someone else's evil.

Yes, eventually there would be a deeper conversation. But not here, not now. Not with enemies to vanquish and lives to protect.

Time. My gift to him was time.

Selfishly, it felt wonderful to have him back.

The village was quiet, a single stretch of road lined with cottages worn by the years. We passed only two residents—humans—one perched on a porch, another plucking tomatoes from a vine. Neither paid us much mind.

"He's been in there a long time," Rafe noted.

"He has."

And the thought of Windley using his power on someone else twisted something uneasy in my stomach.

When he finally emerged, he carried a large pack, its weight evident in the set of his shoulders.

"Holy hell, what did you do to them?" Rafe asked.

Windley shrugged nonchalantly. "Let's just say they took me up on my offer." His gaze flicked briefly to me. "And no, I didn't bed anyone, if that's what you're wondering." He shifted the pack higher, expression casual—but something beneath had shifted. "Now come on. I used enough power to give away our location. We'll travel through the night, make camp at dawn." He pointed eastward. "The coast is that way."

By the time we stopped for camp in a hilly stretch dotted with farmhouses, Luna still hadn't shown herself.

"Are you sure this is a good idea?" I asked. "We're less than a day's distance from where you used your power."

Windley stretched his legs out casually. "Ascian has no

reason to suspect we're headed toward the coast. If anything, he'll assume I went south to see—" He cut himself short.

"To see whom?" I pressed.

He hesitated. "A friend. Er, my keeper's daughter."

The one who had told him stories. The one who had helped him escape. His savior.

"Merr? You're leaking again."

This time, it was both wrists. I shoved them quickly into my pockets. "Must be tired."

"Pity." Windley reached into his pack. "Because I brought us these." Triumphantly, he produced two bottles of mead.

"You brought booze?" scoffed Rafe incredulously. "There had better be a tent in there, or so help me—"

"Relax, chap. There's a tent." Windley tossed the pack at Rafe's chest with careless ease. Then, lowering his voice conspiratorially, he turned back to me. "I know you haven't been sleeping since I told you everything. Thought this might help." He handed me a bottle. "Though, frankly, I'd rather be the one sending you to oblivion. Sadly, we can't risk it here."

I eyed the bottle cautiously. A drink sounded dulcet after everything we'd endured, and he wasn't wrong—I hadn't been sleeping. The echoes had been particularly loud lately, restless with thoughts of revenge. Still, the idea of losing my wits in a foreign land with wraiths and Ascian prowling nearby left me uneasy.

Windley, reading my hesitation perfectly, tapped the bottle in a coaxing rhythm against my knuckles. "I wouldn't suggest it if there were a chance of danger. Rafe's feather cloak has masked his scent, Luna won't appear with the sun so close, and Ascian has no clue what we're after. He'd never think to head east. We're safe, lion queen—and you desperately need sleep."

True. The first blush of dawn was already creeping across

the horizon. True. We were needles in a vast haystack. True. We'd put good distance between ourselves and the village.

"Rafe?"

"Do whatever you like, Your Majesty," he replied distractedly. "Better to drink it now than carry the extra weight." But he was only half-listening, already intent on pitching the tent.

I hesitated—then thrust the bottle back toward Windley. "Fine. But I'm not drinking alone."

Windley accepted, tipping the bottle in a jaunty salute—clearly delighted with his victory.

Rafe took first sleep while Windley and I settled on the hilltop, watching the sun edge over the horizon. I'd join Rafe in the tent once sufficiently drowsy; meanwhile, Windley and Dandelion would keep watch.

"This feels like old times on the tree fortress veranda," I reminisced, watching the deep blues of the sky lighten. Only back then, there hadn't been a massive gray beast curled up at Windley's side.

"It was all I could do not to pounce on you back then." He tinked his bottle playfully against mine. "You have no idea how much I suffered."

"I'm sure you didn't suffer that badly. You had Beau's handmaids to play with, didn't you? You must have."

He turned up his nose, feigning offense. "They meant nothing."

"Ha! And you kept accusing poor Rafe of being a bounder, when you're the real charmer, aren't you?"

"That was merely practice," he corrected, dragging the back of his finger along my arm—drawing a shiver right along with it. "You'll be glad I did."

The glide of his nails against my skin felt even better than usual, as if he might split me open. I swallowed a particularly large gulp of mead—sweet at first, bitter at the finish.

"Can I ask you something, Wind? Something I've been wondering about?"

He drank deeply, the mead making a lovely sloshing sound. "Mm."

"It doesn't...upset you to use your powers now? After being forced to wield them against people you didn't want to? It doesn't bring back painful memories?"

He considered carefully. "I understand why you'd think so. But in this particular case, it's rather like asking if I no longer enjoy food simply because I was once forced to eat something unsavory."

"So humans really are just prey to you, after all," I concluded.

He tapped his chin thoughtfully. "Yet somehow, it feels as though you've caught me."

The first artful brushstrokes of orange painted the horizon. I took another sip of warm mead, letting it settle comfortably within me.

"That reminds me," I said, swirling the bottle absently. "The night before you told me everything, after fighting the wraiths, you said something else I've been wondering about."

Windley tilted his head, amusement flickering in his eyes. "You've been wondering about multiple things? Shocking."

I shot him a look, but he merely chuckled into his drink. "Go on, then."

Truthfully, I'd been wondering about this for longer than I cared to admit—ever since...

It's not in our nature to love humans—even if he's convinced you otherwise.

Blame the mead for my asking now.

I avoided his gaze. "You said it isn't easy for a Spirite to fall in love. What did you mean by that?"

"Naturally, because I don't have a heart."

I nearly spat out my drink.

"Kidding," the conniver clarified quickly, obviously pleased with himself. "I mean, it can be difficult to differentiate love from lust when it's between a human and a Spirite." He cast a thoughtful look at the rising ochre sky. "We might develop mimicking feelings, but once we taste our prey, they usually fade. True coupling between a human and Spirite is incredibly rare—not unheard of, mind you, but scarce enough that some regions won't even recognize their unions. People tend to doubt the sincerity of both sides."

"Oh."

I hadn't meant to sound quite so downtrodden, but there it was, clear as dawn.

Windley's face was suddenly much closer, his hand gliding to the small of my back. "My feelings for you have only grown since tasting you, Merrin. That's how I know you're unique." His voice dropped to something almost reverent. "I love you in a way that has nothing to do with lust. I've known it for a long time." His breath feathered against my cheek. "I lost myself in you instantly, and I've spent every day since making sure I never find my way out."

His lips brushed my shoulder—a kiss meant to soothe or claim, I couldn't tell which.

"I want to serve you. Love you. Beguile the shit out of you." He released another slow breath against my skin. "I would do anything for you."

"Windley..." I pressed my forehead to his.

"And the fact you haven't fled for the hills after what I told you..." His fingers tightened at my waist, a silent admission of barely-checked hunger. "It's amplified something I thought couldn't be amplified further. I'd devour every inch of you if it didn't mean losing you forever."

Dangerous words, especially with the mead half-emptied.

Mustering the last shreds of sense, I grabbed for a safer topic.

"Y-you said Pip was like a brother to you. What about Charmagne?"

Windley went rigid, his mouth hovering at my neck. When he spoke, his voice was a glacial whisper.

"Charm's insane." A beat. "If you get the chance, kill her."

The chill in those words sent a tremor through me. I sat frozen, heart hammering, heat blooming across my cheeks—painfully aware of the sky brightening by slow degrees.

Windley kissed my cheek—then my jaw—and my pulse stumbled, terrified and yearning all at once.

"Feeling sleepy yet, lion queen?"

No. I was flushed, heavy, possessed by something profound, undeniable, and—

"I want you," I whispered, fingers fisting into his shirt.

"Not here." His lips skimmed my face, a ghost of promise, a promise of restraint. "The first time I make love to you, it shall be in a bed."

Yet he took my earlobe gently between his teeth. Yet his hand slipped beneath my shirt to the flesh of my lower back, caressing as though it were the finest silk.

A moan slipped free—unbidden, unrestrained.

Windley faltered. Just for a breath.

Oh no. The mead was nearly finished, and I was nearly drunk. Windley seemed to realize it at the same moment.

Just as effortlessly as he had slipped it under, he withdrew his hand.

"Sorry, queenie." He sat up and swallowed deeply, making his Adam's apple bob. "I drank more than I intended." He edged forward onto the slope, patting the ground. "Let's watch the sunrise. I'll behave myself."

But as he turned to extend his hand to me, his silhouette outlined by the rising sun, something happened. His eyes went wide, his mouth parted in awe.

"What is it?" I shot a glance behind me, certain there was something there.

There wasn't.

"Goddess damn," he murmured. "The way the sun's hitting you..."

I felt it—the heat of dawn's first rays kissing my skin, turning me molten, golden, radiant.

Beautiful. Powerful. Yet...

To have him look at me like this—so openly, unabashedly— I could hardly bear it. I met him with eyes that had defied goddesses and brought wraiths to ruin, but he didn't break. And though dawn unraveled in a breathtaking display of fire and gold, he never took his gaze from mine.

"You're so fucking beautiful," he breathed. "I can't believe you're mine."

My fingers curled reflexively into his, and he drew me down onto the hill beside him. Everything about him was temptation—the way he chewed his lip, the dark promise glinting in his eyes.

"I won't take you here," he said, rolling smoothly atop me, his knee slipping deliberately between my legs. "But I'll come close."

This kiss was unlike any before, ravenous and devouring. I tangled my fingers into his hair, gripping tight as his hands captured my waist, thumbs pressing into my hips.

He tasted delicious. Smelled intoxicating. Felt devastatingly good. My blood raced through every vein; inside, a thousand serpents writhed in ecstatic chaos. I had never been wanted like this, tasted like this. Windley held me like someone battling to contain his own hunger.

I didn't notice the moment he slipped.

The instant traces of his predatory nature emerged.

The moment his eyes flashed emerald.

I didn't notice—but across the fields, mounted upon a beast swifter than any wallop, a certain lavender-eyed villain did.

IO

WE F*CKED UP

I awoke from sleep the way a child stirs from a nightmare —sharply, confused—to find solid arms carrying me like a damsel.

"Heya...lion queen. Lion queen? Lion queen."

It was Windley's voice, but odd, as though he questioned both the lion and the queen.

I blinked to be sure it was him. Yes, I knew that face, had memorized every shadow of it over the last eight years.

The uncertainty was likely due to the mead. Strong stuff for such a rural hamlet. Once, a similar concoction had made me repeat "clandestine" over and over until it no longer sounded like a real word.

"Windley, I think I'm drunk."

"Oh?" he purred. "Excellllent."

A strip of warm light passed overhead—a lantern?

A few strides later, another lantern swayed gently, fighting the meek night wind.

Night?

But the sun had only just risen. We'd been on the hillside

drenched in its first glow, wrestling, indulging, skirting the borders of innocence...

"Are those streetlamps?" I asked. "Where are we?"

"I'm taking you home, lion...queen?"

Perhaps I hadn't fully woken up. My dreams were always extra strange after a night of indulgence, and Windley was a frequent guest these days.

I reached up to stroke his face—solid, not a phantom—and he startled, surprise flashing brighter than the lantern flames overhead.

"Windley, you smell strange. Did you buy cologne at that trader's post?"

"Do you like it?" he asked.

No. It masked his natural scent, which I much preferred.

"It's...different. You've never worn cologne before." I tried looking around him but found only darkness interrupted by flickering lanterns. "Did we sleep through the day? Where's Rafe? And what do you mean home?"

As I began to push from his arms, I felt a sudden swell of familiar power.

"Windley, what are you doing?! They'll sense you!"

"Too late for that," he said, mouth curling at the corners.

"Too...late?"

In that instant I knew something was terribly wrong. I know Windley's essence—his scent, the exact way his heat blooms under my skin. But the power sliding through me now felt wrong: not warm and satiating, but foreign, manufactured.

Like a kiss from a stranger.

The figure holding me might look and sound like Windley, yet my deeper senses could not be fooled.

"Who are you?!" I demanded, struggling fiercely against the impostor wearing Windley's face. "Unhand me at once!"

I was met with glowing eyes of punishment—further proof,

as they weren't the green Windley reserved for me. These were red, cherry-like, shining like polished rubies in the dark. Unfortunately, I could no more escape their power than Windley's emerald stare. They held me in place, turning me limp in the stranger's arms.

"Now I understand why the others are so up in arms about you," he said, voice deepening...

Deeper...

Deeper...

Until it was no longer Windley's voice.

"You taste damn good."

Yet it was a voice I recognized.

Must taste damn good if he guards you so fiercely.

The hooded rogue who'd accompanied Charmagne and Pip in the forest. The one Windley hadn't recognized. The one who'd gripped my shoulders in that infuriating, possessive way.

Forget the rest of this. Why not come with me—slip into the woods and get good and lost...

I'd never gotten a proper look at him.

"Oh my goddess!" I breathed. "Are you Windley's long-lost twin or something? He never mentioned—!"

Wrong. The deep-voiced stranger corrected me with a low, mocking laugh.

"No, hon, I'm merely mimicking his flesh."

"Oh."

Hon.

For a fleeting moment, curiosity overcame my other emotions.

"You can do something like that? But I thought only your eyes and hair could change."

"Is that what he told you? Charm said he was a bit of an ascetic. Truth is, we can change almost anything, provided we consume enough vitality beforehand. This façade only took two human life forces. Doesn't last long, but it was worth it to avoid getting blasted by that smoke magic of yours when you woke."

This villain had drained two humans just to temporarily appear as Windley?

Unconscionable!

"One without merit! Let us strip his flesh and melt his bones! Let us turn him to nothing!"

The echoes battered my ears, thirsty for vengeance, but their efforts were useless. The impostor's ruby-eyed stare held me captive, preventing me from spilling into shadow and unleashing my wrath.

The mead wasn't to blame for my heavy limbs. This fiend had been draining my energy as I slept!

If that wasn't violating, I didn't know what was.

"Where's Windley?" I demanded weakly.

"Who?"

"Windley."

"I know. Just fucking with you. Every time you say his name, you release a burst of life force. It's incredibly crisp. Say what you will about the halo-hugger, at least he knows how to pick a good pet."

I'm not a pet.

The words never left my tongue, clinging there like honey.

From the tapping of his feet, we walked along a cobbled street, akin to the market road back home. The oil lamps lining our path meant we were in a city larger than any we'd encountered in days. A lazy breeze carried the wet scent of petrichor, suggesting recent rain or rainfall soon to come. A shame I was in such a compromised state—rain in the night was one of my favorite ambiances, the glow of damp cobblestone one of my favorite sights.

"You're cute for a human, you know," remarked the false

Windley. "My offer still stands. Become my pet, and I promise to go easy on you. Can't say the same for the others."

If I could've spoken, my response would've been no—perhaps the tartest refusal I'd ever uttered.

"You look like you're trying to speak. Is that a yes?"

No. No, no, no, no.

"Blink once if you'll be my pet?"

With every ounce of strength, I kept my eyes propped open.

"Shame. Submission can be sweet, you know. Maybe you'll change your mind once you see what lies ahead." He shook me roughly. "By the way, your name isn't actually *lion queen*, is it? Heard Windalloy call you that, but it doesn't sound real..." Another shake. "Hey! Don't fall asleep on me. I'll ease up a bit. Tough, though—you taste so...addictive. How'd he get you willing? Those guys always talk about him like he's some legend. Maybe there's something to it after all."

"Where...Wind?" was all I could manage.

"Maybe I killed him."

"No."

I would've felt it.

"Well, lucky for you, Ascian wants you both breathing. After that smoke bomb, I planned to nab your friend and use him as bait—but then there you were: alone, unconscious, just where my master said you'd be. Almost a gift." He tilted his head. "Why'd he leave you unguarded—gone to empty his bladder? You sure about a man who slips off and abandons you? If you were mine, I wouldn't let you out of my sight."

Ruby eyes held me silent.

"If he's smart, he'll come after you on a prancelope this time. That's how I found you so quickly."

Prancelopes—lightning-fast, untamable beasts well known in the north.

Well, untamable unless you had the knack for charming animals, apparently.

"Shouldn't take long," he added. "Maybe you two'll muscle out of this mess like last time. Guess we'll see...*highness*."

His voice was unreadable, stranger still coming from Windley's mouth.

"By the way, feeling faint? I dosed you pretty hard—protective measure against your magic. Seems to have worked. Haven't seen that green glow of yours."

Green glow? He must've thought it was part of my magic. Good. Let him assume it was my source of power, that without it, I was powerless.

"Give...it...back."

He chuckled. "Do you always get whatever you ask for? I'll bet you do—got both those men dancing on a royal string. Where'd the curly-haired one spring from, anyway? I only expected two of you. He's going to feel like a fool when he figures out it was *me* skulking around your camp, not Windalloy."

Windalloy.

Windley.

Wind.

"I said no falling asleep...lion queen."

That name was Windley's alone.

"Merrin," I whispered, head heavy as stone.

"Merr-ín?" he tried, oddly stressing the second syllable.

Good enough; I was too drained to correct him.

He looked like Windley, even felt distantly like him—and the ache of that hit hard.

"Whoa, what's that?" he asked, eyes dimming for a breath. "Haven't seen that look before."

Love, I thought. Longing for the real Windley, miles away and blaming himself.

If only I could tell him: *stop blaming yourself.*

Maybe these villains had sealed their own fate by taking me.

My power could crumble mountains, exile gods.

I would carve the path to his revenge.

I reached for the impostor's cheek again. "Wind...?"

"Loopy, huh? Not Windalloy—name's Edius."

Right. Not Windley.

His magic was tugging at my hands, coaxing me to touch. I had to resist, gather my wits, escape his snare—because wherever he was dragging me, there would be more glowing eyes waiting.

"*M...err...In...*" echoed faintly in my ears, my Crown distant.

Ruby power drained away the last of my strength.

"Where you from, Merrín? Your accent's sorta...rustic."

"N...orth."

"Ah. Charm suspected as much. You really a queen?"

"Mm."

"That Windalloy guy's got game, that's for sure."

Windalloy.

Windley.

Wind.

The impostor—Edius—stopped walking. "A word of advice, Merrín," he said, almost solemn. "When the time comes, don't resist. You'll want it to be me or Pip who hexes you. Don't let it be Charm. Things won't end well if Charm's the one to do it." He leaned forward, pushing something open—a creaky iron gate by the sound of it. "And don't go trying to run, either. Ascian wants whatever power you're hiding, but he wants to hurt Windalloy just as badly. He'll kill you if it suits him. Your best bet is to play nice. Let him get a taste of you, and he's more likely to keep you alive."

Not that I could bolt now—we'd already reached our destination.

Against the rain-kissed night, the bright windows of Windley's childhood home made it seem as though the place were hoarding every bit of life and light.

Soon, I'd learn just how accurate that observation truly was.

II

GODDESS SAVE THE QUEEN

Windley's childhood home—though I didn't know it then—was a two-story brick building with a neat row of shrubs lining the front.

To me, the design seemed boxy, foreign—a brick rectangle topped with a slanted roof. Houses didn't look like that in the queenlands. Ours were lower, cozier, with crooked chimneys and thatch tucked between every crevice. Windley had once called them gnome homes, though I hadn't the faintest idea what a gnome was.

Through a veil of eyelashes, I took in as much of the foyer as possible: a stand for coats, portraits decorating the walls, floors of gleaming wood. It was warm inside, enough to pinken my cheeks as a fire blazed in an adjoining room.

The clear tap of shoes against the polished surface announced someone approaching.

"Edi! Did you bring him? Did you bring—! Oh! You brought *her*."

I recognized that playful tone.

It looks more like a magical reaction to me. Master Ascian, let me taste her and find out? Please?

"Pip," said Edius. "Where's Master?"

"Not back yet," Pip replied cheerfully. "He sent me and Charm ahead to prepare the house... Hey, what's wrong with your face?"

"Just changed back. Wore a mask so the human wouldn't curse me. Still got the wrong nose."

I fought my eyelids, desperate to catch a glimpse of the impostor's true face, but it was no use. The warmth from the fire conspired with the beguilement already swimming through my veins.

"Good call! Oh—did you notice? Doesn't she look just like Flo—"

"Where's Charm?" Edius cut in sharply.

"In the bath."

"And your...uh...creature?"

"Sleeping."

Creature?

"Alright, Pip, listen closely. Until Master Ascian returns, lock yourself in your room with the human. Don't open for anyone but him. Understand?"

"O-okay, Edi," Pip said uncertainly. "But why?"

"I don't want Charm spoiling her before Master arrives."

We started moving, ascending the stairs, Edius's purposeful footsteps accompanied by Pip's hurried scampering.

"But Pip, remember what the human did in the forest?" Edius pressed. "She's dangerous. You have to keep her subdued, alright? Her magic wounded Master—imagine what it could do to you."

I'd wounded Ascian? What a lovely surprise.

Pip groaned anxiously. "But Windalloy will be mad if I do that..."

"He'll be even madder if she gets loose and Charm ruins her, won't he?"

We paused in front of a door.

"I guess," Pip mumbled reluctantly.

Edius carried me into the heart of a warm room, laying me gently upon a quilted bed. "Got your key, Pip?"

"Right here!"

"Good. She's full of my power at the moment, shouldn't stir. But if she moves—even an inch—give her more. Watch her breathing. You know the signs, right?"

Pip must've nodded because Edius's steps receded toward the hallway.

"And Pip—one more thing. Once you taste her, it'll be hard to stop, but you must. Think what Master will do if you drain her before he returns. And imagine how heartbroken Windalloy will be if you devour his special snack. Got it?"

"Yes, Edi."

"Good boy."

The door shut firmly, followed by the satisfying *thunk* of a heavy key turning in the lock.

Afterward, silence settled except for the subdued crackle of another fireplace.

The shuffle of Pip's nervous feet approached slowly, stepping carefully over a creaky board.

Pip.

The boy Windley had left behind, source of his deepest guilt. The one he'd nearly betrayed my spell for.

My first impulse was to steal a glance at him and the room.

My second was wiser. If I stirred, Pip was instructed to placate me further. I needed to keep my heartbeat steady, my breaths even, and listen carefully for the echoes. If possible, I needed to find a way out without hurting the boy still so precious to Windley.

I felt Pip leaning over, his imprint pressing into the mattress.

"Q-Queen lion?" he whispered fearfully, prodding my cheek with a pudgy finger.

He leaned closer.

"Windalloy never liked pets. Guess he does now."

Through nearly closed eyes, I glimpsed his silhouette, head tilted curiously.

"You smell like him. Your spirits mixed a lot. Are you why he stayed away so long?"

The tone in Pip's voice was unexpectedly gentle—the same affection Windley had used when recounting memories of him.

These two shared something deep and painful.

I'd absolved Windley of his crimes; was Pip innocent too?

Were all of Ascian's stolen children?

Pip withdrew slightly. "Windalloy will be mad I helped."

He was talking to himself rather than to me now. What had Charmagne called him? "Impressionable"? I saw it clearly. Pip sounded easily swayed—like someone teetering on a tightrope, ready to topple with the faintest breeze. Yet after all these years, he still cared what Windley thought of him.

The diplomat within me wanted to reason with him, but the risk was too great. I needed more of his heart first. Eight years was ample time to change—Windley himself was proof of that.

Raindrops pattered in a hush against the glass, prompting Pip to straighten. "It's starting again," he said toward what I assumed was a window. "Been raining off and on all day. Too bad Edi didn't bring Windalloy. Rain's his favorite, 'specially at night."

Windley had never said so directly, but I knew. I'd seen contentment on his face when rain pattered chaotically against our fortress's belvedere—a symphony of disorder, somehow comforting no matter its intensity.

"Queen lion?"

Pip's voice drew near again.

"I know you're awake. Have been for a while, haven't you? I'm good with heartbeats—better than Edi and the others."

Again, he leaned close.

"That magical reaction may have faded from your feet, but there's still magic inside you. You understand, right? I have to do it. So you don't hurt us."

His fingertips trailed slowly from my inner elbow to wrist, igniting warmth through my blood.

There was no use biding my time now.

I opened my eyes to find him staring down at me. His were dark, the way Windley's usually were. Pale cheeks glowed faintly in the firelight, hair a spun-sugar blue. He regarded me as a stray animal might, curiosity tempered by caution.

"You taste nice," he admitted shyly, tracing circles on my palm. "Clean, innocent...but a little spicy." A quiet chuckle escaped him. "So, that's what Windalloy likes." His other hand slipped cautiously beneath mine. "T-tell me about him? I'll let you stay awake if you promise not to hurt me."

My throat was dust-dry, but I managed a slight nod.

"That's a yes?" Pip prodded gingerly.

Another careful nod.

"Okay—but—" His eyes flashed golden, locking mine in place. "Try moving, and the deal's off." His grip tightened slightly. "Mmkay?"

I closed my eyes, steadying myself beneath his power. "De...deal."

When I opened them again, his irises were still glowing faintly, casting an eerie light in the dim room.

"P...Pip?" I swallowed against the dryness. "I'm M...
Merrin."

"Merrin," he repeated, tasting the name. "How long have
you known Windalloy?"

I considered lying but found no point. I didn't know Pip
well enough to craft the perfect deception, and truth could cut
deeper than falsehood.

"More than eight years," I answered carefully.

Pip stilled. "Since he left us?"

I nodded. "After he fled, he traveled north, beyond the
Emerald Wood. He trained to become a royal knight—my best
friend's knight. She's a queen, like me."

His eyes widened. "You really are a queen. Charm said
that's why you smell different." But he quickly discarded this
thought as something more enticing captured his attention.
"A royal knight? For a queen?" Admiration brightened his
gaze.

Pip idolized Windley.

"Want to hear more?" I asked, hoping to distract him
further. "Wind's a brilliant fighter—fast, precise, artful. He's
brave, almost recklessly. He's risked his life for me countless
times."

"Because he's your knight too?" Pip asked, intrigued.

"Er—No."

"Because you're his pet?" Pip pressed eagerly.

I shook my head. "Because..."

Windley's voice whispered through memory, aching:

I'm in love with you, darling... Tell me you know that.

Our monster stirred. Love hurt most vividly when
remembered.

Pip's fingers twitched. "Oh. Your heartbeat changed.
What's that feeling?"

Heartache. Worried, unyielding.

"I miss him," I admitted quietly. "We haven't been apart in ages."

"Oh." Pip leaned back, disappointed. He'd expected something juicier. "That's his power. It'll fade."

"It won't," I whispered. "Windley doesn't protect me because he must—he protects me because we love each other."

Reality iced over me.

I'd known since waking in Edius's arms that I was in danger, that our quest had derailed, that fighting was inevitable.

But now, as a tight band cinched around my chest for Windley, the true weight crushed me: I was bait.

Windley would come for me—straight into danger, into the grasp of his tormentor, into memories he'd buried for years.

I had to escape before then.

Pip stared doubtfully. "He loves you—even after tasting you?"

"He does," I affirmed.

Pip's head tilted. "You're human, right? Then...you're his wyrdbound one?"

I didn't recognize the term. But before I could ask, chaos erupted in the hallway outside.

A woman's voice pierced through the door—singsong and dripping with malice. "Oh, Pii-iiip! Open up! *It's my turn to play with the royal.*"

Before I could fully process this, another voice followed—lower, more exasperated.

"Pip, stop it! We can feel you in there, and you're doing too much. Make sure that creature of yours doesn't wake up!"

Edius.

Again, the mention of a creature. What creature? There had been nothing else in the room—at least nothing I'd noticed.

"Come on, Pip. Back off."

"Enough, you little cretin!"

Pip flinched, his glow faltering.

I seized the moment.

"Pip, you don't have to stay here," I urged in a hush. "You could leave, like Windley did. You could start over somewhere better. I can help you."

Confusion knitted his brow. "Why would I do that? This is my home."

My heart twisted painfully.

He truly believed that.

"You've been made to do terrible things, haven't you?" I pressed with care. "Ascian—he's hurt you, too, hasn't he?"

Pip's breath caught. "Hurt people? No, no—I make them feel good. See?"

Wrong direction. The conversation was shifting. His stare narrowed, locking onto me as his magic pressed deeper, filling the spaces between my bones, wrapping my muscles like strangling vines.

No.

Desperately, I grasped the only thread left. My gaze darted to his hand, catching a familiar glint—a blackstone ring.

Just like Windley's.

"Pip," I rasped, forcing the words out before magic could clog my throat, "what about your hexes? Those hurt people, don't they?"

His fingers froze.

"Hexes?" He pressed a hand to his temple, wincing faintly.

There.

That gesture—I'd seen Windley do the same the night we'd encountered Ascian.

Pip wasn't stable.

"Pip," I whispered, voice taut with alarm, "have you taken a memory elixir?"

His gaze turned vacant, doll-like. He didn't answer.

"Pip?"

"I only hex baddies," he said stiffly.

Based on what Windley had told me, that wasn't true.

"You don't hex innocents with pure spirits for Ascian to drain?" I challenged, wary.

"Nope."

But his fingers twitched, and his breathing accelerated.

He knew.

Somewhere deep inside, the memories were there.

I seized upon it. "Pip, Windley will be furious if he finds out you helped Ascian capture me. But if you help me escape—"

His lips pressed thin. "He'd be happy, but..." His stare turned solemn. "If you're really his wyrdbound one, he'll come for you. And I'd rather see him unhappy than never see him again."

I exhaled, dread pooling heavily in my stomach.

"Oh," I said sadly. "I'm afraid my feelings are quite the opposite."

Firelight blinked across his eyes, a thin wash of gold flickering through the irises—there and gone. His fingertips drifted from the bend of my elbow to my wrist, a slow siphon that lured my pulse toward sleep.

Then, for a heartbeat, his face wavered—cheekbones sharpening, boyish roundness draining away as though every thread of magic aged him a year. The shift was so fleeting I almost doubted it—and in that same instant his gaze sparked with recognition.

One hand splayed against my clavicle, the other cradled my cheek, holding me like something fragile and volatile. "There's...someone else in you," he breathed, half wonder, half fear. "An entire spirit."

Power plunged deeper—too deep, the echoes writhing, pinned beneath the weight.

"E...choes—" I coughed, fighting the choke of his magic. "Ex...it—"

Heat roared through my chest; his pupils glittered with hungry curiosity. "What is that? Tell me."

I tried again. "Ex...i—"—the syllable broke against the vise at my throat.

The echoes bucked, desperate. Black sparks danced at the edge of my vision. Air vanished; stars burst behind my eyes.

"...tium," I forced out.

All at once, something tore loose inside me—shadows racing through my veins and cascading down Pip's arms in blistering rivulets, an arctic flame that swallowed the room. The hearth gave a single, frightened pop, then guttered out.

Pip reeled back, hands charred black where they'd touched me; terror flared across his face, and he crumpled, eyes rolling white as the darkness snuffed him out.

Silence pooled—thick, ringing. For an instant the very air vibrated with the echoes' chaotic energy. My pulse thundered in my ears, my breath spent, yet my limbs felt oddly weightless, as though the shadows had siphoned Pip's magic away, leaving only tingling static.

12
NEGOTIATIONS

"**G**et up, Merrin."
"*MErrIn.*"
"*MerRIN.*"
"*MERRiN.*"

The chamber—dimmed by the darkness I'd unwittingly unleashed—pulsed with the echoes' voices. They prodded at me, whispering from every corner, an eerie chorus weaving in and out of my name. But one voice—clear, more piercing than the rest—cut through them all.

"*I said get up.*"

"Exitium?" I whispered.

"*If you had called me sooner, we could have ended this hours ago.*"

I pushed myself upright, limbs sluggish from Pip's fading magic. My bones still tingled where his power had burrowed deepest. "How did this happen?" My voice rasped, disoriented. "I couldn't summon the echoes."

"*I told you before—you need only speak my name.*"

Had it truly been that simple? A mere whisper, a fleeting thought—and that was enough?

I glanced at Pip, lying unconscious beside the bed. He'd lost every bit of childish innocence; his features looked older, more angular—dangerous. Which was his true appearance?

From the other side of the door, Charmagne and Edius took turns ramming against the wood, their frustration evident as darkness seeped beneath the threshold.

"You moron! Why leave him alone with her?!"

"Because I didn't trust you, obviously! You'd devour her before Ascian even got home!"

"I have more self-control than Pip, clearly! He doesn't even know what he's capable of!"

I pressed my palm against the cool wood, listening carefully.

"Let us in, Merrín," Edius called, surprisingly composed. "Pip's the strongest among us—if he loses control, it won't end well for you."

Too late for that. Surely, they felt the sudden absence of Pip's power. Windley would, too—wherever he was.

My gaze swept the room—quaint, tidy, furnished with applewood furniture, a thick woven rug, and little trinkets over the mantle. Cozy. Too cozy for a queen planning her escape.

I steeled myself, raising my voice. "Edius! Pip is incapacitated and my hostage. I will leave this place on my own terms." Pressing harder against the door, I added, "You have two choices: get in my way and die, or fetch me supplies and leave them outside. Step aside, and I'll spare your lives."

Though my voice remained steady, my legs still felt weak. But they didn't need to know that.

Silence from the hallway, then—

"There are two of us, Merrín," Edius said evenly. "Only one of you."

Wrong.

"THERE IS A LEGION WITHIN ME."

The words emerged like a divine decree. I snapped my mouth shut, chills skittering up my spine. Had I said that—or had Exitium?

A ring of darkness encircled me, shifting, alive, though I hadn't summoned it. The echoes flurried with excitement. I had not called them, either.

"What even is she?" Charmagne hissed.

"A royal?" Edius murmured uncertainly.

"Besides that, you idiot!"

They hesitated.

"If you stall, I will make your decision for you," I warned, stomping a foot to send a surge of shadow rolling beneath the door.

Charmagne shrieked, recoiling. "ARGH! Fine, you royal cow! Run! See how long it takes Master to find you again!"

"Not so fast," Edius said darkly. "Think about it, Merrín. You'll be his pet either way. He'll treat you gentler if he doesn't have to hunt you down again."

I bared my teeth, my tone icy. "I don't fear Ascian any more than I fear either of you. Next time, no one—not even Windley —will be able to betray my spell."

"Tch! Stop calling him that," Charm snapped. "His name's Windalloy." After a long pause, she sighed bitterly. "Fine. Go fetch her a pack, *Ediot*."

"Really? Just letting her go?"

"Unless you'd like to sacrifice Pip?" Charm sneered.

Another pause. Then Edius stalked away.

Now it was just Charmagne and me, separated by a slab of mahogany. I still hadn't glimpsed her face.

Charm's voice wormed through the cracks like oil. "What's

your plan now, cupcake? Run straight back into Windalloy's arms? Trade one evil for another?"

Her fist struck the door, but I held my ground.

"Ironic, isn't it?" she drawled coldly. "He's the worst of us—because he tricked you into thinking he actually cares. That little performance in the forest? Please. He's just thirsty, and even if hades froze over and he somehow cared for a human, I promise you—"

Her voice dropped venomously.

"He wouldn't choose a fat, frizzled human like you."

Something inside me snapped—hotter than fury, keener than rage, more consuming than betrayal.

I'd never hated someone before meeting them. But I hated her.

My voice sliced through the door like steel. "Do not speak his name like you know him, you snide bitch."

Silence. Wicked, furious silence.

"Spending a few traumatic years with someone is nothing compared to watching them grow into themselves, breathing their air, touching your soul to theirs." My teeth clenched. "I suggest you find a bureau to curl up in, Charmagne, because I won't hesitate to unleash every nightmare in existence if you're still in the hall when I emerge."

I was shaking.

Exitium's voice slithered over my skin. *The bloodlust writhes in you now, Merrin. Branded on your soul. Together, we will destroy everything.*

I recoiled inwardly.

No.

I won't let them stain me.

Charmagne tsked, letting out a clipped breath. "Edius should've hexed you when he had the chance." Her voice turned thoughtful, then hardened. "When I find you, cupcake," she purred, laced with malice, "you'll be my pet—and I'm far less delicate than the others."

Her fist slammed the door again. "You'll regret ever raising your voice to me."

Then she stormed off.

I forced myself to breathe—in through my nose, out through my mouth—exhaling the rage clawing my ribs. Being this powerful was both blessing and curse: while I felt safe from the world, I felt unsafe from myself.

Once Rafe pacted his goddess and Windley defeated Ascian, then it would be my turn. I needed to do something better with the Nemophile's Crown before Exitium's voice grew louder, before the echoes twisted something inside me beyond repair.

With Charm gone and Edius fetching my supplies, I knelt beside Pip. He was breathing steadily, unconscious, features soft again, looking almost harmless. His hands remained stained black.

I found the key in his pocket. This had likely been his room, though the furnishings were generic enough to belong to anyone.

Finally steady, I crossed to the window. Rain pounded the glass, wind wailed down empty streets. I wouldn't make it far without leaving a trail or drawing attention. Perhaps that was for the best.

If Windley felt Pip's power, he'd find me. Better to wait somewhere close.

A curt knock rattled the door.

"Heya, Merrín?" Edius called through in a slow drawl. "Gotcha a pack. Canteen, blanket, knife—not that you need one—bread, cheese. You like cheese?"

"That's fine." I adjusted my grip on the key. "My cloak?"

"Out here."

"And coin?"

"Coin?"

"Currency."

"Oh, *farthings*. Look, the more shit I give you, the madder Master gets."

"Not your concern."

"Like hell it isn't! When Ascian learns we cut you loose, whose back do you think he'll flay?"

I pressed my fingertips against the ground, shadows seeping beneath the door.

"Alright—stop that if you want my help! And what are you, anyway, besides a royal?"

I knew better than to answer. But Exitium spoke through me again:

"*We are she who wears the Nemophile's Crown. We are eternal. We are Destruction.*"

Not my words, not my voice.

A heavy pause. "No shit?" Edius sounded more intrigued than fearful. "Thought that was a myth. No wonder you taste like dessert."

"Enough idle chat, Edius. Retreat so I can leave. If you try anything, I won't hesitate to end you."

"Sure, sure." His tone was light but unsettling. "Don't expect me to be so *nice* next time, little human queen."

I pressed my ear to the door, listening until his footsteps faded down the hall.

Only then did I turn toward the waiting darkness.

I tipped my head back into it—and a wisp curled into my palm, black and pulsing, like a living thing awaiting my command.

With one final glance at Pip, I turned the key, stepped over the threshold, and entered the hall.

The second floor overlooked the first, enclosed by a waist-high banister on three sides. A candle-lit chandelier hung from the ceiling, its flames flickering as though disturbed by something unseen. Mahogany doors lined the hall, all closed except for one at the far end.

In its frame stood two figures.

Charmagne.

Edius.

Charm and Edi.

As I collected my cloak and the pack at my feet, I finally laid eyes on the rest of Ascian's so-called family.

Bitch or not, Charmagne was beautiful.

Unfairly so—gorgeous in the most irritating way possible. Her skin shone like burnished copper, hoarding daylight beneath its surface; dark, thick-lashed eyes glimmered with mischief, and her short, glossy hair caught even the dimmest light.

And here I'd hoped her exterior would match the rot within, but no—the only ugly thing about her was the sheer disgust carved into her expression. *Crusty* was the right word for it. She wore all white, the fabric draping effortlessly over a physique as honed as Sestilia's.

No wonder she thought I was thick. Anyone would be, standing next to a silhouette like that. For now, Charmagne's hair was rose gold—but knowing their kind, I doubted it would remain that way the next time we met.

If there was a next time.

They'd be wise to avoid it.

Beside her, Edius stood taller, broader than either Windley or Rafe, his frame built for strength yet carrying it with ease. His dark hair was half-tied, careless strands falling across his face—an afterthought or perhaps an act of rebellion. Men in the queenlands didn't wear their hair long, but I doubted anything else would suit him; he had a presence that demanded a touch of wildness.

He was older than I—perhaps even older than Windley, edging toward Ascian's years. Like most incubi, he seemed artfully engineered to draw the eye: powerhouse shoulders, long limbs, skin a tawny-gold glow. Every angle of him lounged in effortless confidence, yet his smoky eyes lingered with a depth that suggested he was cataloguing secrets none of us could guess.

A flicker of amusement crossed his sharp features, though his mouth remained impassive, when I passed.

At the base of the stairs, I didn't bother looking back, though I felt their stares on my neck.

I wrapped my cloak tightly around me, grabbed an umbrella, and stepped out into the storm.

A city, indeed.

Though the rain had extinguished the street lanterns, sporadic lightning illuminated the boulevard in jagged flashes. Rows of houses—identical to Ascian's—lined the road, neat yet lifeless.

If there was one thing to be grateful for, it was that the storm had clogged the sky enough to obscure the moon.

No Luna. No threat of her power finding Rafe while we were separated.

Ascian was mortal. Luna was not. I feared her far more than I feared him.

Still, I needed cover. I wouldn't make it far in this rain without drawing unwanted attention.

I slipped into a neighboring shed, settling between stacks of hay, sacks of seed, and abandoned gardening tools. It wasn't much, but it would keep me dry.

I curled up, listened to the rain beat against the roof, and waited.

Waited for the storm to pass.

Waited for the sky to lighten.

Waited for Windley.

Only when the last drops of rain kissed the earth, when the sun began to paint the horizon pale gold, did I finally see the city for what it truly was.

Gray.

Silent.

Desolate.

And entirely, entirely wrong.

13
KIND AND WARM

I've wandered through countless settlements—hamlets, villages, sprawling trade towns—and every one of them, even the sleepiest, shared the same tell-tale pulse of life: children laughing, merchants barking prices, the warm drift of fresh bread on the air.

This city should have been no different.

At dawn, I gathered myself—drew up my hood, ate the breakfast Edius had packed—and waited for the city to awaken.

Gradually, shutters eased open. The cramped, cobbled streets—lined with brick houses—welcomed their earliest risers: a parcelman, a patrolwoman, a shopkeep.

At first glance, it was a city like any other: medium-sized, dense with shaded alleys, orderly signs etched in an alphabet I couldn't read. Chimneys exhaled smoke into the early-morning chill.

But something was off.

A hush clung to the stones themselves, the air too thick for morning—carrying neither birdsong nor the clatter of dawn cookware.

Even the chimney smoke seemed to rise unnaturally straight, reluctant to bend or mingle with anything else. I caught myself holding my breath, afraid the simple act of exhaling might shatter the fragile trance holding the city together.

It was in the way they moved—the courier, the guard, the merchant—walking as if guided by invisible strings, drifting through routines without intention or destination. As more residents emerged, the feeling only deepened.

No conversation.

No smiles.

No eye contact. The quiet felt contagious, poised to sand away every laugh I'd ever hoarded.

A city full of people—yet not a single one of them felt alive —only a two-dimensional portrait of life stripped to its shallowest form.

To test my theory, I entered a bakery and pretended to browse a menu I couldn't read.

"Think more rain's on the horizon?" I asked the balding baker, doing my best to mimic Windley's southern accent.

"Could be," he replied, eyes passing through me on their way to the window.

Moments later, a woman entered in a patterned dress. Silently, she set a piece of parchment on the counter. Without a word, the baker handed her a seeded loaf. She stowed it in her satchel, never exchanging so much as a glance, then left.

I followed her into the street, careful not to stray too far from Ascian's house, observing the same strange, mechanical interactions among the residents milling about.

This was not a city of life. This was not a city of light.

But I knew better than to ask questions.

Instead, I retraced my steps, returning to Ascian's street,

slipping into the shadows with an unobstructed view of the house.

I waited.

Waited for Windley and Rafe.

Waited for something—anything—to happen.

But as day melted into night, no one approached Ascian's house.

No Windley. No Rafe.

The only visitor was a lamplighter, moving sluggishly through the motions of igniting streetlamps.

Was Ascian even inside?

The house was still, its windows dark—no sign of movement, no ripple of activity. No Spirites raging down the street in pursuit of me.

Couldn't I just blast the place to smithereens and be done with it?

But that would mean blasting Pip away, too.

And I knew how Windley felt about Pip.

As the city fell asleep just as dully as it had awoken, doubt began to gnaw at me.

What if Windley hadn't felt Pip's magic at all? What if he wasn't coming?

Or worse—what if something had detained them?

Something big, bad, and orby.

Last night had been too cloudy for Luna's interference, but...

I clenched my fists. I needed answers. Tilting my head back into the shadows, I whispered, "Little terrors?"—then slipped beyond my eyelids into the void, letting the swarm of bodiless hands catch me.

"*MerriN!*"

"*MeRRIn!*"

"*Ones without merit! Let us tear them! Let us rip them! Let us turn their teeth to gnashing! We hate them! We loathe them! They are the filth of the earth!"*

They were still thrumming with fury from last night.

"Not yet," I pressed into them. "I need something else—a means to an end. If I spread you over the city, can you see if Windley is near?"

"MerRin?"

"mErrIn?"

A pause. The echoes shifted, murmuring among themselves.

And then—

"Why keep up this game, Merrin?"

The voice was clearer, defined. *Exitium.*

"Their purpose is destruction. Feed them as you should have done last night. You only delay the inevitable by sparing your enemies."

"I wasn't asking you," I said coldly. "I was asking them."

"You should be asking me." Exitium's presence swelled, pressing closer. *"I am the one who can help you."*

I hesitated. Desperation, maybe, but I took the bait.

"Fine," I said. "Is Windley near? Can you see him?"

"The beastling is not in this city."

Beastling was not a word I recognized. Not northern. And not one I had ever heard Windley use.

"But there is someone here looking for you," Exitium purred. *"A female. The next street over. She whispers your name into the shadows."*

I stiffened. "A female? You mean Charmagne?"

"Not a beastling. A hume."

A human? The only plausible 'female' was Beau, but if she had dared venture this far into danger for me—

I would never forgive her.

Exitium's voice slithered through my mind one last time:

"*It may prove worthwhile to see what the human female is after. She does not sound hostile.*"

Then, like a tide receding, the presence fell away, leaving only the unquiet murmurs of the echoes.

"*See what she is after. We will see what she is after. MeRRin, MErRiN, see what the human female is after...*"

I braced against the lingering unease. "Thanks," I muttered, dragging myself back into my body. The echoes stirred, restless.

A human looking for me? All the way down here?

There was only one way to find out.

I shifted from my hiding place, muscles stiff from stillness, and crept into the alley leading to the next street over. It was just as deserted as the last—save for a lone figure moving briskly beneath the lampposts.

My knuckles curled, pulling a small collection of shadow into my palm.

Just in case.

The figure noticed me immediately—then vanished into the gloom.

A sudden rush of footsteps. Quick. Intentional. Approaching from the unlit side of the street, weaving through debris, slipping between waste bins.

They stopped just a short distance away.

I couldn't see her face. Just a hooded silhouette against the dark.

I hesitated, then slowly lowered my hood.

A soft gasp. "Your hair!" she breathed. "You're...Queen Merrin of the north?" Her voice was like honey.

And definitely not Beau's.

I narrowed my eyes. "Who are you?"

She said nothing.

Instead, she stepped closer, though her hood remained drawn. "You are Merrin, right? He said you'd have wild hair."

He.

"Yes, I'm Merrin," I said again. "Who are you?"

"We aren't safe here. I've got a stag waiting. Come quickly!"

The figure seized my arm, her grip firm, urgency sharper than the cool night air. She stumbled over an uneven cobble but caught herself quickly, yanking me after her into shadows and down the street.

"I'm a friend," she said, voice hushed.

I anchored my heels, refusing to be dragged farther. "A friend?"

"Of Windalloy's." She glanced behind us into the dark, as if afraid something might materialize and give chase. "With their network of hexes in place, he can't enter this city—they'd detect him immediately—so he sent me to find you. I'm just glad you weren't inside that house! I don't know if I'd have been able to get you out. Maybe if it were just Pipsqueak, but not with those other two there. Charm is perfectly wicked."

"What do you mean, their network of hexes?" I asked, pulse quickening. "If that's the case, why didn't Windley—er, Windalloy—send Rafe to find me?"

The woman led me toward the city's gate, grip unrelenting. Even without visible pursuit, she didn't slow or let go. Her voice eased, shifting as though she spoke more to herself than me.

"Rafe? The magician you traveled with? He isn't here. Windalloy will explain once we reach my cottage. It's just a short ride..." She hesitated. "I didn't want to move too far away. In case he ever came back."

In case he ever came back?

Even as doubt roiled inside me, I followed her beyond the city walls, where a massive white stag stood tied to a post beneath the glow of a solitary lamp.

"Good boy, Boomer." She patted the beast's flank affectionately before effortlessly swinging herself onto his back. "Come on up. He can carry us both, easy."

"What kind of stag is this?" I asked warily. Too large to be a wind stag. Not malevolent enough for a blood stag. Maybe a water stag? It matched none of Mother Poppy's vivid descriptions.

"A spring stag," the woman answered. "Bred in the west. Now hurry! Windalloy will be panicking by now."

I mounted behind her cautiously, shadows at my fingertips. If this was a trap, it was a terribly thought-out one.

But it wasn't a trap.

I knew that immediately.

This person was good. Warmth radiated from her in waves —golden, comforting, untouched by darkness. She was everything one would hope a friend of Windley's might be.

Yet something deep inside me...

Something nameless, intangible...

Remained uneasy.

"Oh, shoot! I haven't even introduced myself." Her laughter glimmered like sunlight breaking through dusty glass. "It's Meraflora. You can trust me, I promise. Windalloy and I go way back. You might even say we saved each other."

Meraflora.

Windley had never mentioned that name before. Obviously, he'd known people other than his adoptive "family" before fleeing north. It shouldn't have surprised me that I didn't know all their names.

...Right?

I brushed aside the strange prickling settling in my gut and focused on what mattered most: Windley was near.

"I'm glad to meet you, Meraflora," I said carefully. "Windley's other childhood accomplices haven't exactly proven kind."

"Oh, you poor thing." Genuine pity undertoned her warm voice. "Most of their kind truly are good, you know. It's really just a small pocket that are creeps. Hopefully, you'll meet more like Windalloy while you're down here."

Whatever other small talk Meraflora attempted on our ride to her cottage, I didn't commit to memory. My mind was far too busy wondering.

Wondering about this kind stranger whose past was rooted alongside Windley's.

Wondering how they'd saved each other.

Wondering why he'd never mentioned such a sweet-voiced girl.

Meraflora's cottage appeared suddenly, nestled in a wooded nook branching off from a more traveled road. I might have admired its charming wooden construction, the quaint atmosphere, or the rose-filled garden surrounding it.

But none of that mattered to me.

I didn't care about the glowing beetles illuminating the path, drawn to the honey left in tiny glass feeders. Nor the clear, unbroken expanse of star-dappled sky stretching overhead.

Not even the colored bottles and delicate chimes swaying from branches, whispering gentle secrets to the breeze.

I cared only about the figure waiting on her stoop. The one who rose abruptly upon seeing us, his hair as black as doom. The one who set my heart racing.

He rushed toward us and pulled me from the stag into a desperate, crushing embrace.

"Merr." Windley's voice shook, face buried against my shoulder. "It's my fault. I lost control—I gave us away without even realizing it."

If he'd intended to say more, he never got the chance—

Because my lips found his to show exactly how forgiven he was.

Yet the kiss, to my surprise, was one-sided.

"Wind?"

He drew back, breathing uneven. "Sorry, lion queen. Give me a moment. I can't risk losing control again—just let me compose myself before you do that."

When he finally came back to me, the kiss was decidedly two-sided. For a fleeting heartbeat, Windley and I were the only two people in existence. I had never felt happier—or safer —wrapped in his arms.

It was dangerously easy to forget everything else when he held me like that.

Meraflora, ever practical, gently intervened. "Windalloy, we should head inside," she urged, tactfully smoothing the edges of her words. "You need to catch her up, and I'm sure she'd appreciate a chance to freshen up."

Windley didn't set me down until we were inside her cozy log cottage—a place clean and comforting, filled with billowing white curtains that surely fluttered on breezy afternoons. Bundles of dried lavender and star-mint hung from the rafters, perfuming the air with a gentle, soothing sweetness. A place suited perfectly for an angel.

A kind, warm, life-saving angel.

Why was I feeling so prickly?

"I owe you, Flora," Windley admitted, leaning casually against the kitchen counter. A grin teased his lips, that heart-stealing smirk I adored. "Yet again. Though I'm not sure I'll ever live long enough to repay you."

Only...

He wasn't showing off that grin to me.

He was directing it at her.

At Meraflora.

Or, as he'd called her just now—*Flora*.

Now, Flora... That was a name I'd heard before.

Or rather, almost heard.

No wonder Windalloy likes you. You look a lot like Flor—

Did you notice? Doesn't she look just like Flo—

And as kind, golden-hearted, honey-voiced Flora finally lowered her hood—

I was rendered speechless in the worst way.

The thing about Flora was that she looked a bit like me.

Scratch that.

Flora looked a lot like me.

An older, polished version of me.

If my hair were straight and silky.

If my waist were smaller.

If my bosom were fuller.

If my teeth were whiter, my skin softer, my every imperfection ironed into something effortlessly elegant, refined, desirable.

Suddenly, a memory tugged ruthlessly at my mind—words Windley had spoken in the quiet darkness of confession:

My keeper's daughter. The one kind thing in that house.

That foreign, ugly feeling swelling inside me—the one causing friction with our inner monster?

Its name was jealousy.

And jealousy is perilous indeed with darkness coiled in your heart.

14

WINDLEY'S SECRET

"**M**errin?! You're leaking again!"

Yes, shadows were rising around us, spilling from my wrists, thick and slow, curling like ink through water. And for a treacherous moment, I didn't even want to stop them.

The only person Windley had ever spoken of with such open admiration just happened to bear a suspicious resemblance to me?

Not to mention our names—*Meraflora. Merrin. Meraflora. Merrin.*

Had he called her Merr, too?

"Oh my goddess, Windalloy! You were right! She really is the Nemophilist!"

And he had told her that? Only my greatest secret?

I may have been a queen raised to lead thousands, trained to remain calm amidst chaos, expected to wield diplomacy with a steady hand.

But it took every shred of my restraint not to slap Windley in front of Flora.

Meanwhile, Windley pressed a hand to my forehead, as though I were some fevered child. "Merrin, what's wrong? Your spirit feels..."

Even if Flora hadn't shared my face, jealousy would have already taken root—but the fact that she did look so much like me? That Windley had neglected to mention it?

It made everything infinitely worse.

Because it meant he'd hidden her.

And if he'd hidden her, he had something to hide.

Perhaps I was partially to blame. I'd given him permission to lie to me, to skew truths, to tell me easy versions—but I hadn't intended for him to hide the fact that I was some sort of surrogate!

Flora was his true desire.

I was just the next best thing in her absence.

My anger surged, feeding wild, irrational theories about Windley's intentions. People often told stories to fill gaps in their understanding—to quiet fears.

And my mind was weaving an exceptionally painful one.

The darkness spilling out of me quickened.

Clutching my mother's necklace, I forced my voice into something falsely pleasant. "Meraflora? I am so sorry to do this after you've shown such kindness, but I need to speak with Windley alone."

"Oh my! Of course!" Flora smiled sweetly, entirely unbothered. "I actually need to prepare the bedroom for you two anyway. Go ahead and talk. When you're finished, I'll fix you both a meal, alright?"

She was so understanding. So soft, warm, *kind*.

The darkness around me swelled.

"Merrin?" Windley's voice pitched in worry. "Why did you just use that voice—the one reserved exclusively for tenuous coin negotiations?"

"Windley..." I pressed my palms flat against the table, bracing as if the ancient wisdom etched in its rings might grant me enough strength not to strangle my lover with my bare, shadow-coated hands.

"Queenie?" he prompted cautiously.

"She looks exactly like me."

Windley's brow furrowed deeply. "Who does?"

If I'd been holding a drink, I'd have asked someone to hold it.

"Flora, Windley. Flora looks like my elder sister!"

He closed his eyes, visibly picturing it, then opened them slowly. "Huh. You know, you're right. You two do sort of look alike. I never really noticed."

My jaw clenched painfully. "Are you seriously gaslighting me right now?"

"I—I'm not! I really didn't notice!" He paused, studying my face as though decoding a puzzle. Then, slow as sunrise, his lips curved upward. "...Are you jealous?"

"Windley!" I threw up my hands. "Why are you being dense?! Obviously I'm jealous! Anyone in my position would be!"

He squinted like I'd just posed an impossible riddle. "...But you're a queen."

"So?"

"Flora's just a normal woman."

"So am I, Windley!"

His perplexed expression deepened, as if he were solving a particularly vexing equation. I could practically see him carrying the one in his head.

"Think like a human," he muttered to himself.

"No need," I snapped. "Let me spell it out. The fact that I look like her? It's cruel, Windley."

That struck him. Windley visibly flinched, his bravado

cracking. "Cruel?" His voice fell, sincerity creeping in. "I think I understand why you're upset, but...this whole thing is different for me than it is for you." He swallowed roughly. "I told you—I connect with spirits before bodies. When I look at you or Flora, I see your spirit first. I'm not blind—I do see you—but physical appearance is secondary. It's hard to explain to a non-mythic."

That excuse wasn't good enough.

"Pip noticed. Twice."

Windley ran a hand anxiously through his hair. "Yeah? Well, you can't compare me to Pip. Pip's...incredibly powerful. He manifested five years earlier than the rest of us. He sees heartbeats. He's gifted."

I stared at him, searching his face.

Windley took my hand and knelt so we were eye level. "Merrin, when I met you, I couldn't even recall Flora's face clearly. But even if I had, it wouldn't have mattered. I never loved Flora. She was my friend, yes—a comfort when I had none—but I never desired her the way I desire you."

His voice dropped, raw and earnest. "I liked you from the moment I saw you. And as much as I enjoy your...shell, that isn't what I fell in love with." His fingers tightened around mine. "What I feel for you? I could never feel it for someone else. There isn't enough life in me."

He was telling the truth. I knew him well enough to recognize it.

But even still—

The bloodlust from the Nemophile's Crown was strong.

But the pounding ache in my chest was stronger.

I released my anger, and in the emptiness left behind, another emotion swiftly took root.

She had been his only comfort during a time filled with cruelty.

And I had wanted to punish him for it.

What kind of monster had I become?

Windley's thumb traced slow, steady circles over my knuckles. "Merr, I've been around humans long enough to know how you function. I should've realized how it might look to you. That was my mistake." He shook his head at himself. "But I meant what I said—love is different for us than it is for you. There will never be anyone else but you."

His voice dipped lower, something unguarded and visceral slipping in. "Quite literally, my heart isn't the sort that can love more than once—none of ours are. A Spirite gets one shot, and that's it." A single, humorless chuckle escaped him. "That's why I was living in torment when I thought I'd never get to have you."

My sternum tightened, snagging a breath, as the universe re-balanced around his vow.

Oh.

Oh, my heart.

A million strings plucked deep in my chest.

"You can't say things like that to a human," I whispered. "We'll explode."

His grin returned, sly now. "Seems to have worked. You stopped leaking."

Satisfied, he sank into the chair opposite me, lacing his hands behind his head. "I have to say, I'm a mite flattered. You being jealous over me and all." His smirk sharpened. "You do know you're a teensy bit out of my league, right?"

Because of me, the pain of his past had crept in—and now he was deflecting with humor. I owed him for indulging my darkest feelings, so I indulged his in turn.

"Didn't you know? Lions can be quite ferocious when guarding their prey."

His smirk turned devastating. "Oh? So you'll be nibbling on me, then?"

The thought was particularly tempting after being apart—I would've liked to reacquaint myself with the contours beneath his shirt—but it was difficult to fully recover from the ugliness I had just shown.

How could I stop it from resurfacing?

If we spun stories in the absence of understanding, perhaps understanding was the key.

"Windley...you do enjoy when I touch you, don't you?"

I'd seen how he looked at me, felt how his body responded. He'd called me beautiful, traced my skin with reverent fingers, yet—

"That much is obvious, isn't it?"

"But if bodies don't matter to you...I just want to understand better. I feel like I know you so well, yet know so little about how you see the world."

Windley considered, tapping his fingers thoughtfully against the table. "Bodies do matter," he admitted. "It's like getting cake with frosting. The cake's the main attraction, but that doesn't mean I don't want to lick the frosting."

I arched an eyebrow. "That's your analogy?"

"You're lucky I didn't go with stew."

I sighed. "So the cake is the spirit, and the frosting is the body?"

"You've got it." He pointed at me proudly, like a tutor pleased with his student. "Now, for me, your frosting's especially desirable because I know there's cake underneath—the best cake, actually. Some people don't have cake at all under their frosting—just a slice of shit. And if I know there's shit inside, I'm not going to bother licking the frosting."

That...made a troubling amount of sense.

Come to think of it, I'd been surprised Windley hadn't shown interest in Sestilia, despite her dazzling exterior.

"And since I desire your cake," he continued, "I notice your frosting above all others. I have no reason to bother with anyone else's." He leaned forward, smirking gently. "That's why it didn't occur to me your frosting and Flora's might look similar. I had to picture you side by side before it clicked."

"But isn't Flora's cake good, too?" All that kindness and warmth had to count for something.

Windley shrugged. "Sure, it's good, just not the kind I'd want to eat for the rest of my life. Some cake's too sweet, you know? It's rare to find a slice that gets better the more you taste it."

His gaze flicked up, watching me closely. "You're smiling. Does that mean you understand?"

Finally. I nodded, letting him know.

Relief relaxed his features, and he slumped back into the chair. "I've always found it strange that humans go straight for the frosting," he mused.

"It's because it takes us a while to figure out if we like the cake." I tilted my head, thoughtful. "The frosting's easier. For what it's worth, I noticed your cake before your frosting, and I enjoy both...even if you're occasionally full of shit."

His grin stretched wider.

"You know, Edius said I was cute for a human. Does that mean he was talking about my cake?"

Windley's smile dropped immediately. "Edius?"

Oh, right. There were far more important matters than cake, and poor Flora was still politely tucked away down the hall.

I quickly recounted everything that had happened during my encounter with Edius, Pip, and Charmagne, making sure to emphasize that Pip had survived my darkness.

In turn, Windley detailed what transpired after we'd collapsed on the hill.

Edius had been right: Windley had wandered off briefly, not realizing his power had flashed the night before. He hadn't realized his mistake until I'd been taken. Knowing he needed swift transport, he tried securing a prancelope, but they couldn't bear the weight of both him and Rafe, nor could they be controlled without beguilement.

In the end, Rafe had reluctantly agreed to head toward the coast alone, tasked with pacting Soleil and securing her support against Ascian.

"I wasn't too disappointed to part ways," Windley admitted. "Give him time to cool off. He was rather grouchy about my slip-up and losing you. Chap's no fun when he's in a mood."

My stomach twisted. "But what if Luna comes for him while we're separated?"

Windley's expression darkened. "It's a risk we had to take. She hasn't reappeared since you fought her, so we're betting you wounded her enough to keep her down for a bit. Let's save our panic for when she returns to the sky. With any luck, we'll reunite with Rafe before that happens."

Not the most comforting plan, but we had little choice.

"I suspected Ascian would take you somewhere familiar—Abardo, where we once lived, being a top guess. When I felt Pip's power, I thought maybe he was helping me out...until I reached the city gates. Turns out Ascian had hexed damn near the whole town. If I approached one of his pets, he'd know instantly. I needed to be sure you were inside before risking it. That's why Flora volunteered to scout. She was only supposed to check the house, but she did one better—she brought you back."

So, Flora was brave, too. Brave, kind, and warm.

Worthy of my respect—and from now on, she would have it.

"That reminds me—Flora mentioned you two 'saved each other.' I know how she saved you, but how did you save her?"

"Oh. Well..." Windley made a face. "I told you she allowed me to escape while her father slept? Truth is, I didn't leave immediately. Instead, I entered that bastard's chamber and drained him while he slept. I hadn't done it sooner because drinking even a little of him made me sick—his taste was rancid —but I couldn't leave Flora alone with him if I was leaving for good, so I powered through. His energy was what got me to the Emerald Wood."

Something unreadable churned in my chest. "...You killed her father?"

Windley's voice quieted. "He didn't treat only me badly."

A chill slid up my spine. "Why didn't you tell me before?"

"Shame?" His usual smirk was gone. "I've taken plenty of lives out of necessity. That was the only one I also took for pleasure."

However dark, it was honest.

"I understand," I said softly—because the thought of killing Charmagne was more enticing than it had any right to be. "So, what now? Do we truly need Soleil's help to defeat Ascian? With them all cooped up in that house, I could probably eliminate them with one blow. Edius even mentioned I wounded Ascian last time."

"No, Merr—and not just because Pip's in there." Windley sat forward, all humor abandoned. "Considering the state of Abardo, Ascian has more minions than those three. No way could they hex an entire town alone. We shouldn't confront him until Rafe completes his pact."

I didn't entirely agree, but I'd respect it. I didn't yet understand Ascian's true threat, nor the extent of his coven.

"Fine. Then we rest here tonight and set out for the coast tomorrow."

With that settled, Windley went to fetch Flora, who cheerfully offered me a bath and clean clothes.

Her washroom was small but suffused with gentle heat, a space lovingly cultivated over years of quiet, comfortable living. Candles of varying heights lined the shelves, their dried wax drippings evidence of many unhurried evenings. Jars of colored oils and soaps crowded the wooden ledge above the basin, blending into a sage-and-floral aroma that seeped into my skin as the water surrounded me.

I tried to let the bath soak away the jealousies still staining my soul.

Flora was a good person. A friend to Windley.

Only a troll would fault her for that.

Yet, as I scrubbed my arms, my gaze drifted to the blurred reflection of my face in the water. My hair, wet and flattened, sharpened my features—made them appear more delicate, more refined. More like hers.

Maybe that was why my hand paused a moment too long on the antique knob of her washroom door.

It lingered even longer when I heard their voices drifting faintly from the kitchen.

"You're a man now, Windalloy. And you've returned with a queen on your arm—who would've thought? If you marry her, will you become a king?"

Windley let out a low, mellow laugh. "No, it doesn't work that way. The north doesn't have kings. Royals partner with other royals, mostly to produce royal offspring, but they don't grant the male a title. It's not like the storybooks."

"Offspring?" Flora repeated curiously.

"Er...yeah..."

Her voice lowered. "She doesn't know much about your kind, does she?"

There was a note of wistful sadness in her words.

"I'm trying to tell her," Windley admitted quietly, "but slowly. I know it isn't fair, but I'd forgotten a lot of it myself until recently. And besides, we would never be allowed to wed. If she keeps me, it would be as a paramour."

A pause stretched taut. Then—in an even more hushed tone —"Windalloy...I fear you'll have your heart broken in the end."

Something thick lodged in my throat.

Why would she say that?

Worse—why didn't Windley disagree?

"I know," he said, voice like midnight rain. "But it's worth it, even if it's fleeting."

Silence filled the cottage, broken only by Flora's movements as she presumably prepared our meal. I imagined she was as wonderful a cook as she was a homemaker.

Then—

"By the way—" Windley cleared his throat. "She thinks you two look alike."

"We do," Flora replied lightly. "But then, you wouldn't know that, would you?"

So, my jealousy hadn't vanished after all.

Neither had my guilt.

Flora's reaction was far more reasonable than mine had been. She understood him worlds better than I did. And here I was—ignorant, jealous—though I'd once fancied myself a champion for lofty ideals like acceptance and justice.

I was quickly learning we couldn't always control our feelings.

Sometimes, the line between heroine and villain blurred.

I resolved to accept these feelings quietly, burying them

deep where no one could see. I might not control my jealousy, but I could control how it influenced my treatment of others.

"Thank you, Flora," I said when I rejoined them at the table. "I haven't felt this clean since leaving the castle. I meant to say before—I'm envious of your cottage. It's lovely and rustic, like the forest hideaway I use to conduct business with my neighboring queen, Beau."

Windley snorted, eyes twinkling wickedly. "Conduct business? Don't you mean drink mead and flirt shamelessly with guards?"

"Quiet, pinkie."

His hair had now shifted to a shocking shade of fuchsia.

Flora giggled, filling the cottage with warmth. "Please, Queen Merrin, won't you have some pheasant pie? The carrots and potatoes are from my garden—I'm told they're quite flavorful."

Damn it all, Flora was an excellent cook—this was easily the best meal we'd enjoyed since leaving Sestilia's palace, and mercifully free of the spider queen's oppressive tension.

After dinner, thoughtful Flora even offered to braid my hair, looping it around my head like a wreath, reminiscent of the way girls wore it during the Clearing's gilded lunar festival.

"There," she said brightly, stepping back with an approving smile. "Now you have a crown, as every queen should." She gave Windley a knowing look. "Don't you agree?"

"I prefer it untamed," he replied lazily, flicking his wrist with mock disdain.

Then he turned to me, extending his hand gallantly, like a prince plucked from a fairy tale.

"Well, my queen, may I escort you to bed?"

In reality, it was well past midnight, closer now to morning —but time had little meaning anymore. Our sleep schedules hadn't been right in weeks.

Flora was busying herself at the sink, so she didn't see the heat blooming across my face as I stared down at Windley's outstretched palm.

But Windley saw it.

And it made his mouth curl into its most dangerous, delicious smirk yet.

Because I was suddenly remembering the promise he'd made that night on the hill.

The first time I make love to you, it shall be in a bed.

15

HAVE YOUR CAKE

Windley didn't release my hand the whole way to the bedroom Flora had so graciously offered us weary travelers—a room boasting long, flowing curtains, fresh flowers on the nightstand, and a quilt Flora had surely patched herself.

He didn't walk beside me, either; he led me, drawing me along gently while I trailed behind on unsteady feet that seemed suddenly complicit with my hot, flushed cheeks.

Windley and I had spent several nights side by side, curled tightly together—but never behind sturdy walls, and never in a proper bed. The thought proved rather unnerving. I, the lion queen, was suddenly reduced to a mouse—meekly scurrying about, searching desperately for a hidey-hole.

Squeak. Squeak.

At the end of a hallway much shorter than it had appeared, Windley eased the door shut and set his lantern on the bedside table. He moved the curtain aside with the back of his hand, peering out into the waning night. Beyond, incandescent beetles drifted lazily, casting a muted glow in the moonless dark. Thankfully, no Luna in sight.

Flora's floors were polished wood. I stood near the door, awkwardly tracing circles with my toe, fidgeting with my hands, and eyeing the bed.

The room stilled, the closed door severing us from the pulse of the world. Alone together, wrapped in shadows, the ambiance set my chest aflutter, my skin ashiver, my stomach askew—

—and made my armpits distressingly clammy in a most unqueenly fashion.

I steadied my breath and straightened my shoulders, willing myself dry before Windley could notice.

He kept his eyes toward the window. "Do you feel recovered, Merr? From our tiff?"

"I do."

"Any lingering doubts as to my intentions?" His voice was tender, careful.

My cheeks heated further. "No."

"And do you forgive my part in it?"

"Of course. Do you forgive mine?"

Windley let the curtain fall and faced me with an easy curve of his mouth. "Always. And...is this all right?"

Moving with deliberate ease, he peeled his shirt up, muscles flexing as the fabric cleared his shoulders.

I swallowed a lump that felt suspiciously like half a dinner roll. "It's...fine."

The lantern flame danced, casting warm light and shadow across the taut lines of his chest. Lean. Sculpted. Strong. And a slew of other very appetizing adjectives.

"What?" he said. "I get hot under covers."

He knew very well "what," or he wouldn't be grinning at me like that.

Windley's frosting was delicious frosting indeed.

Though I noticed he carefully kept his scarred back turned toward the wall.

"I've never been alone in a room with a shirtless man before," I said lightly, trying to mask nerves with humor. "Albie would faint if he knew."

Squeak, squeak.

He arched a brow. "You look upon my exposed torso, and your first thought is of Sir Albie? We might have a problem, lion queen."

My first thought was, in fact, far more indecent—but that stubborn lump in my throat kept me silent.

"May I ask what you're doing all the way over there?" he continued, dark eyes glittering playfully. "Wasn't the lion going to bite her prey? You can't do so from across the room."

He was toying with me because I was acting every bit the mouse I felt. My lion's fangs had shrunk to a twitchy nose and quivering whiskers.

His sharp edge melted into subtle wickedness. "Or is it that you're afraid of my bite?"

"As if I would fear something like that!" I squeaked—then grimaced at my telling reaction.

Windley immediately relented. "I'm teasing, Merrin. My only intention tonight is to hold you and sleep. Nothing more."

Relief and an odd flicker of disappointment fought within me. "You don't mean for us to—?"

He shook his head, pulling back the quilt in invitation. "I'll put my shirt back on if it helps. Though it'd be a shame; I rather enjoy the way you're looking at me." He flashed me a devil's grin. "It's not often my wits are sharper than yours."

Just like that, the tension loosened, leaving only my bruised pride.

I straightened.

I was no mouse.

I was a fearsome queen.

"Sharper? Only through trickery! You purposely led me to believe one thing was happening when it wasn't!"

"What thing would that be?" he cooed, all innocence and roguery.

Squeak.

He laughed again as I deflated. "No, lion queen. If you haven't noticed, I've something of a weakness when it comes to you. If we were to become physical right now, I doubt I could resist using my power. Trust me—you're handling this better than I would be if it were your shirt strewn over the dresser."

He folded the garment, set it aside, and perched on the mattress, gaze softened to quiet resolve.

"Truth is, you're not ready yet—and that's all right. I've already waited years for this moment. Now that you're mine to cherish, I want to savor every breath along the way. If it takes a lifetime, I'll wait a lifetime."

Oh, my chest tightened.

He tilted his head, a spark of mischief lighting his eyes. "Now," he winked, "would an incubus say something like that?"

"A particularly scheming one might."

He chuckled softly. "If you're worried, I can always sleep in the living room instead. Though, I believe that's where Flora's sleeping..."

"Get in," I grumbled, pushing at his chest since he was still strategically keeping his back angled away from me.

With teasing ease, he pulled me down with him, wrapping his arms around my waist and nuzzling his fuchsia hair against my neck.

It was so classically Windley—something we'd done countless times—yet...

He must have sensed me stiffening, because his touch gentled even more. Mouse whiskers threatened to sprout anew on my burning cheeks.

"You're so nervous," he whispered against my forehead, then caressed his lips there. "It's just me. I'll never do anything you don't want."

The problem wasn't him.

The problem was the bed.

Because somehow, a bed made it feel like we were back home. And who we'd been there was far different from who we'd become out here.

Thinking back to the guard who'd burst into my chambers all those nights ago...

"Sleeping in a bed after all these years," I murmured, "it feels like suddenly bridging two different worlds."

"You find the bed intimidating?" he interpreted quietly.

"It just feels...different. Like a collision of past and present." And for all my dirty thoughts and daydreams these past weeks, suddenly I didn't know what to do with myself.

He shifted onto his back, drawing me in with a hush of tenderness and guiding my hand to rest over his steady heartbeat. "I'm the same person in a bed or a tent, Merr. There's nothing to fear here."

And yet, my heart still raced, utterly unruly.

This was undeniably different.

"I just feel awkward. I know it's silly after...after everything on the hill."

Unwed queens didn't typically caress the bare chests of handsome young guards. He knew that—knew I was inexperienced in a way even the most innocent handmaid likely wasn't.

Windley carefully guided my fingers across the smooth expanse of his chest, his touch reassuring.

"It's okay, love," he murmured, lullaby-soft. "Intimacy isn't the same as being sexual. I don't expect anything of you now just because of what we did then. Take your time. Get used to the feel of my skin. All I want is for you to feel safe against me —no matter where we are."

Windley closed his eyes, surrendering himself to the mercy of my exploring touch, letting my fingertips glide slowly over the lines of his body, learning them, memorizing them. His bareness was warm and inviting beneath my palm.

The curve where his shoulder met his arm became my favorite—built of protective muscle and sinew, stronger and more comforting than I'd imagined. My fingers skimmed lightly across his collarbone, drifted up the telling thrum of his neck, then traveled down, tracing the contours of his stomach.

"You feel good to touch, Windley," I whispered, as if sharing a secret.

A measured smile spread across his mouth, its edges soft in the lantern's shimmer—only to fade almost immediately.

"Not all of me." His eyes lifted, fixing on something far beyond the room.

"You mean what I saw while you were bathing?"

He slid a hand behind his pink head, feigning casualness, eyes locked to the ceiling. "You weren't meant to see it. It's grotesque." He bit at his lip, thoughtful. "Though, given your unfortunate spooning habit, I suppose it was inevitable."

In truth, I'd already gotten a closer look back at the ruins in the forest.

"I've been dreading this moment," he admitted in a hum, still staring upward. "I had planned to ease you into it—let you feel it quietly in the dark—but..." He let out a sigh, heavy with acceptance. "It's only fair you know all of me. I can't expect you to feel safe if I won't allow myself to feel safe with you."

My breath caught. This was no small gesture; it was an offering of trust. A big, meaningful moment.

Then, in Flora's borrowed bed, beneath the comforting glow of a single flame, Windley slowly, awkwardly turned onto his side, baring the scars fully to me—deep, jagged marks of torn flesh, healed and reopened countless times.

My brave knight.

Swallowing the ache in my chest, I spread gentle fingers across the damaged skin.

"Don't force yourself, lion queen," he said thickly. "I know they're offensive."

He spoke with shame, as if somehow he deserved them.

"They're from Ascian, aren't they?" I asked delicately.

"The longer ones. The shallower ones came from Flora's father."

Windley held perfectly still as I carefully traced the grooves carved cruelly into his back, each scar a silent tale of endurance and resilience. I imagined the suffering he'd borne, the darkness he'd faced, the strength it must have taken to survive and overcome.

Grotesque. Offensive. Those were not the right words. What surged through me wasn't pity either—it was something fiercer and stronger.

Respect.

Respect filled my heart as I leaned forward, pressing my lips reverently against the scars.

"M-Merrin?"

"These aren't offensive, Windley," I assured him. "They're proof of your strength." I kissed him again, higher up, at his shoulder, then once more, softly, at the side of his neck.

"You've looked into the eyes of evil and come out on the other side. That is commendable. That is powerful." My fingertip traced tenderly along his spine. "You'll never be rid of these marks, so you should reclaim them. Take back the power stolen by those who left them, and never hide them from me again. There is nothing about you that is grotesque."

He didn't speak, didn't move. A new truth seemed to settle in him.

"I should have known you, of all people, would feel that way," he finally said, voice barely above a whisper.

"Don't put me on a pedestal, Windley. What I said was the truth—and that truth has nothing to do with me. The triumph belongs solely to you."

When he finally turned back to me, the charming glint had returned to his eyes. "Gross. Stop being so regal."

"You know how I get when I feel conviction."

"More than most."

And with that, all was right again.

No mouse tails or whiskers remained—just a lion and a devil, settled softly in the quiet dark, happy to simply be together.

Windley extinguished the lantern and coaxed me tenderly into his arms.

But things were different now.

The bed no longer intimidated me.

And Windley had nothing left to hide.

We didn't sleep immediately. Instead, we lay facing each other in the hush of the room—Windley sketching lazy circles over the small of my back beneath my shirt, while my fingers wandered feather-light along the column of his neck.

Though my soul felt at peace for the first time in days, it was impossible to shut my eyes with a face like his inches from my own.

"It will be difficult to sleep like this," he murmured eventually.

"Like what?"

He tugged me even closer. "With your eyes piercing into me. Close them."

I obeyed—but secretly delighted in having caused him trouble.

"Good queenie," he murmured in playful praise. "I'll reward you."

He brushed a kiss to the corner of my mouth, savoring it, then claimed my lips in a deeper, heated press. When he withdrew, his breath hovered against mine, as if weighing the temptation of a third.

My mouth quirked deeper.

"Quiet, you," he whispered.

"I said nothing."

"Your smirk says enough. Perhaps I should sleep somewhere else after all. You're too distracting."

"No." I pressed my nails lightly into his shoulder. "I like the feel of you. Your...frosting."

"And I like yours far too much," he murmured, fingertips dancing along my side. "That's the problem."

It felt good, powerful even, to be so desired—to know I had such a hold on a creature designed to hold power over others.

A controlled inhale slid past my lips while I tilted just enough to feel his grip adjust.

A quiet sound escaped him, part growl, part sigh, and his hand slid higher beneath my shirt, dangerously close to new territory. I didn't object.

"You're so soft," he breathed. "It almost feels wrong to touch you."

No. Wrong wasn't what it felt like at all.

To prove as much, I slid my palm to the small of his back and coaxed him closer, hips meeting with deliberate insistence.

"Lion queen..." His voice was strained, half warning, half plea.

I met his gaze silently, challenging.

"We should stop. For all the reasons I mentioned before. Remember those?"

So he said—but his thumb was pressing with unrelenting intent against my spine, his hand sliding steadily downward.

"You're the one doing it," I whispered.

"You know full well you're doing it, too. Temptress."

"Incubus."

"Wayward queen."

"Devil."

"Shhh." This time when he kissed me, he captured my lower lip in a tender bite between his teeth. "You're playing with fire."

Because he was, after all, a predator at heart.

But so was I. My hand found the back of his head instinctively, fingers threading through the silken ruff of his hair, pulling him deeper into our kiss.

"*Fffff—*" He sighed against my lips. "Fine. But only kissing, and only a few minutes. You need rest, and I need control."

With that, he rolled onto his back and pulled me atop him, guiding my mouth to his, opening warmly beneath mine. Straddling his hips, I cupped his jaw, savoring every delicious movement of his tongue while his hands explored dangerously close beneath my shirt.

I wanted to capture this moment—bottle the liquid tension, the intoxicating apprehension forever. Flesh and bone, muscle and sinew. Windley struggled to keep his promise, and before either of us spiraled beyond reason, he took my wrists gently in hand.

"I take it you aren't nervous anymore?" he teased breathlessly.

No. The night's truths, our vulnerability, had set my mind

at ease, my body craving nothing more than to explore him endlessly.

Holding my wrists, he pressed a firm kiss against my forehead, whispering roughly, "Goddess damn, lion queen. All that talk earlier about licking frosting..."

"You started it."

"*You* started it. Trailing your scent past me without regard for my instincts." His eyes darkened with feral promise. "Would you like to know what those instincts are telling me now?"

I gave him a nod, swallow thick as molasses.

"To beguile you. Steal you away to a secret place and do whatever I please with you. You've no *idea* the thoughts I've had." He drew my thumb slowly across his bottom lip, then took it between his teeth, pressing a sharp eyetooth delicately against my nail. "Oh, how I'd devour you, my queen."

That hardly seemed like a bad thing.

"Now, go to bed." He eased me from his chest.

In defiance, I promptly returned to him, clinging to his back like the turtle shell I was. This time, he welcomed me, guiding my arm around him and pressing my palm against his chest.

Whatever sort of heart he had, I felt it racing beneath my fingertips, satisfying proof that he suffered the same rush as I did.

Though a daunting task awaited us beyond the walls of this room, for this brief moment, everything felt perfect. More perfect, perhaps, than any night we'd shared before. Our bond had deepened—queen and guard, lion and devil, friends and lovers.

Yet, just as sleep brushed my eyelids, a snaking voice hissed at me from beyond, threatening to unravel all we'd built.

"*A word of caution, Merrin: that beastling harbors a considerable amount of lust, and beastlings were made to feast upon the vitality of humes. Are you sure you know what you're doing?"*

Exitium, whatever they were, clearly hailed from a time before Spirites had evolved. I refused to lend their whispers any credence.

Still, I couldn't ignore how the distant echoes grew frantic afterward, buzzing insistently in my ear.

"One without merit? One without merit? The beastling is one without merit?"

"NO," I pushed firmly against the void.

I was grateful that darkness concealed the shadowy clusters already beginning to gather around me.

16

DIRTY LITTLE SECRET

Windley and I slept well past the morning sun and straight into the thick of day.

We woke to the sound of birds fluttering outside the window, feasting on whatever seed Flora had left for them.

Feasting.

Beastlings were made to feast on the vitality of humes.

Not this beastling.

This one was too busy devouring Flora's pancakes.

With the sun and the birds came brighter spirits for Windley and me.

He'd shared his last secrets. I'd embraced his scars.

I'd confided my worries. He'd put them to bed.

We'd spent the night wrapped in each other's arms, safely behind walls—a preview of many future days, we hoped.

The thought was intoxicating.

Windley seemed especially puckish as he teased me over breakfast, holding the syrup just out of my reach—a playful reminder of simpler, happier times.

As I watched him cast wicked glances my way, a secretive twitch at the corner of his mouth, I wondered—how had I not realized my love for him sooner?

Eight years.

He'd loved me for eight full years.

Eight years' worth of missed opportunities, lost moments we could've spent just like last night—feeling his warmth, listening to the truths of his heart.

"You're staring again," he said, snapping me from my thoughts.

"I wasn't."

"You absolutely were."

"Only because you're hideous."

Flora stiffened at the stove, clearly unused to our particular flavor of flirtation.

"At least I'm tidy," Windley purred, eyes narrowing with sly amusement. "Unlike the queen of soil."

"Better queen of soil than king of smut."

Flora relaxed, finally catching on, and shook her head with a fond huff, stacking another pancake onto the pile.

"We should have plenty to reach the coast," Windley said, rifling through his pack. "Between what you stole from that great brute—what'd you say his name was? Edmond?"

"Edius," I corrected, hiding a smile.

"With *Edmond*'s contributions and what Flora's donated, we won't need to stop for supplies along the way."

"Thank you, Flora." I caught her eye, letting my gratitude show. "When all this is over, I intend to repay you tenfold." *Once I regain my royal resources.*

"Consider it thanks for taking care of Windalloy." Flora wiped her hands on her apron, her voice softening as she regarded him. "I've always thought of him as a little brother. I've worried what might've become of him, but it comforts me to know he found someone worth staying away for."

She was warm. She was kind.

And she might have been telling the truth.

Yet, something told me she wasn't.

It was subtle—the way she nudged his chin with her knuckle as she spoke, something fractionally more than sisterly lingering in her eyes.

Then again, perhaps that was my jealous heart conjuring things from thin air.

Our monster was not the sharing kind.

"Windalloy," Flora continued, her voice low and lilting, "after you face Lord Ascian, will you return here? I'd like to see you again before you head north."

"I was counting on it," he replied with an easy grin. "I doubt we'll find a kinder host."

With him gazing up at her, radiating that unstudied calm, and her looking back with those honey-bright eyes, I had to remind myself firmly—it was *my* cake he wanted.

The sudden flare of darkness in me was not my own.

"Why does this keep happening?" Windley caught my wrist, examining the shadow spilling out of it.

"Anticipation, I suppose." I offered lightly, "Facing off against your former master might have that effect."

A lie—but it would do.

Outside, just beyond Flora's rose-filled garden, the white spring stag from the previous night stood penned beside another beast—one I'd seen grazing the northern plains but had never come close to taming.

A prancelope.

The swiftest of all four-legged creatures.

And famously cantankerous, prone to bucking at anyone who dared approach.

Yet, this prancelope trotted eagerly to the gate when Windley appeared, sleek and spotted, its long legs gracefully carrying it forward with unnatural obedience.

It delicately took a carrot from his outstretched hand.

"You always teased me about Ruckus's terrible behavior," I accused. "Meanwhile, you've secretly been charming wild stags into docility, haven't you?"

"A queen's guard never reveals his secrets."

I knew it.

Which meant he could have easily calmed Ruckus into compliance when we'd fled the woodcutter's hut. He'd deliberately chosen our slower, hidden route through the woods.

"Mayhap I just wanted more time alone with you," he admitted sinfully when I pressed him. "I rather liked the idea of sneaking through the forest, pulling your body behind trees, covering your mouth with my hand..."

Ruck's supposed "unruliness" had been nothing more than a convenient excuse.

A dastard, through and through.

With final farewells exchanged with Flora, whose voice was just as kind and honey-sweet as ever, Windley and I set out from her cottage, past Abardo, and onto the rolling hills.

At last, we were back on course.

Prancelopes were far swifter than stags—so swift I had to cling to Windley just to avoid being swept away with the leaves and petals caught in our wake.

The creature climbed hills effortlessly, leapt obstacles gracefully, and paid no mind to the scents of predators lurking in the brush.

"This is so much faster than the wallop!" I shouted over the rushing wind.

"Unfortunately, it wouldn't let you ride without me."

"So, you're accustomed to mounting whatever you please through your powers of titillation?"

He laughed. "Mercy me, if the other guards could hear such defilement from our noble queen's mouth."

Truthfully, I felt more like myself than ever.

I much preferred the drum of hoofbeats to the clink of fine glassware.

I'd let my braids loose, my mane now wild behind us, whipping free in the wind like a dark-golden cape.

The southern air tasted of freedom and autumn. The horizon stretched wide and full of promise. By nightfall, Windley slowed the prancelope's pace to study the sky.

"I see chap's lover still hides her face."

"Luna's avoiding him, isn't she?"

"She doesn't strike me as the sulking type."

"Perhaps I wounded her more gravely than we thought."

It was unsettling, the thought of having injured an immortal being.

My focus soon drifted elsewhere.

"Windley, do you think Flora and I might share some distant ancestry?" I asked casually. "Maybe generations back in our bloodlines? Surely the north and south have mingled before."

He shrugged. "Couldn't say. The two of you don't exactly smell alike."

Smell?

"It would be fascinating to see the world through your eyes, Wind."

"And yet, all you'd see is you."

I clung tighter to him as we pressed onward into dusk.

As evening darkened the skies, I again searched for signs of Luna's rise, hoping her telltale glow might reveal Rafe's location. Yet again, she remained hidden, withholding her light. Instead, the heavens unraveled into a tapestry of winking stars —lavender mostly, usually a harbinger of rain.

Windley slowed our pace further, tilting his chin upward. "I still don't see chap's sulky lover."

"It's strange," I murmured. "Until meeting Luna myself, goddesses felt so abstract—like a vague chorus in the heavens. But Rafe's people seem to know them all by name. Do your people?"

"Somewhat. We don't name them individually, but we acknowledge four primary goddesses—the moon, the sun, the goddess of beginnings, and the goddess of endings. Lesser, nameless ones drift through the sky like embers. There are also wraiths—monsters that dwell between realms—and angels, although most fell during the dawn of humankind. That was around when the goddesses moved permanently to the celestial plane."

"Leaving their physical forms behind in the Necropolis?" I clarified.

"Apparently so."

"I'd like to learn more about your people's lore, Windley."

"Oh, *would* you?" He smirked, eyes dancing with delight. "And what would you like to know?"

"You mentioned the goddesses don't favor your kind because your foremothers were something else entirely. What other creatures are capable of creating life?"

Windley hesitated, then spoke quietly. "That's an old word, Merrin—rarely uttered even among my kind. They were called the Drakaina."

I'd never heard the term before.

"They were among the first beings to emerge from the

void," he continued. "According to legend, they warred against the goddesses for dominion over the mortal world. The Drakaina lost and were exiled to a realm beyond reach—neither living nor dead—but their offspring were allowed to remain, adopted in a way by the goddesses. They tolerate us, though they view us as burdens." His aura darkened slightly. "I never put much faith in those stories—not until I stood face-to-face with Luna herself."

"But what exactly were the Drakaina?"

"Celestial-born beings, much like the goddesses. But serpentine in form."

"Snake women?"

He nodded. "Some had wings. The ancients carved their likenesses into caves along the far southern shores. My pop saw them once and painted what he remembered, but those paintings were lost when I was sent away."

Windley, then, was doubly orphaned—first of family, and now, it seemed, of race.

"By the way, are you getting cold back there?" he asked.

I was, but I didn't want to stop for camp. Every stride toward the coast was another stride closer to confronting Windley's abuser. Revenge had never tasted so tempting.

"My cloak is warm enough," I fibbed.

"Tsk." He shook his head. "I can feel your chill through my cloak, Merrin. If you don't wish to stop for camp, at least dismount and walk a while. You'll warm up if your legs are moving."

He didn't leave it open for discussion, sliding smoothly off the prancelope and pulling me down before I could object. Turning to the creature, he patted his knee, whistling.

"Come on, Dandelion."

"You named this one Dandelion too?!"

"I got lazy," he admitted with a sheepish shrug.

"Remind me never to let you name our children."

Windley froze. "Come again?"

Oh.

A terribly forward thing for an unwed queen to say to a non-royal guard she'd only recently begun courting.

"You'd...bear children with me?"

I swallowed. "Only if you prove yourself worthy," I teased, determined to lighten the sudden tension. "Now, tell me—have you ever wiped an ass?"

But my joke fell flat.

Windley was staring deeply into my eyes, and I quickly averted my gaze, studying Dandelion II instead. "Well, obviously it's a bit soon to talk about that, but...I suppose I wouldn't mind it...someday," I confessed.

"Oh." His voice drifted skyward, strangely wistful. "That's...disgustingly nice."

"Windley?"

"I guess you truly do love me."

His strange mood confused me. I couldn't tell if he was jesting.

"I suppose...perhaps a little."

"Merrin." Windley caught my hands, gravity settling over his features.

"Your kind and mine—we can't create life together."

Somewhere a cricket chirped, absurdly loud in the hush that followed. My pulse stuttered, like it had missed a stair.

All I could do was echo him. "Spirites and humans...can't conceive?"

He shook his head. Regret flickered in his eyes while he watched me for any sign of hurt. In that instant, the conversation I'd overheard between him and Flora snapped into focus.

"But if you ever wanted children with someone else, I

wouldn't stand in your way," he added, as though he'd already given it careful thought.

How could that possibly work—watching your partner raise children with another? Shadow curled at my wrists.

"Why can't we?"

"I don't know," he sighed. "It simply never happens. The effort is the same, no matter the pairing, but the outcome always differs."

Committing to Windley meant forfeiting a royal heir—at least one born of us both.

"It's not a decision for today," he said carefully, "but you had a right to know."

Then the full picture set in: Windley had always meant to fade into the backdrop—my twilight paramour while I wedded for lineage.

The notion burned; darkness tingled at my fingertips.

"Oh, Merr!" He reeled me in, wearing a rakish grin to hide the worry in his eyes. "I swear I'll put in the effort to make a child with you every single day, but—"

"It's not that," I said, voice low. "It's picturing you tucked away like some scandal while a Cacti prince stands beside my throne. How could I—"

"Plenty of queens have managed the arrangement," he replied, half-shrug, half-challenge.

I wouldn't know. My mother never spoke of such things, and she was gone before I was old enough to ask them.

Fingering her necklace, I wondered: did she keep secret lovers, or had she truly cared for my father—the Cloudfall royal no courtier ever mentioned? The one who had died at sea.

My silence told him enough.

"Merr." Windley drew me into a shield-tight embrace. "I told you—I'd surrender anything for you. I made that promise knowing I might never be yours in full daylight. If loving you means taking whatever place I can, I'll take it." A rogue gleam sparked in his eyes. "I'll happily remain your whispered sin."

But even if he could live in shadows, I wasn't sure I could bear him there.

And the one person who might understand—Beau—was miles away, carrying a magician's unclaimed heir.

"Then it's settled," I said at last, summoning a smile. "If anyone was born to be a delicious scandal, it's the Clearing's naughtiest guard."

His answer was predictably flirtatious—something about midnight visits and overturned crowns—yet the words blurred as we walked on beneath the stars.

He'd told me Spirites love only once.

Did that mean if I broke his heart, he'd be condemned to solitude forever?

Unfair. An impossible weight to carry.

Still, watching him—remembering every stolen glance, every playful nudge, every excuse he'd invented just to stand a breath closer—I knew the truth:

I could no more have stopped myself from loving Windley than halted the tides. And I had no intention of trying.

Maybe I had loved him at first scent too. Maybe I was willing to give up everything for him too.

These were dangerous reveries for a queen—and something inside me didn't like them.

"When we smite the world, the beastlings will be the first to go."

17
BEASTLINGS

It was a bright afternoon when we reached the coast. Like visiting the Queendom of the Cove, I tasted salt in the air and heard the distant crash of waves before glimpsing the broad patches of sand, interrupted by gnarled driftwood and jagged bits of rock. These were the markers of the sea beyond.

It felt like home, smelled like home, tasted like home—so I spent some time carrying my shoes, digging my toes into the cool sand at the water's edge while Windley released finicky Dandelion II back into the wild, where the first Dandelion already grazed.

"Now what?" I asked, shaking sand from my skirt. "Did you and Rafe agree on a meeting spot?"

"Not exactly," Windley admitted. "The Edge of Nowhere isn't a place you can find on a map. You sort of...stumble upon it by walking, so the plan was to meet Rafe there."

"Assuming we're both capable of stumbling into it."

"...Yes, assuming that."

"And if you'd failed to rescue me and bring me to the coast?"

"Then chap was supposed to use his newly formed bond with the goddess to come find us."

"Assuming she could even locate us," I added dryly.

"Yes, assuming that." Windley hooked his arm around my neck, ruffling my hair. "You know, Merr, it almost sounds as though you're questioning the impeccably strategized plan devised by two experienced royal guards who've planned countless military maneuvers."

"Not at all," I feigned ignorance. "I'm merely wondering how long we'll be expected to bimble along until we conveniently stumble into a picturesque sunrise or sunset—seeing as it's currently the middle of the day."

"Fine, cheeky queen." He threw his hands up dramatically. "Perhaps I was a mite frantic when I realized you'd been taken. If you've a better idea, I'm all ears."

Actually, I did. "One moment."

"Oh, here she goes again, turning all *witchy*." Yet his expression was undeniably intrigued as I sank into the shadows.

"*MerrIn.*"

"*MeeeerrIn.*"

The darkness welcomed me with open, albeit intrusive, arms. I willed them to spread wide and make way for the one voice among them that was more self-aware than the whole.

"Where is Exitium?"

A ripple shivered through the void, whispers knotting and unknotting in the dark.

"*I am here,*" they hissed at last. "*I assume you require my aid once again.*"

"Yes, but I don't want to hear anything about Windley being a beastling or whatever, understood?"

Silence answered.

"Exitium?"

"That is what he is."

"I don't care. I have no intention of destroying him—or anyone else but Ascian."

"We shall see..."

Frustrating, but I wasn't in the mood to argue with a phantom. "Look, when we face Ascian, I promise I'll unleash every bit of bloodlust within me and reduce him to ash. Would that satisfy you?"

If not Exitium, the rest of the echoes certainly riled hungrily at the thought.

"We will tear and feast and burn and bury!"

"Yes, we will do all those things and more. But only to Ascian...and perhaps Charmagne, if she isn't careful."

"And the spider queen!" the echoes howled.

Sestilia again? They were still stuck on her?

"No, not the spider queen. Forget her. I promise someone far better to destroy—someone lacking in any merit—but first, I need to know how to find the Edge of Nowhere."

As always, the echoes erupted into chaos, churning restlessly and asking each other the same question I had posed.

"Exitium," I insisted.

One hand—Exitium's presumably—answered the call, shooting from the darkness to seize my throat. *"She will have noticed the conjurer already, but she will not sense you so easily. Walk barefoot so she might feel your royal blood through the sea."*

"G-Goddess Soleil, you mean?"

"That is she." Exitium's grip loosened.

"Wait!" I rasped. There was another question I'd been longing to ask. One I had avoided, fearing its answer—but something was beginning to frighten me even more: the growing difficulty of keeping the darkness contained within my soul. Leaky wrists weren't a good look.

"How is it that you always seem to know what to do when the others welter about aimlessly? You're separate from them, aren't you, Exitium? What exactly...are you?"

Unfortunately, just because I'd dared ask didn't mean I'd get an answer. Silence returned as Exitium's shadowy hand dissipated back into the tenebrous void.

Lovely.

"Well, your plan is as good as any," I sighed to Windley upon returning to the bright world of the living. "The echoes say Soleil might notice us if I keep my shoes off while we walk."

Windley frowned gently, studying my expression. "You okay, lion queen? You look morose."

"Yeah," I lied. "Just a bit jarring moving between realms, that's all."

He didn't press further, though his concerned gaze said he wasn't convinced.

"In that case—" He bowed theatrically. "Would the lady accompany me for a stroll along the beach?"

But when I took his hand, he immediately propelled me toward the water, drenching me up to my ankles—clearly attempting to distract me from my troubles.

I'd reward his efforts.

"Schemer!" I splashed water at him, and he laughingly kicked it back at me.

"Careful, lion queen. Are you sure you want to start this?"

"I was hardly the one who started it!"

But if I didn't end it quickly, we'd soon be soaked through.

"Move along, schemer," I laughed, nudging his back to urge him forward along the wet sand.

He halted suddenly. "What did you just call me?"

"Schemer?"

"No, after that."

"Schemer again?"

He shook his head slowly, eyes serious. "No, Merr—you called me 'beastling.'"

I replayed the scene quickly in my mind.

Move along, beastling.

So I had—though I hadn't meant to.

"What's a beastling? Like a tiny beast?" Windley caught my wrist before I could hide it and gently ran his nose along the creases, openly smelling the shadows leaking from my skin. "What's happening, Merrin? Is your power growing so strong your body can't hold it in?"

More troublingly, had that been my voice calling out to him —or Exitium's?

"Just excitement," I said lightly, trying to pull back my hand. "We're getting close to your retribution, after all."

Lies, lies, lies.

He didn't buy it, but he didn't press me for the truth. Instead, he quietly slipped an arm around my waist, guiding me forward along the chilly sand.

I found solace in the deep azure of the waves, sparkling beneath the midday sun, trying to distract myself from darker thoughts. Would another giantess emerge from these waters, a celestial body crowned by the blazing sun, just as Luna had risen from the lake? If she had a face, I doubted I'd manage to gaze at her for long.

We walked with only the rhythmic crash of waves breaking the silence. Tiny crabs dotted the beach, poking curiously from their sand-burrows as our footprints left perfect imprints behind us in the shore. It would have been picturesque, were it not for my wrestling thoughts.

"Let me know when you're hungry," Windley hummed softly, staring straight ahead.

"Mm."

"And let me know when you're ready to tell me what's

troubling you so deeply."

This time, I chose not to insult him with another lie.

Until now, I hadn't told anyone about Exitium's distinct voice within the void, nor their whispered promises of blood-lust and destruction. Perhaps it was because I'd known since the beginning that something sinister lingered behind the echoes—something that should never have been invoked.

The echoes can't cause calamity alone. The oracle's true duty isn't to subdue them—it's to bear them, so no one else must.

Beau's words echoed clearly in my mind now, her warning coming too late.

The truth is the echoes can't exist freely; they need a host. And my family ensures they attach to the next born of our lineage. We train our entire lives to resist their pull. When I whisper my intentions into the forest, I'm not doing so to silence the echoes—I'm doing so to silence myself.

Even you need to be careful, Merrin. They are dangerous...

I had needed Exitium's strength then, to rescue Beau from Luna. And I needed it now, to destroy Ascian once and for all. The trouble was keeping myself from being lost in the process.

But what if I couldn't stop it on my own? What if the next time something foreign escaped my lips, it wasn't just a cruel word but an even crueler deed?

Windley had trusted me with all his innermost secrets, yet I was still holding back my darkest truth.

"I need to tell you something, Windley," I finally said, drawing a breath. "About the echoes."

"Wow." Windley gave a low whistle. "I knew something serious was going on inside you, Merr, but I didn't know it was all that." He scratched his forehead thoughtfully. "So, do you think

Exitium is part of the Nemophile's Crown? Or more of a... hitchhiker?"

"I'm not sure. I get the feeling they might be some sort of warden for the other echoes."

"Well, they clearly don't like me. But then again, few do." He flashed me a crooked half-grin. "Can't imagine why."

"It's only recently they've started calling you *beastling*—but that wasn't the first time Exitium spoke through me without my consent."

He tilted his head. "Does Exitium live inside you?"

"I'm starting to fear they might. Pip sensed something within me when he was beguiling me—he called it an 'entire spirit.'"

Windley considered that carefully. "So, when you close your eyes and visit that dark place...could it actually be your soul?"

Goddess, I hoped not. But something deep inside whispered that it might be true.

"I'm frightened, Wind. Exitium keeps saying I'll inevitably embrace my true nature and bring ruin upon the world. They claim a bloodlust writhes within me and that I can't stray from the path I chose when I first invoked it to save Beau. I've committed myself to something I don't fully understand, and if Exitium can make me say things against my will, who's to say they won't soon make me act against my will?"

Windley paused, then squeezed my hand reassuringly. "Let's not fret too much before we know more, Merr. If you ever lose control, I'll subdue you. And after Rafe pacts the sun, we won't need to hide our location. I can beguile you anytime, anywhere, if necessary." He playfully drew a finger along my shoulder. "You said Luna recognized you had the Nemophile's Crown. Did she say anything about Exitium?"

"No—but she wondered aloud if I'd fulfill the Crown's

'long-awaited purpose.' Your lore doesn't mention anything about that, does it?"

Windley shook his head. "But maybe Soleil will know more. Luna took the time to speak with you; I expect the sun goddess would do the same."

It was something. Based on the way he furrowed his brow and chewed reflectively at his lip, Windley was already planning his next moves.

It felt comforting having someone to share my burden.

Maybe fear was like a fire, spreading fastest when left unattended. Maybe speaking it aloud was like dousing the first ember before it could ignite.

My thoughts were interrupted as I noticed the sun behaving oddly, sinking lower than it should have at this time of day.

"W-Windley! Look!"

"I see it."

Together, we watched as the sun plunged toward the horizon, igniting the sky and sea in breathtaking pastels—colors I'd never known existed. A blue so intense it was almost orange; another shade that tasted like spring. They bled together like watercolor paint, mixing with the palest pink, a hush of yellow.

Tufts of clouds hovered delicately at the edges of this sky, cautiously keeping their distance from the dazzling white sun, which now seemed to rest both above and beneath the waves. A thin sheen of water along the sand mirrored this stunning panorama, and behind us, the mortal realm faded entirely, leaving us adrift in a watercolor dream.

The Edge of Nowhere.

If it wasn't heaven, it certainly seemed close.

Yet if this was heaven, then why was a familiar, wavy-haired magician with weary amber eyes sitting hunched atop a nearby rock, looking as though he'd been dragged through hell?

18

SOLEIL'S WISH

"Rafe!"

"You two have some nerve showing up here after all this time!"

I froze at the sight of his furious face, more livid than I'd ever seen it. "Er...Rafe?"

He sprang up from his rock and lunged at me. "What the hell took you so long?!"

"Oi!" Windley shoved him back, placing himself between us. "That's your queen you're yelling at, nitwit!"

Rafe shoved Windley in return. "I expect this is your fault, gallivanting off with Her Majesty while I rotted away! I've been trapped here for over a year! Beau probably thinks I'm dead!"

"Stop it!" I wedged myself between them, forcing them apart. "It hasn't been a year, Rafe—it's only been a few days! We came as soon as we could!"

"A few days?" He searched our faces desperately, eyes wild with confusion. Finding no deception there, he turned to the ocean and threw up his arms, shouting, "IS THAT TRUE,

SOLEIL?! Another of your cruel tricks, you treacherous goddess!"

"Rafe!" I grabbed his arm, pulling him back down. "Don't anger her—we're here to make nice, remember? Have you forgotten why we came?"

"ARGH!" Rafe clawed his fingers through his hair and sank onto the rock again, defeated. "I just want to get the hell out of here."

Windley huffed impatiently. "Chap, get your shit together and tell us what's happened."

Rafe grumbled under his breath, shoulders slumped like he'd just endured a never-ending lecture. His eyes were heavy, and his face worn. "It's really only been a few days?"

"Swear it, mate."

"She's been messing with my head, making me believe I've been stranded here for ages. It's not the first trick she's played."

"Does she not want to pact with you?" I asked cautiously.

"Oh no. She wants the pact—she just demands something in exchange."

"Your heart again?"

He shook his head firmly.

"Then what?"

Rafe's expression turned stubborn. "I'd rather not say, Your Majesty."

Windley studied him closely, searching his eyes. "Ah. A matter between men, then?" He draped an arm over Rafe's shoulder, steering him away. "Excuse us a moment, queenie."

They huddled conspiratorially a short distance away until—

"Ha!" Windley's laugh burst through. "Is that all? Why, that should be easy for a bounder like you!"

"You're confusing me with yourself," Rafe snapped.

"Oh, for goddess's sake," I interjected, impatient. "Just tell me! There's nothing men can handle that women cannot!"

"It's delightfully droll, really," Windley called back, voice crackling with wicked amusement. "Our chap here is having a conniption because the goddess wants his seed."

"His...seed?"

Devilry flickered in Windley's eyes as he spread his hands. "His man-seed. To birth a half-god."

Oh.

OH.

"She wants you to have relations...with her? With the sun? But—how would that even work?"

"She has a body," Rafe explained bleakly. "A giant. Fucking. Body."

"I believe it is you who have the giant-fucking body, isn't it?" Windley mused.

Rafe shot him a venomous glare. "Shut up. You're not helping."

"She doesn't just want me to father her child," he continued bitterly, eyes back on me, "she also expects me to raise it in the mortal world. Imagine me returning to Beau with another woman's child! She'd have my head!"

Would she, though? I paused, thinking it through.

"Well, these circumstances are extraordinary. Not ideal, certainly—but if you explain it carefully, I believe she'd understand. And Windley and I can vouch for you." I worked through the possibilities aloud. "Beau might even raise it alongside her own babe—as twins—assuming it looks human enough."

"With *her* own?" Rafe rasped. "What are you—?"

Oh stars.

I hadn't meant to let that slip; heat rushed up my cheeks, impossible to hide.

"Your Majesty?" Rafe prompted.

"Lion queen?" Windley tilted his head.

They both stared, waiting. I flailed for a cover. "Hypothetically—if Beau were to be expecting, I mean."

Too late. Realization flashed across Windley's face first, then crashed into Rafe's.

"Well," Windley drawled, half-awed, "congratulations seem to be in order, chap—assuming the babe's yours. Queen Beau never struck me as one to keep multiple lovers...though, to be fair, I didn't peg her for sneaking around with brooding magicians either."

"You're fucking with me," Rafe said flatly, though his eyes begged otherwise. "Beau wouldn't... She would have told me."

"She doesn't yet know herself," I confessed. "Luna revealed it to me. That's why Beau lost the Nemophile's Crown—something about magician's blood interfering."

Rafe looked stricken. "How...?"

Windley's smirk returned instantly. "How? Shall I explain it, chap? First, you insert—"

"I meant, *how long*?" Rafe interrupted, glaring daggers at Windley.

"The last night we spent at the treetop fort," I revealed gently.

"Is that where you disappeared off to, chap? Scandalous Queen Beau..." Windley mused.

I shook my head, remorseful. "I'm sorry, Rafe—I truly didn't mean to tell you. I wanted Beau to be the one. I wasn't thinking."

A myriad of emotions swept Rafe's face in quick succession —disbelief, dread, panic, and finally—

"Beau's with child?"

Wonder softened the sharp edges of his whiskey-brown eyes.

I nodded, unable to hold back a smile. "She is. Congratulations, Rafe."

But his awe quickly dissolved into dread. "What happens when the court finds out it's illegitimate?"

"We'll cover it up," I reassured him swiftly. "We'll declare it belongs to a royal suitor, hold a quick wedding—people rarely question the timing of a royal birth. It'll be fine, Rafe. Albie will know how to help, and I'll assist however I can."

Rafe's voice grew quiet. "Thank you, Your Majesty."

"And we'll transfer you permanently to the Clearing—I'll decree it upon our return. She'll need you close."

Rafe was terrified, overwhelmed—but beneath that, he glowed with anticipation. He'd never missed his queen more. I smiled, watching the gentle wonder on his normally stoic face.

Yet while I was watching Rafe, someone else was watching me—and when my eyes caught Windley's, I knew he wasn't sharing in my joy.

The shadow over his expression told me clearly he was battling regret—undoubtedly because he could never give to me what Rafe had given Beau.

It was too soon in our relationship to fret over something like that.

I leaned closer, kissing him softly and whispering quietly enough for only him to hear, "Be happy for them."

"Well, that settles it," said Windley. "You'll have to do whatever it takes to gain the sun goddess's favor. With a little one on the way, you can't risk returning home with a gaggle of wraiths on your tail. Make sure your agreement includes Soleil's protection for both babes, so they'll be safe from harm."

"Good thinking." I patted Windley's arm, proud of how quickly he'd steadied himself. "Rafe, you said you were promised to Luna from birth. Perhaps you should form a similar arrangement with Soleil, extending her protection to your descendants. If it helps, I could negotiate the terms."

Strictly speaking, it wasn't my place—but Rafe seemed far from eager to handle the matter alone.

Rafe stared at us as though we'd gone mad. "You'd both have me commit adultery against Beau?"

His reluctance was charmingly steadfast.

I asked, voice low and cautious, "You know her better than anyone—do you think the goddess can be reasoned with?"

Rafe let out a weighted sigh. "No. I've tried everything. This is the only thing she wants."

"I don't suppose you know any other goddesses we could petition instead?" Windley suggested.

Rafe shook his head. "There are only three powerful enough to invoke by name: Luna, Soleil, and Vita—the moon, the sun, and the giver of life. Others have long since faded from memory. Vita hasn't been heard from in ages, so finding her would be impossible."

"You sorcerers don't speak of a fourth?" Windley pressed. "The goddess of endings?"

"I only know those three," Rafe repeated. "Your guess is as good as mine."

Then Soleil was our best hope.

"I'm sorry, Rafe. I don't see another way."

"If it helps," Windley offered with an impish glint in his eye, "I could amplify your lust and remove any hesitation. You wouldn't even have to think."

"I've seen him use it on cavalry members," I added helpfully. "It certainly makes things...easier."

Possibly the most awkward suggestion I'd ever made to Rafe.

"Great," Rafe muttered dryly. "So I get to be seduced by him and betray Beau?"

"For all you know," Windley said smoothly, "it might not even resemble intercourse as we understand it. Who knows how celestials reproduce?"

Whether or not it resembled intercourse, we never found out. Rafe never volunteered details afterward, and we never asked.

Correction: I never asked. Windley certainly did.

"Would you mind if I spoke with her first?" I asked. "Just to understand her motives, you know—between women."

Rafe nodded bleakly.

Luna had been kinder than anticipated; perhaps Soleil would prove similarly reasonable. With Rafe's consent, I stepped barefoot into the shallows, staring into the luminous horizon painted with pinks and seafoam greens. The Edge of Nowhere's ethereal beauty filled me with longing for a place I'd never known.

One day, I would reflect on how absurd it was to serve as ambassador between realms—to bargain with goddesses, speaking of them as casually as old acquaintances.

But not now.

"Goddess Soleil!" I called clearly. "I am Merrin, Queen of the Crag, bearer of the Nemophile's Crown. The conjurer Rafe is my guard, under my protection. I request an audience with you!"

What followed felt plucked from dreams.

Within moments, the sea quaked. A deep, gong-like boom rolled through the water, rattling the air in our lungs. From its depths rose a colossal figure, radiant as the sun itself.

Soleil breached the waves—impossibly grand. Skin gleamed molten gold; hair fanned out in fiery torrents beneath a halo of light. Steam hissed where brine struck her shoulders, veiling her in vapor that smelled faintly of salt and hot iron.

The very sky paled; color drained from the world until only

her brilliance remained. Each stride churned the ocean, flinging walls of water that exploded on the sand like white-hot fire.

I stumbled back, toes scrabbling in the trembling surf, one arm flung up to shield my eyes. Beside me, even Windley lost his grin, lips parted in mute wonder.

"Greetings, little royal."

Her blazing regard pinned me; warmth rolled from her voice like midsummer noon. When she extended her vast hand, the air shimmered with heat. I flicked a look at Rafe, then stepped gingerly onto her palm, gripping a ridge of gleaming knuckle as she lifted me skyward.

High above the sea, her brilliant face was almost painful to behold.

"Hello, Goddess Soleil. Thank you for meeting with me."

She studied me like a curious seashell. "Ah! It is as you said. The Crown of the Wood truly adorns your brow. The Crown has never sought me out before. Tell me—are you the royal who possesses the conjurer's heart?"

I drew a steadying breath. "No, but she is dear to me. I'm here on her behalf. You see, the royal who holds his heart now carries his child."

Soleil's immense golden eyes drifted past me to where Rafe sat, head hung low. "So that is the reason for his refusal."

A reluctant laugh slipped out. "It's...a formidable request." Even the bravest man might balk at bedding a living sun. "Is there truly no alternative, Goddess?"

"None," she replied firmly. "I've had my fill of mortal hearts. The conjurer possesses something I cannot take alone. My power could scorch your world if given freely; thus, it demands a price."

"I understand. But may I ask—why a child? What do you intend?"

"To watch it grow, naturally," Soleil said serenely. "To witness what it becomes."

"Half-mortal, half-immortal beings must be rare."

"Unheard of," she corrected.

"So—it's an experiment?"

"No more than mortals experimenting with life each time they reproduce," she replied sensibly.

Fair enough.

"If Rafe agrees, will his descendants carry your blessing? When Luna ended their bond, he became vulnerable to attack. I fear for his children without your protection."

"If he accepts, my power will live in his blood, blessing his lineage anew," Soleil promised.

"Including Beau's unborn child?"

"Yes."

"And how...would this birth happen?"

Soleil's laughter shook the very heavens. "The same as all mortals. Once conceived, I shall place it within a surrogate."

"Could Beau—already carrying his child—serve as surrogate?"

"If he wishes."

"And you won't interfere beyond observing?"

"That is my vow."

Then they truly could be raised as twins. Beau would bear two children—both Rafe's, both protected, their true parentage forever concealed beneath royal pretenses.

It was a weighty choice—one Beau wasn't here to make—but knowing her, I believed she'd do anything to safeguard her child. Without divine protection, the child would enter the world as prey for darker things.

A pact-less conjurer is as ripe as the fertile grounds of spring.

"Very well," I decided. "I'll relay your terms. But before I go, I must ask about the Nemophile's Crown. Goddess Luna hinted at a greater purpose—do you know what she meant?"

Soleil paused, thoughtful. "I cannot say. My sisters crafted the Crown while I painted the skies. Its secrets are not mine."

I was alone, then—unless I sought Luna's forgiveness.

"I see."

Soleil's gaze intensified. "Is something else troubling you, little royal? Your heart races."

The question I dreaded most.

"Yes, actually." I inhaled sharply in preparation. "Have you heard the name Exitium?"

She stilled. "Where did you hear that name?"

Carefully, I chose my words. "In the darkness, on the edge between realms."

"Does the conjurer hear it?" Her tone made it plain: a *yes* would end both the audience and our bargain.

"No. Only me."

"Forget that name," she commanded severely. "It's a grave better left untouched."

Her reaction confirmed my fears. Exitium was dangerous— a viper coiled around my soul. A mistake.

I'd gained little but dread from our exchange. The Crown suddenly felt heavier.

"I do not wish to frighten you," Soleil tempered slightly. "But that name should never enter the mortal world."

"I understand," I lied easily. "I'll never speak it again."

Soleil tipped her great head in silent assent. "If our terms are settled, I shall return you now. This must be quite high."

Indeed—far, *far* too high.

Slowly, she lowered me back to solid ground, and I clung gratefully to her thumb until safely ashore.

She left her palm open, golden eyes expectant as they fixed upon Rafe. His normally ochre-brown face had turned ashen. I couldn't blame him—this solitary magician whose greatest joys came from quiet moments in the courtyard.

"Everything's arranged, Rafe," I explained with unruffled tact. "Your descendants will be blessed, and Soleil promises not to interfere. She merely wishes to observe the child grow. If you choose, Beau can bear both children together—I think it's the best way to keep their origins secret. But the decision must be yours."

"She's going to kill me."

"She won't," I assured him. "Beau is reasonable."

"And terrifying," Rafe muttered.

Windley chuckled. "Sounds like the good queen's shown him a hidden side."

"You have no idea," Rafe groaned.

"If Beau refuses, my court can raise the child. Its parentage will remain secret," I offered.

Windley clapped Rafe's shoulder. "You're already having one spawn—what's another?"

Rafe hesitated, burdened with an impossible choice.

"If it were Windley—if protecting him and our child meant this—I'd agree. Beau isn't here, but as her friend for over twenty years, I believe I know her heart."

Windley flexed his fingers. "Say the word, mate."

Rafe sighed heavily. "No tricks. I do this willingly."

Windley nodded, unoffended.

We stepped back, watching solemnly as Rafe climbed into the goddess's waiting palm, carried upward into the shimmering sky.

19
HEARTS IN THE SAND

"How long do you reckon this will take?" Windley asked, sitting boredly on a smooth boulder, cheek propped in one hand and a stick dangling from the other, with which he'd drawn a lazy heart in the sand.

"I'd think you'd know better than most."

"Heh."

I stole the stick from his fingers and added M + W inside the heart.

"Aw," he cooed dramatically. "Does that stand for Meraflora and Windalloy?"

"No, it stands for Murder Windley. Or maybe Mangle Windley. Or Maim Windley. Take your pick."

"Scaaary," he teased, pretending to cower.

I snapped my teeth at him, and he grinned, snatching the stick back to draw a bigger heart around our names.

I gazed out across the sherbet-hued shoreline, swirling in soft pastels. "Are you still feeling negative?"

"Negative?" he echoed innocently.

"About Beau's news?"

"What, you think I'm jealous of some slimy, wriggly little creature?"

I eyed him skeptically. "Babies aren't slimy, you knave."

"They certainly start out that way..." He cocked his head, studying our sandy heart. "Do you think I'd look good with a tattoo?"

"You might want to fix your horrid personality before you start working on your horrid appearance."

"Mean!" He pawed playfully at me. "You owe me three sweet comments to make up for it."

Feigning deep consideration, I studied him openly—taking the opportunity to admire him more closely. "Well...I think it's cute, the way the tips of your ears are pointed. And I like the way the corner of your mouth twitches when you're feeling mischievous." I waved vaguely at his torso. "And all of...this is rather nice."

He sighed, unable to suppress a smug grin. "Goddess, you're completely obsessed with me." Suddenly, he stiffened. "Wait—goddess. Did you ask Soleil about Exitium and the Crown and all that?"

I recounted our conversation, and Windley listened attentively, his face darkening slightly with each word.

"Egad, Merr. You're doing surprisingly well for someone who should be panicking right now."

"I don't have a choice," I said, exhaling slowly. "I'll need Exitium's strength when we face Ascian. After that, I'll just have to find a way to rid myself of them. I already knew they were dark—I just underestimated how dark. They seem to have grown stronger since encountering your former master."

"This is all my fault. If I hadn't dragged you into the woods with me—"

"Then you'd be out here alone, and I'd be worried sick, wondering what became of you."

"It isn't your fight, lion queen."

"If it's your fight, it's my fight."

He released a resigned breath. "Those are supposed to be my lines. You're making me look bad." His voice trailed off as he tucked a coil of hair behind my ear. "You know, there's something I've been meaning to tell you. Something you should know. You'll either find it charming or scandalous. Let's hope for charming."

His eyes fell gently to my mouth. "I kissed you once before, you know. Before the Necropolis."

"...What?"

Windley nodded slowly, swallowing hard as his gaze traced over my nose and cheeks. "It was during one of my visits to the Crag. I fell asleep in the throne room after an evening spent drinking with that stocky guard of yours—what was her name, Saxon? Back when she was just a castle grunt. That woman can drink an army under the table. Anyway, you came to find me but fell asleep yourself, kneeling beside the settee, your head on the cushion. Your cheeks were rosy from the firelight, your eyes half-lidded and sleepy. You'd had meetings all day and looked utterly exhausted. When I woke up and saw you there, I couldn't stop myself. I stroked your hair and kissed your cheek because the thought of leaving without doing so was unbearable. I think that was the moment I realized I would never escape loving you. I loved you long before, but in that moment...I knew it would never leave me."

Oh, my heartstrings.

I remembered that night vividly. A fairyfern shortage had forced us to improvise, doubling our work with remedies, and I'd spent the day in endless meetings. I'd wanted to find Windley and Beau afterward, but Beau had already gone to bed. Knowing Windley's habit of sprawling drunkenly in the throne room, I'd sought him out, planning to tease him—but the warmth of the fire had lulled me to sleep first. I'd dreamt of him that night, and when I awoke, he was gone.

I touched my cheek now, warmed by the memory. "I never knew…"

Windley swallowed again, his voice soft. "And now you're tangled in my problems, directly in harm's way. It's killing me, Merrin. I never wanted this for you."

I took his face between my palms, hoping my eyes conveyed the warmth swelling in my chest. "I'd rather be here, facing evil by your side, than safely tucked away in the throne room enduring my council's endless squabbles. No one knows me like you do. No one else makes my soul catch fire and feel so wildly alive. I love you, Windley. My only regret is not admitting it sooner."

It was easier than I'd imagined, and yet, far more painful.

Loving him hurt beautifully.

Windley held me close, our feet sinking into the sand at the Edge of Nowhere, for moments or centuries—time had no hold on these pastel shores. That was when I knew, without question, that I would never escape loving him either. Like the deeply entrenched roots of a mammoth tree, he was woven irreversibly into my heart.

We could never return to how things were.

I want you, and I would give up everything to have you. So… think about that and let me know, lion queen.

I wouldn't tell him. Not yet. There were still battles to fight.

Windley kept me wrapped in his embrace for what might have been an hour or an age, until Rafe finally returned from the distant horizon.

"Rafe! You're glowing!"

Soleil's radiant essence still clung to him, but it faded quickly, taking with it the colors of the Edge of Nowhere. The sky dimmed, and in moments we found ourselves back on the mundane coast beneath the onset of dusk.

After the brilliance of Soleil, the mortal world felt oddly dim and muted. It would take time to readjust.

"It's done," Rafe muttered, dazed.

I wondered if Beau sensed any difference yet. I hoped dearly that I knew her as well as I believed.

Windley leaned in, curious. "So, how was it, chap? As terrible as you imagined?"

"It was...warm," was all Rafe managed.

Yet the encounter had clearly worked, for when he unsheathed his sword, it blazed with vibrant flame. He swung it experimentally, casting sparks where frost once formed.

"Incredible!" I marveled. "You'll never need flint again."

Rafe examined the blade thoughtfully. "It'll take some getting used to. Spar with me, Windley." He shed his cloak eagerly, no longer needing its itchy feather lining to mask his scent.

"What, you don't want to spar with me, Rafe?"

"I prefer to survive our duels, Your Majesty."

Windley laughed, arching an eyebrow at Rafe. "Surprised you've any strength left in you, honestly. But sure, I'm game."

He drew both hatchets from beneath his cloak, spinning them expertly in his hands with practiced flair.

Watching the two guards clash for the first time was unexpectedly thrilling—Windley, all taunts and fluid grace, and Rafe, relishing every precise strike. Windley danced more than usual, even leaping dramatically off boulders to strike from above.

By the end, Windley rubbed a burn Rafe had gifted him, while Rafe examined a tear in his shirt. The greatest casualty, however, was a nearby shrub now burning furiously from their efforts.

"How do you like Soleil's power?" I asked.

Rafe held the flaming blade, watching it reflect in his eyes. "It's different—but I think I'll grow fond of it."

"Better hope Luna doesn't hear that," teased Windley. "If she ever shows her face again, that is."

Rafe shook his head. "Soleil said she's still recovering."

Exitium's power was that formidable—enough to force a goddess into days of recovery?

I stared thoughtfully at the darkening sky. "Our plan still stands—lure Ascian here with Windley's power before Luna recovers?"

"Yes," Windley confirmed. "With all of Abardo hexed, Ascian's stronger now than eight years ago. We don't need to give him another ally." He turned to Rafe. "Did your sun mistress agree to help us?"

Rafe nodded. "She was reluctant, but when I explained our child wouldn't be safe unless we eliminated the fiends pursuing the queen, she agreed to protect me when the time comes."

Windley turned up his palm with a roguish smirk. "Courting powerful women does have its advantages, doesn't it?"

"There are some conditions, though," Rafe added cautiously. "She's most powerful along the coast, so we must stay near, and she can only protect us during daylight."

Only during the day? It made sense, but it was another troublesome restriction we had to manage.

Windley thought carefully. "Well, it might work in our favor that they've only ever seen Merrin's power at night. If luck's on our side, they'll fear a night attack based on that alone. If not, we'll just have to stall them until sunrise."

Yet another unsound plan—but it was all we had.

"I'm worried about ensuring Ascian actually shows this time," I said. "Before, he sent Edius in his place."

"Knowing Ascian, he won't repeat the same mistake," Windley said. "Since you escaped last time, I bet he'll come himself. And if he doesn't, we'll just keep dispatching whoever he sends until he shows his ugly mug."

"Planning to start tonight?" Rafe asked.

"Sooner's always better," said Windley eagerly.

"If your magic is anything like mine," Rafe said, glancing briefly at me, "you should use as much of it as you can, over a prolonged time, to send a strong signal."

Windley's eyes glittered mischievously. "Oh, I intend to."

"What I mean is—" Rafe lowered his voice, murmuring something I couldn't hear.

"Blow my what?" scoffed Windley, feigning scandal. "I'm a professional, Rafe. Have some faith."

After restraining ourselves for so long, the thought of Windley using his power without restraint was enticing—but I preferred Rafe to have no further hand in the details.

"Alright, enough of that," I cut in. "We'll set camp here. Windley, find a suitable place for the tent. I'll help Rafe with dinner."

The horizon had shifted to a brilliant cerulean, deepening steadily into blackness overhead. The rain promised by lavender stars never arrived; tonight, they shone golden, trailing tails of emerald.

Rafe had already gathered sticks to feed the shrub they'd set ablaze during their earlier spar. "I can handle dinner, Your Majesty. You should rest."

"Actually, Rafe, the reason I offered was to see how you're doing."

He glanced up from the fire with tired eyes. "Fine."

"I'm serious," I pressed. "I know you don't like sharing your feelings—least of all with me—but I imagine your choice today was exceptionally difficult. You're young. Fathering Beau's child is one thing, but fathering a second of celestial origin... that's an extraordinary burden. So, forgive me, but I doubt you're really 'fine.'"

He was quiet as a tombstone, unwilling to speak.

"I won't force you to tell me anything," I continued with added sensitivity. "But if speaking relieves you in any way, I'm here to listen. I won't judge or even give unsolicited advice."

He remained silent even longer, busily rummaging through Windley's pack, seemingly dismissing the conversation entirely. I assumed that was that.

But then he cleared his throat. "It must be the same for you, Your Majesty. Life has changed so quickly."

"Yes. I scarcely feel like the same person."

He hesitated. "The choice wasn't actually hard, in the end. I'd kill anyone for Beau. Anyone—even you," he admitted, hanging his head. "Dishonorable as that is."

It was off-putting to hear—but I understood.

"I know, Rafe."

He stared at the growing flames. "So, I thought: If I'd willingly end lives for her sake, why wouldn't I create life too? That was my reasoning."

Strange. For as delicate and fair and princess-like as Beau was, it was hard to imagine her with anyone other than this grouchy magician from the distant north who preferred solitude and avoided conversations.

"I'm glad you found each other," I said. "For Beau's sake and yours. And my own too. I might never have recognized my feelings if I hadn't first witnessed them in you two."

Rafe gave a blunt, barely audible laugh. "I doubt that. Windley wouldn't have stopped trying, ever. Everyone knew he liked you—we just weren't sure about you. He's so damn annoying, I don't blame you for outrunning him as long as you did."

"You say that, Rafe, but you don't really mean it."

The waves quietly kissed the shoreline behind us, while the fire greedily consumed the kindling Rafe offered, growing into a tall, crackling pillar of flame.

Rafe released the longest, heaviest sigh yet, though his expression stayed blank. "Fine. He does keep things lively, I suppose. He's a decent fighter. And he keeps a secret."

I knew it.

Rafe considered Windley a friend.

"Has he explained the situation with Ascian any further?" I asked.

"A little. We're not supposed to kill the round-faced boy? He's Windley's brother or something?"

"Or something," I said softly. "From what I understand, the coming battle will be emotionally charged. Thank you for staying with us to see it through."

"I'm still your guard, Your Majesty," Rafe said simply.

"I'm glad you are, Rafe."

I gave him an appreciative smile and turned toward Windley to check his tent-building progress, but Rafe's voice—rarely candid—stopped me.

"Good luck tonight, Queen Merrin," he murmured dryly. "To me, he's looking a little...ravenous."

Ravenous.

Raaavenous.

Rav-en-ous.

20

BAIT

After dinner, the three of us sat around the fire, watching tailed stars streak across the coastal sky. The heavens seemed endless here, over this wild, unbound land beside a restless, unexplored sea. My heart beat freely, unrestrained.

Windley had lounged behind me for some time, chin balanced on my crown, arms draped over my shoulders. When Rafe rose for firewood, Windley shifted. With slow intent he swept my hair aside, exposing the tender arc of my neck to the chill.

A draft kissed my skin, and a shiver chased up my spine.

"Wind?"

His reply unfurled, low and unhurried. "Even if they left Abardo now, riding hell-for-leather, they won't reach us before midday."

He was suggesting we begin the next phase of our plan: luring Ascian by drawing on Windley's full Spirite power—and, as his chosen focus, he was courting my consent.

He brushed a kiss along my shoulder, breath trailing heat. "Any hesitations, Queen Merrin?"

"N-no."

He gathered my hair, wrapping it lazily round his fist, tugging just enough to spark across my scalp. His mouth grazed the nape of my neck, slow, deliberate, leaving wildfire in its wake.

A shaky breath escaped me.

"I'll try to keep my promise," he murmured.

"Promise?" I asked.

A dark chuckle vibrated at my ear. "I told you—I won't make love to you on a tent floor. Not the first time, anyway."

Heat flooded my cheeks; I steadied my breathing. "You're making me nervous again."

"Good." His hand glided up to cradle my throat, tipping my chin higher. His teeth caught my earlobe in a coaxing nip. "If I can wind you this tight now, imagine the rest."

He toyed with me, breath tracing from ear to shoulder, inhaling my scent like the Spirite predator he was—stoking every ember beneath my skin.

Never had I imagined how exhilarating—how *arousing*—it might feel to be...sniffed.

Perks, perhaps, of loving a creature bred for temptation itself.

In another age, on this very spot, he might have drained me dry. Even now, with his power reined in, I was an apple poised between his teeth—skin stretched, waiting to be bitten.

Windley was danger rendered irresistible.

"I can hear your heartbeat," he murmured, voice dark velvet. "Are you frightened?"

No. Perhaps I should have been—but trust eclipsed fear, and exhilaration took root. I felt chosen, desired, deliciously exposed beneath his unblinking attention.

"My heart's racing," I whispered back, "and I like it."

"You give me wicked thoughts, Merrin—things I'll never say aloud."

I fought not to shiver, sure he'd feel even the slightest quake. Salvation arrived as Rafe's boots crunched through the undergrowth, arms full of firewood. Windley noticed at once, smoothing my hair back, sliding his hands down my arms before strolling off to sip from his canteen.

Rafe clocked everything—my flushed face, Windley's predatory grin—then folded his arms. "So the seduction's officially under way?"

Windley smirked. "Volunteering as bait, Rafe? I'm flattered. Shall we begin?"

"You're dreaming."

Still, Windley's gaze never left mine.

Rafe flicked a dismissive hand. "Do it elsewhere. The last thing I want tonight is a front-row seat."

"Why do you think I pitched the tent?" Windley drawled. "Be a good lad and stay out a while, yes?"

Rafe faced the fire. "Say the word, Your Majesty, and I'll gut him for you."

"Don't worry," I replied, half-sweet, half-threat. "I'll gut him myself if he misbehaves."

An outright lie, and Windley knew it. The amused gleam in his eyes, the confident curve of his mouth—everything betrayed him. He lounged against the tent's entrance, stance arrogant, posture cocky and inviting. Tousled hair, eyes dark with intent, sleeves rolled to bare sculpted forearms, top button undone—had he boosted his looks with magic? Was he laying a trap, making himself impossible to resist?

I'd never seen him more enticing.

He merely dipped his head, a silent summons I couldn't

have resisted even if I'd tried. I was already caught—long before any beguiling power touched me.

Eyes still locked on his, I crossed the cushion-soft sand, chin lifted in challenge. He met it without a flicker of doubt. When I reached him, his hands claimed my waist—firm, commanding.

"I'm going to enjoy this, lion queen." With slow precision, he brushed a teasing kiss across the bridge of my nose, then drew me into the tent's shadowed interior.

Firelight seeped through the canvas, casting undulating silhouettes. The autumn sea chilled the air, yet the heat rolling off him chased every trace of cold away.

"First things first." He touched his lips to mine, feather-light; sensation pricked like static. As he withdrew, his hair bled to deep scarlet. Three deliberate kisses trailed down my throat —each spot tingling—and emerald eyes greeted me when he lifted his head. "That's the look you like best, yes?"

Answering was impossible; he was undeniably captivating —more alluring than Sestilia, more enchanting than any Spirite or mortal I'd ever seen.

Sensing my stunned silence, he squeezed my hand. "Still me, queenie. Maybe a bit...pent-up. But still me. If it's too much, tell me and I'll back off."

Hearing Windley's familiar voice from such a devastating guise felt surreal.

"I dialed it down," he added, gesturing to his eyes—their gleam intentionally muted. "Didn't want to entrance you. Not yet."

"Goddess, Windley. I'm always drawn to you, but now..." I bit my lip, words failing.

His focus snapped to that small gesture; he swallowed, throat working. "One nibble of your lip and you take control again."

Emboldened, I slipped the next button free.

"W-wait, Merr," he laughed under his breath, voice husky. "You're putting me off my game—I'm supposed to beguile you, not the reverse."

"So I'm meant to stay submissive?" I teased, working another button free.

"Not exactly...well, perhaps a little." He captured my wrists —equal parts restraint and invitation—then sank to his knees.

Air lodged in my throat.

Seeing him kneel awakened something fierce. Wrong, always, yet sinfully right—like I was queen of a secret court; he, my most dangerous, most devoted subject.

"I've always considered you my true queen," he murmured, tone rough with reverence, "and I'll kneel anytime you wish." He kissed each finger, drawing just enough of my spirit to cool my skin and send my pulse skittering. "But right now, your flavor alone nearly unravels me." Emerald light flickered in his eyes. "I'm not sure I can hold the line."

His jaw flexed, as though picturing exactly how the line would break—how *he* would.

Now I was picturing it too.

I wanted to rip him open—thoroughly, scandalously.

Still kneeling, he slid warm hands beneath my shirt, thumbs tracing the finest hairs. "Last time I did this, it was...less than gentle. Let me remedy that."

I could only nod. My breath hitched as he lowered his mouth, planting a kiss just below my navel, lingering there while a tremor went through him.

Our fingers laced as he skimmed upward along my ribs, leaving streaks of heat. Then, with deliberate slowness, he rose, eyes dark as stormglass—tempo of my heartbeat hitching higher.

This time his power felt deliberate, enchanting. He drank

from me, yes, but he also poured back—filling every hollow with a need that flared along my nerves.

I tried to stay composed while he explored exposed skin: fingertips skimming my ribs, palm cradling my cheek, mouth wandering from jaw to throat.

We sank to the bedding just as his eyes flared. My senses unraveled beneath his single-minded touch. He lowered me, pinning one wrist in a light but iron claim; a thrill shot through me at the dominance in that *wolfish* gaze.

For a single heartbeat I surrendered—then the lioness refused to stay leashed. I surged up, rolling him onto his back, feasting on him as he'd feasted on me—nipping at the curve of his shoulder, teeth closing over tempting flesh.

"O-ow!" He jolted, laughter rough at the edges, and in a blink flipped me again, reclaiming command. Pressing me into the blankets, he murmured at my ear, "Careful, lion queen. You bite; I bite back."

"Prove it," I dared.

He did. His mouth crashed onto mine—breath for breath, heat for heat, spirit threading with spirit—until I could no longer tell where his magic ended and mine began.

I felt his muscles bunch, our breaths tangling, bodies sliding in a decadent rhythm—almost too much to bear.

Desire and magic collided, the monster between us swelling into a rhapsody of emerald light until Windley tore his mouth from mine with a guttural gasp.

"I have to stop," he rasped, braced above me, every sinew taut. "One more moan, Merrin, and I'll break every promise I've ever made."

My pulse thundered in answer. "What if...I don't want you to stop?"

"I want our first time to matter," he breathed, thumb

grazing my trembling lip. "Not rushed. Not stolen. Not on a tent floor."

"It would matter anywhere."

His gaze flickered, hunger veiled for a moment by something raw. "When you say things like that, I—"

He swallowed, confession snagging in his throat.

"Say it," I whispered.

"You ruin me," he managed, pressing a reverent kiss to my brow. "You ruin me for anyone else."

He drew me against his chest, holding until the beguilement ebbed and our breathing slowed in tandem.

"There's so much more," he murmured into my hair. "So many things I want to do with you. *To* you. But not yet."

"I'll hold you to that," I promised, lungs finally steady.

He sealed the vow with soft kisses across my cheekbones, my eyelids, my nose. "Until then."

Wrapped in his arms, I drifted toward sleep, safe in the cradle of his bones, lulled by the measured thrum of his heart.

That night, I dreamt the sky was falling.

21

THE HURTFUL TRUTH

"Wake up, Merrin."

In the morning, I was alone, disheveled among the heap of blankets we'd accumulated on our journey to the coast.

None of last night felt real.

But my skin was sensitive, my chest fluttery—a lingering symptom of Windley's magic still dancing in my veins. He'd taken a considerable amount from me this time. Was it his power that made me crave giving even more?

I was fortunate to be beyond normal human limitations. Without the echoes replenishing me, I might have needed a full day or more to recover from what he'd spent.

Speaking of the echoes—

"Merrin!"

Exitium buzzed at the edge of my awareness, but I had no interest in a lecture about freely giving myself to "one of the beastlings."

No entire people deserved to be branded by the acts of a few. Whatever Exitium believed, I regretted nothing.

The feeling of Windley devouring me was worth it.

My Windley.

My devil.

I was anxious—eager, even—to face him after witnessing the full extent of his power, though I reminded myself that last night's bliss served a purpose: to lure our enemies closer. Despite my fluttery heart, this was not a honeymoon. This was a trap for our foes.

And they were probably already on their way.

Outside, I found Rafe beside a dying fire, and Windley a short distance away, arms folded as he studied the sunlit sky.

The daylight was reassuring—proof that Soleil watched over us, ready to lend aid if needed. My plan was to cast my echoes over the area to detect enemy movements, though we still likely had time.

"Your girl's awake," Rafe called over his shoulder, voice looser than usual.

My, my—the magician sounded quite informal this morning. Oddly warm, even.

Windley turned, lips curved into a dangerously inviting smile. "Merrin," he purred, eyes bright with an unfamiliar glint.

A shiver crawled my spine; something in that brightness felt...sharp.

I ran to him anyway, throwing my arms around his neck. "Last night was..." Words failed. "You did exceptionally well."

"You think so?" he murmured, voice dark as tar. Tar, not velvet—a first rust-note of disquiet.

"Very much," I said, though my brow furrowed against his shoulder. "Oh! Windley, that's quite a lot of magic. Don't you need some recovery?"

He gave an exaggerated sigh. "I suppose you're just hard to resist."

Behind us, Rafe chuckled.

"Shut up," Windley snapped, irritation flashing. *Too sharp*, I noted—Windley's barbs were usually wrapped in humor, not steel.

"W-Windley, have you sensed Ascian or any of his rogues nearby?" I asked.

"I haven't caught even a hint of them yet." His grip tightened again, power pressing more insistently into my skin—almost painful.

"Hey—easy," Rafe said, the corners of his mouth drawn taut in something nearer concern than amusement. His knuckles whitened on the stick; a silent *Enough*.

"Jealous?" Windley shot back, voice like broken glass.

"Hardly," Rafe muttered, flicking an uneasy glance at me before schooling his features.

"Jealous?" I laughed, trying to cut the tension. "Rafe is probably disturbed, not jealous."

"It was a joke," Windley said flatly, tone devoid of the usual swagger.

"Your delivery's slipping," I teased, though the words tasted wrong even to me.

He stared at me, unblinking. "Blame whatever you did to me last night. I'm hardly at my sharpest."

Whatever I did to him?

"Er, anyway," I said, shaking off the wording, "I'll spread a net of echoes around to alert us to any approaching trouble. With Soleil awake, I'm less concerned about an immediate threat—it's nightfall we have to prepare for."

As I tilted my head, about to reach into the shadowy realm, Windley abruptly stopped me.

"Before you do that, let's talk."

A dozen tiny alarms rang in my gut, but I held them quiet.

"...About?"

He didn't answer, simply grabbing my hand and guiding

me toward the windswept shore. The sea breeze tossed sand playfully at our feet, shaping miniature dunes as we passed. I glanced behind to see Rafe following at a distance, poking lazily at the sand with a stick—attempting subtlety, but clearly unwilling to leave us entirely alone.

The salty mist sprayed us as Windley brought us near the water's edge, positioning himself beside me as if preparing for a romantic revelation. But hadn't we already shared all our confessions? Something small knotted uneasily in my stomach.

He looked upon the horizon, a stiff silence hanging between us until he finally spoke.

"Do you ever think maybe you shouldn't have left your home, Merrin?"

"Never. Do you?"

"All the time."

I laughed, but his expression remained oddly severe.

"I can't tell if you're joking or not today," I admitted lightly.

He didn't smile. "Maybe it's because I can finally be myself now that I got what I wanted from you."

An awkward beat passed.

I studied him carefully. "And what is it you wanted from me exactly?"

His lips curled cruelly. "Your virtue."

My *virtue?*

Wording aside, I believed I knew what he meant. But...he hadn't taken that step last night. He'd explicitly held back, wanting better circumstances than a tent floor.

Was he attempting some sort of boast in front of Rafe? No, that wasn't Windley's style, and besides, Rafe appeared distracted, poking at shells far behind us.

"What's gotten into you?" I asked quietly, my discomfort growing. "If you're aiming to irritate me, you're succeeding."

"Oh, Merrin." He gripped my shoulder too tightly. "I'm not

trying to irritate you—I'm telling you the truth. Spirites are masters of seduction and deceit, after all. Isn't it time we shattered this fantasy of yours?"

His laugh rang hollow.

"Imagine me taking a human for a mate—it'd be like courting a dog."

And there it was—not the familiar pine-and-amber musk that belonged to Windley, but a silken drift of rosewood, polished and expensive. Lovely...yet utterly foreign to him, and achingly out of place on this windswept coast.

My stomach dropped.

I tried to pull away, but he clamped down, forcing me to meet his eyes.

"It's not your fault you were gullible. I'm exceedingly good at what I do, after all," he drawled coldly. "It may have taken forever, but I've finally accomplished Master's task: I've ensnared a royal. And now, having wrapped you so tightly around my finger, it's time for my reward."

He leaned close, voice venomous.

"I'm going to break you into irreparable pieces and feast on your shattered soul until you're nothing but ash. How does that sound, sweetheart?"

The tone was alien—nothing like Windley's easy mischief, his wit-edged affection, his warmth.

The trust built over years and weeks stood firm. Memories fought each other, trying to reconcile the man I knew with the creature beside me.

The woodcutter's cabin hadn't broken us.

Flora's likeness hadn't.

Each challenge had only strengthened our bond, teaching me more clearly who Windley truly was.

And this—

"RAFE! THIS ISN'T WINDLEY!"

This truth rang through me, clearing the lingering magical daze from my mind in a rush of dread.

The impostor shifted swiftly behind me, twisting my arms into a locked position. "Argh! Already?! That didn't take long at all! Thanks for the disappointment, cupcake."

...Cupcake?

CUPCAKE?!

I didn't know what had happened—where the real Windley was, or how she'd found us so quickly—but I knew one thing for certain: of all the people to wear Windley's face, she was among the least worthy.

"*I knew it!*" I seethed, my muscles twining in anger. "*Charmagne.*"

"Ding, ding, ding."

"How dare you mimic him! You don't deserve to copy a single freckle or strand of his hair, you vampiric tramp!"

"My, aren't you bold for someone with their hands *wrenched* helplessly behind their back?"

The blast of Spirite magic Charmagne hit me with next was unlike anything Windley had ever unleashed upon me. It wasn't gradual or gently tingling—it was knife-edged and fierce, sending an icy numbness through my back and shoulders.

If Charmagne sought war, I'd end it before it even started.

All morning, I'd held shut the floodgates against the whispers lurking just beyond the veil. But now, with my permission, they surged forth in a landslide, Exitium at the forefront.

"*Why do you insist on insubordination, Merrin? I've been trying to reach you for the last hour!*"

"*MErrIN!*"

"*meRrIn!*"

"*Ones without merit, MeRRIN! Ones without merit!*"

The echoes were screaming, trembling in their fury, but it was nothing compared to the tempest roaring within me. What-

ever had brought us here, I would blast Charmagne into frag-
ments of hair and cinders. I'd separate her bones from her flesh.
I'd make her rue the day she crossed paths with me.

My fury eclipsed all reason.

*"It is time, Merrin. Give in to your bloodlust. Do not stop
with the beastling. Speak my name—give birth to destruction!
End this world of lust and pain!"*

Disembodied hands crawled across my skin, pulling me
toward the edge between their realm and ours. For the first
time, Exitium's offer held appeal.

But running toward me was a reminder of everything we
were fighting for.

"Stay back, Rafe! You'll get hit!"

Rafe didn't listen.

Determined, he ran straight toward us. He was—

Inspecting the ground around my feet?

"Did you do it?" he barked at the fake Windley. "Is she
hexed?"

"Not all the way—the cow has a thick aura. I'm having
trouble penetrating it. Help me."

A sickening wave of disillusionment crashed into me as
Rafe seized my throat, one hand adorned with a blackstone ring
identical to Windley's. Leaning close, he whispered darkly:

"Heya, Merrín. Too bad you didn't take my offer. I warned
you I wouldn't be so nice next time."

22

A SMIDGE OF
FONDNESS

"**E**-Edius?"

Rafe's face smiled at me, darker than it had ever looked before. "Miss me?"

"How did you get here so fast?!"

"Simpleton!" Charmagne spat, still wearing Windley's face. "As soon as you escaped, we set up camp at that little hill Ediot found you at last time. We knew you'd have to pass by on your way to wherever you three dolts were going."

Meaning they had been close—far closer than we'd realized —when we set off our beacon.

It was a detail we should have considered, but Windley and I had been distracted by our own indulgences, and Rafe by thoughts of returning to Beau. We were, after all, imperfect beings.

"Soleil!" I shouted to the sky. "Where are they? Where are Windley and Rafe?"

But the goddess didn't answer, leaving me shouting desperately at the indifferent sun.

A dull tingling sensation had begun in my feet, rising slowly through my legs. I had no idea how long it took to fully hex someone, but I was sure I could call forth the echoes faster.

This time, I didn't merely listen for them—I closed my eyes fully, plunging headlong into the boiling dark. They were frantic with ire that matched my own.

"Exitium! Where are my guards?"

"The bright one pulled them into her domain upon sensing danger. She intended to take only the conjurer, but the beastling was nearby."

"They're safe?"

"For now. They are attempting to convince her to release them, but her priority is protecting the conjurer so that her child will have a father."

"That's the 'protection' she promised Rafe?!"

"You should expect nothing less. Goddesses are wicked. Every last one."

Not ideal. That meant I'd be alone against two Spirites, but at least Windley and Rafe wouldn't be harmed when I unleashed my wrath.

"Is Ascian close?" I demanded. "With any luck, I can defeat all three at once."

"I cannot say. A male draws near, but his figure eludes my sight."

"Then I'll handle these two first and deal with him afterward."

"You only delay the inevitable by choosing enemies selectively. True destruction lives in you. The sooner you accept that, the better."

"I'm not destroying the world!"

"Fate cares little for your desires, Merrin."

"Argh! Just answer when I call you!"

Exitium didn't reply.

No matter—I would force them out. I had done it before, and I would do it again. I'd use the Nemophile's Crown to end Edius and Charmagne, then it would be Ascian's turn.

And I'd accomplish all of it without destroying the world.

With echoes amassing in my core, I opened my eyes to the world of light—and found myself face-to-face with Edius's true appearance.

I had glimpsed him only briefly from afar at their manor, but up close...

He was thickly muscled and would have towered over Windley and Rafe by a full head. Yet his powerful frame had the sculpted grace of a predator. My gaze traveled up to meet his sphinx-like eyes, arrogance dancing in them as he looked down without the slightest effort. His hair—still the same deep shade—fell wild and unruly around his broad shoulders, as though he'd just returned from a hunt, giving his imposing form an undeniable, primal allure.

But none of that mattered.

What mattered was the color of his stare—red, glittering, and dangerously captivating.

I tried quickly to avert my gaze, but Charmagne still restrained me tightly from behind, forcing my head forward until my eyes locked with Edius's.

"You've got a feisty stare," Edius noted. "Charm, hurry this shit up. She should be hexed by now."

"You're not helping, *gnat*! Her aura is as thick as pitch. I'm barely halfway rooted!"

"Told you we should've waited for Pip," Edius snapped back. "That little freak would've wormed in easy."

"Let me go, Edius!" I seethed.

Though his mouth stayed neutral, amusement danced wickedly in his crimson eyes. "Nah."

"You don't want me for an enemy," I warned.

He brushed off the threat easily. "Funny thing—got all my stuff back, y'know. Everything you made me pack for you. How's that feel?"

This Spirite would do well not to antagonize someone so deeply entangled with darkness. I was about to show him precisely how I felt.

"Oh, shit—she's starting!" Edius kicked his feet at the smoke beginning to curl around me.

"Well, do your job and ensnare her already!" Charmagne hissed. "Are you even trying?"

"This is your fault!" he argued. "I told you to hex her while she was sleeping, but you wanted to play with her first!"

Because once hexed, I'd become an empty shell—no longer fun for Charmagne's twisted games.

"Oh try me, cupcake. We aren't afraid of your little shadows."

"Speak for your fucking self."

Cupcake.

Cupcake.

Goddess-damned *CUPCAKE*!

"EXITI—"

The sudden press of a foreign mouth stopped the invocation.

Because Edius was kissing me.

He was still kissing me.

If ever there was a kiss without reciprocation—

The Spirite's mouth might've been designed to seduce humans, but I found nothing tempting about it. I tightened my lips defiantly, prepared to bite off his tongue if he dared force it past my teeth.

"She's got zero fondness for me, Charm," he muttered against my unresponsive mouth. "This is gonna be near impossible."

"Then build some fondness, you dolt! I've got half a hex at best. If you screw this up and she escapes again, Master Ascian will castrate you!"

The chill creeping up my back from Charmagne's hex felt like frostbite, numbing my senses—but it couldn't dull my fury.

"We will fillet her, rip her, bite her, tear her! We'll curse the ground beneath her feet until the earth swallows her whole!"

The echoes surged in our realm, thickening the swirling darkness around us.

"EXITI—"

"Ah, ah, ah." Edius's oversized hand clamped harshly over my mouth, sealing my jaw shut. His ruby eyes flared brighter. "Some kind of invocation? Don't fight me, Merrín. I'm not such a bad guy."

In my experience, only villains felt the need to declare their goodness aloud.

"This is pathetic," Charmagne spat. "Woo her, fool! Treat her like any other prey!"

It was impossibly strange hearing Windley's voice speak with such toxic disdain.

But speaking of voices—while Edius silenced mine, he couldn't suppress the raw, surging power in my core.

With a sharp exhale through my nose, I commanded the darkness around us to rise and whirl.

Edius's grip on my mouth remained firm, but I felt his stance shift subtly, his fingers tensing as he recognized the storm gathering strength around me.

"Wait." His free palm slid over my heart in a condescending caress, as though he could soothe me into compliance. "You like other humans, right?"

An attempt to find common ground? Shallow. *Laughable.* There was nothing common about us.

"In that case, you should know, I didn't really kill those two humans—the ones I used to impersonate Windalloy. I just implied it to make you fear me. I mean, I drained them, but I left them alive. Same with the ones from today. I try to leave them breathing if I can help it."

"Are you serious?" Charmagne scoffed, her stolen voice grating to my ears. "I didn't know that. *Pathetic*, Edi."

That hardly made him a saint.

The darkness swelled, pressing outward, whispering and writhing, desperate for release. I was close. I only needed a moment—one small opening to unleash it.

"I told you I find you cute for a human, didn't I?" Edius murmured. "I really wouldn't mind making you mine. I'd take care of you—in exchange for a little of your magic." His fingers splayed over my chest, sending unwelcome tingles sinking beneath my skin. "Guarantee my power's stronger than your boyfriend's."

I sliced him with a glare sharp enough to split stone.

"What? He's okay, and I'm not? Because he fed you some tragic backstory—a convenient excuse for all his evil?" Edius leaned in, voice charcoal-rich, eyes narrowed in cold scrutiny. "You strike me as someone who likes *broken boys*."

I refused to humor him.

Edius angled closer, dropping to a darker hush. "Ever wonder why I might run errands for Ascian? Maybe he's got someone I care about in chains—maybe I don't have a choice. But it's easier for you, isn't it, to paint everything in black and white and pretend the gray doesn't exist?"

Charmagne had put it plainly: they were master deceivers.

"What if I took you away for myself right now?" he mused, eyes suddenly aglow with a reckless promise. "Swept you off to some dark cave, got to know you better. Found out you're lovely enough to switch sides for. Protected you from the others. It'd all begin with me stealing you away. You'd feel small in my arms. I can picture it. Can you?"

I could.

But not by choice.

Even as I fought to focus on the shadows swirling within me, my mind strayed traitorously. Was there a grain of truth in his words? Could he truly be acting under duress?

Were all Ascian's "children" worthy of redemption?

No. Some were irredeemable.

"I bet you could fix me," he whispered.

Doubt crept in, subtle and insidious.

Edius's lips twitched. "Hah. Look at that—one little taste and the leash is already tightening, *highness.*"

"Good. Finish the hex," Charmagne demanded. "See if you can slip through."

Edius scowled past my shoulder. "Can't do anything yourself, can you?"

Had I not been so drained, I might have enjoyed his biting remark. But then his gaze took on a lethal shine—because, somehow, he'd managed to humanize himself, if only for a heartbeat.

My resolve wavered.

One of his hands remained firmly over my mouth, silencing me. Without my voice, I couldn't call Exitium. Simply thinking the name wasn't enough—I had to say it.

So I did the only thing that came to mind.

I imagined his touch was Windley's.

Edius's crimson eyes narrowed. "Yeah, I can tell that's not meant for me. You can't force the real thing, but...if you're giving it freely, I'll take it." He shot a smirk over my shoulder. "I think she's trying to seduce me. I'm getting in, little at a time. Shouldn't be much longer now."

Damn it. I should have left seduction to the experts.

I was running out of time.

Windley and Rafe were trapped in Soleil's domain.

Charmagne was draining my strength.

And Edius was close to completing his hex. Once he did, Ascian would have access to my power.

The echoes had always been my easy way out. I had foolishly overestimated myself.

But I had underestimated someone else.

"STOP! Windalloy will be mad if you do that!"

That piping voice—Exitium's sensed male presence—wasn't Ascian at all.

Pip burst onto the beach, breath labored, wide-eyed face flushed with panic, damp strands of baby-pink hair plastered messily across his forehead.

Charmagne shrieked, her stolen Windley-voice cracking. "Pip! What the hell are you doing?!"

"Windalloy won't come for her if she's broken! Stop it until we get him back!"

His boyish frame slammed into us with surprising force, nearly knocking me free from Edius's iron grip.

The distraction was enough.

Edius swore, spinning me around to reassert control, quickly reclaiming me in his oversized hold—but he made one crucial mistake.

He broke eye contact.

I seized the opening.

With every ounce of fury I possessed, I unleashed the echoes.

"We will wrench them, tear them, burn them alive!"

They erupted from my core like a tidal wave of black-violet flame, shrieking through the night air. The ground trembled.

Sand lifted in spirals. Power slammed into Edius and Charmagne with bone-splintering force.

Charmagne's scream tore across the beach. She doubled over, silver bracelets clinking uselessly as her fingers clawed at an agony no mortal hands could dislodge. The dark surge rippled, and for a heartbeat I saw it—cracks of violet light spider-webbing beneath the skin of her stomach, as though something inside her wanted to burst free and devour her from within.

Edius staggered, boots skidding, sand exploding at his heels. He kept a tenuous grip on my arm, but the tremor in his knuckles told me the cost. No matter. I was no longer under his spell, and I intended to finish this for good.

I inhaled, ready to hurl the echoes again—

But a piercing cry fractured the chaos.

"You...you hurt me!"

My head snapped toward the voice.

Pip.

He stood there, eyes wide, cradling his arm. My stomach lurched. Where my echoes had brushed him, the length of his forearm was already blackened, blistered, and scabbed.

"You're a baddie! You hurt me!" Pip's voice trembled, and for the first time, fear glazed his expression.

Edius groaned, pressing his fingers to his temple. "Oh, shit."

Charmagne, despite her obvious pain, managed a crooked grin. "Oh, *perfect*."

Pip was terrified of me—and I'd given him every reason to be.

"SHE HURT ME, EDI!"

Charmagne gasped dramatically. "She did, Pip! And what do we do to people who hurt us?"

Edius's jaw tightened. "Charm, stop it. Heya, Pip?

Remember how sad you were after executing all those soldiers from the north? You don't want to feel like that again, do you?"

Executing all those soldiers.

The creature who had slaughtered Beau's cavalry—

Was Pip.

A chill pulsed through me, cold and numbing.

Well.

That complicated things.

23
THE BOY AND
THE BEAST

"**K**ill her, Pip! Then you can have Windalloy back!"
Charmagne hissed.

"Shut up, Charm," Edius growled, annoyance biting at his tone. "Goddess, you're insufferable. Ascian'll have our heads if Pip loses it before he gets his taste of the Nemophilist. Pip, control yourself. Keep that creature inside you asleep!"

Again with the "creature"? Windley had warned me Pip was no ordinary youth—an early bloomer, dangerously powerful.

I studied his slight, wiry build, trembling under the weight of his fury, wondering what kind of beast Edius believed lay hidden behind that innocent face.

Meanwhile, Edius was clearly plotting his next move. Before I could muster another word, his hand clamped back over my mouth—reasserting control with a bruising certainty.

"Merrin," he murmured urgently at my ear, "if Pip unleashes that monster he's got inside, we're all doomed. I need to move my hand so you can calm him—but if I do, promise you won't fry me with your smog. I'm not dying for this shit."

Just a few paces away, Charmagne crouched in the sand, fueling Pip's rage with every barbed word. The round-faced young man stood rigid, fists clenched, white-hot anger radiating from his frame.

Edius pressed, "Do I have your word?"

I nodded sharply.

"And are you a queen of your word?"

I nodded again, more fiercely.

He loosed a gale of exasperation. "You know, if you'd just agreed to be my pet, we could've skipped all this mess. Freed her and left these idiots behind. But since you refused...guess I have no choice but to trust you, huh?"

A fleeting thought crossed my mind about the mysterious "her" Edius wanted freed, but I pushed it aside. I nodded a third and final time.

His hand hovered, ready to let me go.

And somewhere behind us, Pip's ragged breaths grew harsher, as if wrestling something feral inside.

I steadied myself, throat tight, preparing to face the tremor-wracked youth who had already killed so many.

I foolishly hoped I could save him—and all of us—before it was too late.

Slowly, as though signing his own death warrant, Edius removed his hand.

"What are you doing, you idiot?" Charmagne screeched.

Edius ignored her, gripping my shoulders. "Don't make me regret this."

I shrugged him off impatiently and turned to Pip. "Pip! I didn't mean to hurt you, truly! It was an accident! Please, stop whatever you're doing. Windley—*Windalloy*—wouldn't approve! He wants us to be friends!"

Pip didn't relax. "You're a baddie! You hurt me before, and now again! You probably hurt Windalloy too! That's why he isn't here!"

"No! I'd never hurt Windley—I *love* Windley! You said yourself I'm his wyrdbound one, aren't I?"

"Wyrdbound one?" Charmagne scoffed cruelly. "Pipsqueak, don't tell me you actually believe that drivel. She's obviously lying! She tricked Windalloy, and now she's trying to trick you!"

Charmagne's poisonous words fanned Pip's anger. I had to switch tactics fast.

"Soleil!" I screamed into the empty sky, desperation knotting my throat. "If you must keep Rafe, at least release Windley so he can help me defuse this madness!"

Silence. Not even a whisper from above.

"Come on, Soleil!" My voice strained. "You're causing more harm than good! I promised I'd take your child if Beau wouldn't—but if I'm defeated here, my queendom falls and your child with it!"

"Damn. She's actually crazy," Edius muttered.

"See, Pip? She's rabid!" Charmagne jeered. "End her before she ends us!"

I probably looked the part—hair tangled from a night of passion, clothes rumpled from battle, cheeks streaked with dirt, feet bare in the sand. I had no choice. I'd have to unleash Exitium and face the heartbreak it might cause Windley.

"EXITI—"

But I was cut off by a figure launching ashore from the sea, appearing like a miracle in the surf.

"Wait, lion queen!"

That voice. Playful, utterly captivating. My heart stalled mid-beat. For a breathless moment, chaos faded into nothingness.

Windley stood ankle-deep in surf, dripping seawater and adorned comically with ribbons of seaweed like some mischievous sea god. Sunlight painted him golden, every droplet a tiny star.

I tore away from Edius and ran, barreling into him with a hug fierce enough to knock him backward, heedless of the madness unfolding behind us.

"Thank goddess—she finally let you go!"

Windley caught me, dripping and breathless, eyes sparkling mischievously. "Only because I threatened to stab Beau through the stomach if she didn't. Sorry about that—wouldn't actually do it, of course."

"You have no idea how good it is to see you," I whispered against his salt-kissed skin.

"I might have some idea." A grin lifted his lips. He looked down at his soaked form with mock disapproval. "Not my best look, though."

I couldn't disagree more, but I forced myself to concentrate. "Ascian's not here yet."

"Good." Windley hastily pushed me behind him, turning toward the others with perky confidence. "Whole gang's here, huh? And Charm? Looks like Merrin got you pretty good."

Charmagne crouched, seething and clutching herself. "Perfect!" she snarled. "Now Pip can exterminate you both—you *and* your plump pet!"

Windley dismissed her, gaze locked warily on Pip. A brittle urgency threaded his hushed question: "What's wrong with him?"

Pip's whole body quivered, strung too tight to breathe, as though something nightmarish brewed beneath his skin.

"I accidentally hit him with the echoes," I admitted regretfully. "He snapped. Edius implied Pip's hiding something—some kind of *monster*?"

Bewilderment creased Windley's brow. "A monster?"

"Yes. Edius said Pip was the one who massacred the cavalry."

Windley snorted incredulously. "Pip? That timid kid? Don't believe Edius's rubbish. Pip's strong, yes, but dangerous?" He moved forward. "I'll talk him down. Mind handling the others for me?"

"Be careful, Wind," I urged. "Edius freed me, knowing what I'm capable of. He fears Pip more than he fears me."

"I'm always careful," he said, casting a haughty wink. Then he drew his hatchets and approached the shaking young rogue with caution.

I turned my attention to Charmagne, now fully herself, collapsed in a heap of white fabric. Edius watched warily from afar, arms crossed, clearly uncertain whether I'd keep my promise. I was a queen of my word—I met his gaze with a brief nod, and moved toward Charmagne.

She glared up balefully. "If you think I'll beg, you're even dumber than I thought."

"I don't expect begging." Calmly, regally, I placed my hand atop her rose-gold hair.

"Ex—" The word froze in my throat.

For all my power, I'd never intentionally taken a defenseless life face-to-face.

"*No merit!*" screamed the echoes.

"*Release your bloodlust, Merrin!*" whispered Exitium. "*The beastling has no merit!*"

Charmagne rolled her eyes with bitter contempt. "Are you serious? Too weak to finish it?"

"I'll kill to defend, but never to murder the defenseless." My voice was steel as I withdrew. "You're no longer a threat."

"I *will* be."

"I'll wait until then."

Then would be sooner than expected.

As I turned to help Windley, Charmagne lunged up from the ground with startling force, shoving me back into the nearest trees.

Edius tensed, about to move—then hesitated. Windley wasn't as reserved. "Charm! You're asking for death!"

"Sugarplum's too righteous to kick me while I'm down," Charmagne sneered. "Let's make it easier."

Then, in a desperate grab for power, her lips crashed onto mine—soft, perfumed, nails raking up my throat—but ultimately powerless. There wasn't an ounce of real fondness between us.

Thunk!

Windley's hatchet split the bark above our heads, forcing Charmagne away, startled and bleeding from my earlier spell.

"The next won't miss," he snarled.

Charmagne slumped back with a spiteful laugh. "So the northern queen fancies lace as well as steel—didn't know your lot allowed that up there."

Strange. She'd recognized my royalty instantly, and now she knew our customs?

"Don't worry, cupcake," she added, sagging in defeat. "It's common down here. Once you tire of Windalloy, I'll be waiting."

"Kiss me again," I warned icily, "and you'll die."

Leaving her slumped, I hurried to Windley. He was struggling to rouse Pip from his trance.

"Pip! It's me, Windalloy. Snap out of it! Goddess, what did they do to you?"

Pip stood rigid, unresponsive, muttering nonsense.

I turned on Edius. "What's wrong with him? You said something's inside him—what is it?"

Edius hesitated. "He hexed something horrible a few years

back—none of us could've handled it. Now he can wield its power. Kid wiped out an entire cavalry alone—those weren't your soldiers, were they?"

"Killed how?" Windley demanded.

"They...boiled alive," Edius said with a grimace. "After some spider-thing got 'em."

"Spider?" Windley and I echoed.

"Spider-ish. Extra legs. A dripping horror crawling out of his mouth." He shrugged. "Only triggers when he's provoked—like with those soldiers, or when you hurt him."

"You left me alone with that?" I snarled.

Edius shrugged. "My advice? End him now. I like the kid, but he's lethal. He hexed every soul in Abardo by himself—wiped a whole city the way most folk snuff a candle. That's the scale we're talking about."

"The whole city?" Windley repeated, voice tight.

So Ascian's "army" was just this youth, cursed by a monster. I knew that sinking feeling of darkness within all too well.

Edius studied me grimly. "Merrín, you might be the only one strong enough to stop him—Nemophilist and all."

Windley's expression pinched with alarm. "You told him?"

He couldn't talk, given he'd told Flora without my say.

"Exitium told him," I clarified.

Edius lifted a brow. "Who?"

"Never mind," I muttered, focus snapping back to Pip. "If we can't stop this, we run—right, Wind?"

"If you're running, go north." Edius raked a boot through the sand, scoring a line toward the dunes. "Ascian'll be crawling up from the south."

I shouldn't take strategy from the thug who'd bound me minutes ago.

Yet the swagger had drained out of Edius: salt clung to his

lashes, shoulders sagged in something like resignation, and his boot carved half-hearted lines in the sand.

"Why the warning, Edius? Moments ago you had me at your mercy."

He rolled one powerful shoulder. "Maybe releasing you helps me, maybe it gets me whipped. Either way, it's leverage."

"Leverage?"

"Forget it." His gaze hardened. "This doesn't make us friends. Next time I won't be so generous."

"Fair enough," I said, turning to Windley. "Come on, Wind."

But Windley wasn't ready to abandon Pip so easily. It broke my heart to watch him plead with the unresponsive young man, guilt heavy in his voice—guilt from leaving Pip once before, now compounded by having to abandon him again.

Gently, I touched Windley's shoulder. "I know this is difficult, my knave, but we need to leave him for now. We'll come back—I promise."

He didn't speak. Instead, his thumb brushed the back of my knuckles—one small, anchoring stroke.

My gesture of comfort had the opposite effect on the least stable person among us.

"Don't touch Windalloy!" Pip screamed, voice distorted by a rage that wasn't entirely his own.

His mouth gaped impossibly wide, and one slick, needle-sharp spider leg lurched upward from his gullet, glistening with foul droplets as it scraped free.

Windley sprang back, eyes round as moons. "Goddess-damn—tell me that isn't a wraith!"

Charmagne's laugh was shrill and triumphant. "Too late, fools! Get them, Pip! Crush the royal and reclaim Windalloy!"

At that, something primal in the world seemed to pause.

The coast itself recoiled—wind cut out, waves drew back, and even the sand went eerily still.

Just inland, a scrubby thicket of wind-gnarled brush crouched in silence. As we braced for the thing taking shape inside Pip, a voice knifed through the hush, yanking every eye that way—

"ENOUGH."

A new, deeper stillness dropped as Ascian finally stepped forward—serenely brutal, unshakably composed.

Thwack!

The crack of a whip split the air—instantly recognizable, a sound I'd heard only once before but one Windley knew far too well. He ducked on instinct, bracing for impact.

But the whip wasn't meant for Windley.

It was meant for Pip.

The brutal three-tailed lash struck the youth, blasting him to the sand and strangling whatever creature had been emerging. Pip gasped, wheezing, limbs jerking as the grotesque black appendage snapped back into his mouth with a sickening slurp.

The wielder strode closer—stance commanding, dark, absolute—an apparition pulled from the heart of twilight itself. The dunes fell mute, and the echoes—usually a swarm—hovered in wary suspension.

Then I saw his eyes.

Lavender.

Sharp. Penetrating. Unforgettable.

"HE HAS NO MERIT!"

In that instant, something deep within me shifted.

24
THE THINGS THAT FELL

"Merrin, stop!"

That was Windley's voice, but I couldn't see him clearly through the blackness that welled up behind my eyes. A dense, oily shadow had flooded my airways, and the hands that once caressed me like a lover now forced my mouth wide, expelling choking darkness.

Dark forces I'd invited but no longer controlled were overtaking me.

For the first time in the stark clarity of daylight, I laid eyes on the oppressor responsible for Windley's dark, forgotten past —the one who'd etched cruelty into his skin and soul, leaving scars he fought so hard to hide.

That ugliness was nothing compared to the ugliness standing before me.

Ascian stood casually, his whip dangling like a serpent at his side. Next to him, Pip cowered, bruises already darkening his fair face. Ascian's lips curled into a vile smile, dripping contempt and arrogant self-assuredness. When he pulled down his hood, he did so grandly, as though bestowing a gift upon us all—a gift we should have felt privileged to receive.

He was indeed handsome, and younger-looking than I'd expected someone bearing the title Master to be. I had always associated that word with the aged and hardened, faces carved by wisdom over countless years. But perhaps cruelty aged differently.

Still, I refused to dignify him with any internal praise or acknowledgment of his features. For Windley's sake, I would think of Ascian only as the man with lavender eyes.

"What entertaining trouble you've all managed to stir up," Ascian mused to his gathered followers. "Edius, I see you're no help at all to your brother and sister. Have you forgotten it isn't you who will face punishment?"

Edius released an exhausted sigh. "Sorry, highness." Then, without further ceremony, he grabbed a handful of my hair, tugging me roughly toward him.

Windley didn't react beyond tightening his jaw, his body momentarily frozen, muscles locked by a trauma too ingrained to easily overcome.

And me?

Well, we'll come to me in a moment.

When Ascian noticed Charmagne still wounded on the sand, he crossed to her, lifted her roughly by one arm—like a toddler lifting an unwanted doll—and gripped her throat firmly, steadying her upright.

"Heal yourself, girl. Then tidy up. Your current state disgusts me."

With that, Ascian planted his mouth firmly upon hers.

Apparently, the entire coven favored unwanted kisses.

Under Ascian's lips, Charmagne's injuries began to heal. He had hexed countless people across untold years, and evidently, at least one of those hexed carried sweet breath capable of restoring magical wounds.

Charmagne's blackened injuries faded, and strength flooded back into her limbs. She sprang upright, vibrant once again.

"I was trying to use Pip's creature to—"

"To snuff out the greatest tap of power ever placed within our grasp?" Ascian interrupted, his voice dangerously calm. "Tell me, brainless girl, why you'd do something so foolish?"

Charmagne fell silent, sensing instinctively that the wrong answer could very well end her life.

Ascian, however, had already shifted his cruel gaze toward Windley, who stood protectively between Ascian and me, his remaining hatchet raised, body rigid with defiance.

He was so brave. Even carrying scars of fear and pain, Windley was brave.

If only I'd been a damsel who needed saving. For while Edius gripped my hair, he'd conveniently left my mouth uncovered—likely on purpose.

I made note of that small observation, though it was distant, along with everything else, since Ascian's arrival had reduced the world to little more than a faded, irrelevant backdrop.

Ascian's presence had been a catalyst, shrinking reality into a pinpoint of darkness within my corrupted soul. The darkness I had long harbored was no longer merely an entity—it was alive, clawing at the edges of my will, demanding to be released.

It had a name: destruction.

Born of Exitium, nurtured by whispers of the echoes, and fed by my own simmering hatred, it had become strong.

The darkness I'd inherited—the curse Beau's family had so carefully suppressed for generations—was now awakened and ravenous. It had flourished as I'd selfishly wielded its power, side-by-side with my growing bloodlust.

Now, standing upon this wind-swept shore, I felt utterly alone, balanced precariously on the precipice of worlds, looking down at countless grasping hands of shadow below.

I despised Ascian with every fragment of my being for what he'd done to Windley, to Pip, to the innocent souls of Abardo.

With searing hatred, I aimed the depths of my darkest gaze straight into those lavender eyes that mocked me from across a vast distance.

I hated him.

Loathed him.

And I would be the one to end him.

"Awaken to your true self, Merrin. Speak my name, and together we will harrow the world."

Exitium's slippery voice—neither fully male nor female, clearer and more commanding than ever before—no longer tempted me.

It was inevitable.

How cruelly ironic, that something as pure as love could twist into a force this terrible.

I had never wished to end the world, nor had I ever wished to become destruction itself. But in the presence of Ascian, my desires corrupted—as if the only proper punishment for such profound evil was to obliterate every possible vessel of darkness along with him.

Little did I realize, that was exactly what Exitium had been waiting for all this time.

I was no longer a queen of the people.

I had become vengeance incarnate.

As I teetered on the brink of surrendering myself entirely to molten wrath and ruin, one final lucid thought emerged:

"If you intend to use me, Exitium, then at least reveal your true nature. Tell me, what are you?"

My whisper echoed over the expanses of grasping hands. From the deepest recesses of my being, I finally received the answer to the mystery I had long pondered since first uttering the dark thing's name.

Exitium breathed into me the secret she'd kept buried for eons, and I spoke it aloud, giving it form and life.

"Exitium...you're a goddess?"

The fourth goddess. The one from Windley's tales.

The goddess destined to end all things.

"Angels are not the only things that may fall."

This was the last I heard from the goddess Exitium before the echoes ripped open my throat and poured from me with enough venom to end the world.

"The lavender-eyed man has no merit! Let us scorch him! Let us pierce his eyes! Tear him apart. Rip him asunder. Devastate all who walk and crawl. Filth of the earth! Burn them. Dry them. Kill them. Kill them. KILL THEM!"

"EXITIUM!"

The fallen goddess surged up my throat, riding upon the voices of her lost devotees.

...

...

...

"Merrin, stop!"

That was Windley's voice, though I couldn't feel him through the shadow draped across my skin.

"Perfect. I've backed the losing side—again," Edius muttered, shifting behind me.

Lastly—

"Your Majesty!"

Rafe? Had Soleil finally freed him? I had no time to wonder what bargaining that must have required.

Because in that instant, Exitium devoured my soul, and all became black.

From there, I had to rely on Windley's later retelling of events.

A spear of shadow burst from my eyes, stabbing into Ascian's lavender ones, draining them lifeless and black. He let out a cry—one Windley later described as a coward's wail —and began frantically grasping for any stolen magic he could summon. Blinded, he sent forth a poisonous gale, but Windley and the others dropped to the sand, narrowly evading the deadly blast. Next, thorned spikes erupted from the beach, but instead of striking their intended targets, they only felled the tree still holding Windley's embedded hatchet.

Ascian's final desperate act was to summon the creature lurking within Pip. But as a grotesque, jagged leg clawed its way from Pip's mouth, Ascian himself fractured apart, cracking and disintegrating into ash. Shadow seeped from his pores, each fleck punctuated by another pathetic, agonized scream.

I regret missing the sight.

His end was far too merciful for the villain who'd inflicted such horrors upon Windley. Windley would never have his grand reckoning, never deliver the final blow. Justice, it seemed, had its own agenda.

But Ascian was never our greatest threat—not by far.

My power continued spilling forth uncontrollably, staining the beach black. Shadows spiraled from my open mouth, forming a cyclone—a beacon summoning Exitium's fallen followers. It would soon erupt, consuming the world.

That much I knew instinctively, for Exitium and I had become one.

"Lion queen! You have to contain it!" Windley shouted frantically, though I could not hear him.

"Argh! Rafe, tell your goddess-damned—*goddess* to help us! What was the point of giving her your seed if she won't hold up her end? Once that child is born, I vote we throw it to the wolves!"

"Soleil!" Rafe raised his sword defiantly toward the sun, like a knight demanding divine aid. "Lend us your strength!"

I heard none of it.

Nor did I see Charmagne stumble over Ascian's remains, dropping to her knees beside the drifting gray remnants.

Nor Edius frantically dodging attacks from the nightmarish leg thrashing from Pip's grotesquely stretched mouth.

I heard nothing.

Felt nothing.

Saw nothing.

Before the time of the Clearing,
when the moon hung low, heavy with secrets,
and frost reigned eternal upon the land,
two crowns slipped silently from heaven,
lost among shadows of northern pines.
The forest wept, yet none listened,
ears deaf to sorrow, hearts blind to loss.
Before the time of the Clearing,
when starlight whispered gently through leaves,
and twilight lingered long over frozen lakes,
two crowns awoke, glistening with promise,

found by souls who heard the wood's quiet hymn.
The forest sang, and they listened closely,
ears open to wisdom, hearts warm with grace.

Long ago, beneath a moon that ruled both night and day,
a heavenly crown fell and fractured upon the earth.
One half sank to the sea, the other lost among the trees.
A simple maiden found the forest half,
yet only half its whispers reached her ears.
Mistaking wisdom for warning, she commanded the
   burning of the wood.
Heaven, in fury, reclaimed her crown.
But years passed, and the sea returned the other half,
revealing her tragic error.
With humility, she repented, and the heavens forgave
   her.
Crown restored, she became the eternal guardian of the
   wood.

Within that nothingness—absolute wrath—I heard nothing.
   Felt nothing.
   Saw nothing.
   Until suddenly, there was something.
   A small, delicate something.
   ...
   "M...rin."
   It was gentle.
   ...
   "Me...rin."
   It was tender.

...

"*Merrin! Can you hear me?*"

It was *warm.*

Through the bleakest shadow a voice found me—soft, air-light, comforting in a way I hadn't felt in ages. Whatever raged outside this void, inside it I was simply relieved not to be alone.

"Who are you?" I pushed into the darkness.

"*You can finally hear me? At last! Listen well, little royal. You must end this—I cannot watch the world fall again.*"

End it? I wasn't strong enough. My bloodlust ruled me now.

Even unspoken, the voice understood.

"*Do not lose heart. Time is short, but not gone.*"

"Then tell me how. I feel like a servant to the fury, not its master."

"*Cast the destroyer from your soul. Hurl her into the wastes. Quickly!*"

But the echoes would only hunt another royal.

"*True—but banishing her buys us time to use the Crown for its real purpose.*"

Exitium and the echoes were *bound* to the Nemophile's Crown—drive one away and I'd lose the other, wouldn't I?

"*Not so. There are two halves to the Wood's Crown. The dark half followed you from the Scarlet Wood, lurking in shadow until it found your heart suitable to corrupt.*

"*My half lay silent in the Emerald Wood, waiting for royal feet. When your soles touched that moss, I entered you. Only then did the destroyer strike, hoping her roar would drown my whisper, because I alone can wield the Crown as it was meant to be.*"

"And that is?"

"*To exile the destroyer until the end of days. Destruction is inevitable, but not meant for now. Together we must send her away."*

Trusting another bodiless voice was madness. I knew that. Had proven it.

"Your trust will come in hours and days. Cast Exitium out and my power will pour through you. Together we'll raise mountains, mend springs, and set the world to rights." Her voice softened, bright as dawn. *"I am Vita, goddess of creation. I bring no pain, no ruin—only life. Will you stand with me, Merrin?"*

That name—Rafe's lore, celestial things beyond my ken. If Exitium was the goddess to end things, Vita was the one to begin them.

Another goddess. And so far, goddesses had caused me nothing but grief.

But the alternative was ending everything—and losing Windley, Beau, and Albie forever.

"Yes. Tell me what to do."

See? Some decisions were easily made.

"Feel it—in marrow and muscle. Desire it fully, and it shall be."

I did as she asked—let every fear of what I'd lose flood my mind, conjured a color no eye had ever seen, and drove every shard of will toward one purpose: *out with Exitium.*

In the pit-black that followed, I glimpsed the one thing that can cleave perfect night:

Light.

It poured around me—luminous, finely wrought—and for the first time in an age, my soul felt clean.

But the beach I'd left behind was anything but.

25

UNTIL WE MEET AGAIN

When I returned to the physical realm, it was as though the world had taken a deep, rejuvenating breath.

A dawn-lit thrum stirred beneath my collarbone —Vita's muted resonance settling where Exitium's shadows once coiled. Life, not ruin, now coursed bright in my veins.

My feet felt lighter, as if brushed by wind. Everything sprang sharper, more vibrant—the gleam jittering across the waves, the weather-bleached driftwood, even the charred crater my fury had gouged into the sand.

Only Windley, Rafe, and a few irritated crabs remained. The others were gone, though their footprints betrayed them: Charmagne and Pip had fled one way, Edius another.

Windley spotted me and lunged across the beach, eyes glassy, face streaked with soot from the darkness I'd unleashed. Before he could speak—before I could fully grasp all that had happened—he swept me into his arms as if he'd never let go.

"Your Majesty."

Windley's embrace went beyond love, beyond gratitude—deeper, incandescent, a wonder language could never cage. I surrendered to it: the cadence of his heart against my cheek, the living current racing in his veins, the low hymn of creation in the very air. Vita's power was unlike anything I'd known—radiant where Exitium had rasped their cold, ruinous hiss.

When Windley finally released me, he flicked a wary glance toward the crater where Ascian had fallen—his form half-crumbled into ashy remains. I, however, turned to the wavy-haired, amber-eyed magician who looked as though he'd been dragged through hellfire.

"Rafe." I laid a hand on his shoulder. "You made it. I was so worried about you. Thank goddess—not *that* goddess, though. Maybe you'll fill me in later?"

He hesitated, then did something unprecedented: he patted my back with a stiff, awkward motion—like a distant relative mustering the faintest show of affection. For Rafe, it was monumental; for me, unexpectedly tender.

That brief relief died at once.

Behind me, Ascian's body finally collapsed the rest of the way. Windley stumbled across the scorched ground, dropping to his knees near the charred debris. He sifted frantically through the cinders, ignoring the heat as he scooped and scattered handfuls of soot.

"Where is it?" he muttered, voice tattered. "No, no, no..."

His fingers plunged uselessly into the dust again, and a strangled groan escaped him.

"Ascian's ring—it's gone!"

Alarm jolted through me. I hurried over, my bare feet quickly layered in ash. "What do you mean?"

Windley shook his head, frustration blazing in his eyes. "If Charm took it, she'll have access to every hex he ever stole—including that monstrosity inside Pip!"

Ice pricked along my spine. We had toppled one tyrant only to hand his stolen souls to an even less stable heir: *Charmagne.*

Worse, the echoes were on the loose—slinking across the sand, sniffing for a fresh royal to corrupt. Let them latch onto someone wilder than I'd ever dared, and everything we'd bled for could unravel before dawn.

Unfortunately, they would find *her.*

Although we didn't know it yet, Exitium had already chosen her next victim—a royal as volatile as she was wrathful. A queen beautiful, mercurial, and *magnificently* mad.

With Albie and Beau's whereabouts unknown...

With Edius's true intentions still uncertain...

With magical twins nestled inside Beau's belly...

With an ancient, monstrous creature bound inside Pip...

With Charmagne wielding the might of a hundred hexes...

And with at least three of the four goddesses furious at us—

I, the Great and Mighty Merrin, alongside a flame-wielding magician and a dangerous rogue with a surprisingly tender heart, set out to save the world from destruction's capricious grasp.

Simple enough, right?

Well, captive ones, this feels like a good place to pause. You've survived all the sticky parts and hopefully enjoyed the swoony bits too. I warned you—a little chaotic.

Trust me, it all comes together in due time.

Until we meet again, with all my love,

Merrin

MEET BRINDI QUINN

Brindi Quinn is a Minnesota-based romantasy author best known as "the genie author" behind the wildly swoony Come True series—and for weaving sparkly worlds where romance, banter, and reluctant attraction collide. Since 2011, she's penned 20+ YA and NA novels that blend fantasy, paranormal, sci-fi, and comedy into page-turning mashups filled with morally gray protectors, forced proximity, and plenty of swoon.

Her earlier titles are currently retired while she gives her backlist a full, professionally edited revamp—so for now, her available reads are the Come True series and The Crown Saga.

When she's not plotting meet-cute mayhem, Brindi can be found biking with her soulmate, gaming with her dog, or chatting all things bookish online. She is represented by Eva Scalzo of Speilburg Literary.

Find more at Brindiful.com.

Brindi Quinn

Magical books for magical people.

facebook.com/brindiful

instagram.com/brindiful

tiktok.com/@brindiquinnbooks

goodreads.com/brindiful

bookbub.com/authors/brindi-quinn

youtube.com/@brindiquinn

amazon.com/author/brindiful